CLAIMING THE ALPHA'S DAUGHTER

THE VAMPIRE KING'S FEEDER
BOOK ONE

BELLA MOONDRAGON

CONTENTS

1. Better Than Money   1
2. Take My Daughter   9
3. Not Lola   15
4. I'll See You Again--Someday   23
5. Move the Moon   29
6. It's Best Not to Resist   35
7. She's not in a Room   41
8. The Guards Move In   47
9. In the Bedroom   53
10. The King Has a Fiancée?   59
11. Dinner and a Show   65
12. Opal is Out of Line   73
13. Touch Me, King Kane   79
14. Lustful Thoughts   85
15. Shift for Us, Feeder!   93
16. Just a Taste   99
17. I Don't Love Her   105
18. What Were You Thinking?   111
19. What's Wrong with Me?   117
20. He Came to Claim Her   123
21. She Would Be Dead   129
22. All Alone   135
23. Why He Ran Away   141
24. A Letter From the King?   147
25. The Pain of Dying Prematurely   153
26. Save Her   159
27. Tracking Them Down   165
28. Am I Dead?   171
29. Thank Yous   177
30. Getting His Head on Straight   183
31. Demands of King Peter   189
32. Confrontation   195
33. I'm the King of the World!   201
34. How Did He Escape?   207
35. Saying Goodbye   213

36. The Scene of the Crime   219
37. An Imminent Threat   227
38. This Is War   233
39. Family or Power?   239
40. The Emergence of an Alpha   247

Also by Bella Moondragon   255

BETTER THAN MONEY

Emory

MY STOMACH IS TIGHT, like a fist, as I follow my parents up the walkway to the monstrosity of a stone fortress known as Castle Graystone. Lightning illuminates the sky overhead, which seems to fit perfectly with the scene, though it's not raining—not yet anyway. Something tells me there's about to be a shift in the atmosphere, and as my black boots hit the ancient wood of the drawbridge that has granted entrance here for upward of a thousand years, I can feel the electricity in the air.

Thunder rolls across the blackened sky, the boom echoing deep within me. Lola clutches my hand more tightly and lets out a little whimper. "It's okay," I tell her, forcing a smile to my lips. "Everything is just fine."

She looks up at me, her wide green eyes filled with anxiety, and her head rocks back and forth, but I know she doesn't believe a word I've said. Why should she? I don't believe it either.

On my other side, Colt walks more confidently. At seventeen, my brother is the epitome of the cocky male, ready to attack anyone and everyone who might seem a threat to him. The only problem is, he has yet to meet his wolf, so against the likes of these bloodsuckers, he'd be as good as dead in a matter of seconds.

Even now, I feel their ocean eyes on us as we make our way to the other side of the bridge. My father gives pause, looking up at the mammoth doors that have already been thrown open for us. Castle Graystone is welcoming our party in the same way a shark invites its prey, with a smile, and even though this meeting has been arranged as a way to finally make peace between our two warring sides, the fact that we were only allowed to bring five warriors along with our family feels a bit like a death sentence.

The bloodsuckers would destroy all of us, eat us for dinner and leave us drained and writhing on the floor while our bodies, desperate for any sort of life saving liquid, slowly cease to function.

A shudder goes down my spine thinking of it.

My father had called us all into his office late last night, sat us all down, and explained to us that we were going to Castle Graystone to meet with the Vampire King. He'd said it was time to find a way to peacefully solve our differences. Colt had flown off the handle—just like Darius, who walked behind me now with his parents. His father, Jace, is my father's Beta.

They'd demanded we continue the fight to the bitter end, but my father lamented the loss of so many lives these past ten years or more, saying that we had reached the unprecedented threshold of one hundred thousand dead wolves—and that was enough. No more.

Now, he will negotiate the peace with the Vampire King, and we will comply. Whether or not they had already come to those terms or not, I am not sure, but I've gotten the impression all but one small detail has been worked out. I've seen loads of our natural resources being shipped out over the last few weeks, timber, coal, precious gemstones, even tankers of natural gas, items we need to survive, items we sell to other packs to keep ourselves able to buy other necessities. Why would the vampires need those things? Perhaps to sell them themselves? I don't know the details of the war. I only know that we are losing.

And as I step foot into Graystone, Lola's sweaty hand in mine, I realize that I had been wrong. We aren't losing—we've already lost.

My boots are loud as I follow my father, flanked by two of our warriors. My mother's slippers hardly make a sound. She is no warrior. She is crying even now. I know all of this has been so difficult for her. When I think of everything my father has put her through, I have to wonder why they were still married.

Mates. They are mates. It is the madness of the Moon Goddess that had brought them together and makes them stay.

At the thought of the word reverberating through my head, I turn and look at Darius. He is twenty-one. He should've met his mate by now, if she is old enough. The fact that he hasn't makes me wonder if our suspicions are true.

Was it me?

I won't be twenty-one for six more months. Then, maybe we will know for certain.

It will only be fitting that we would be, considering our stature in the pack. I will be Alpha one day soon, when my father retires, and Darius will be my Beta.

"Emory," Lola whispers, bringing me out of my head. "Look at the paintings."

My eyes follow her gaze up the walls of the hallway we are marching down, and I wish I hadn't looked. More importantly, I wish her twelve-year-old eyes had been spared the gruesomeness. Vampires in various poses sucking the life out of other creatures—mostly humans or creatures in their human forms—but occasionally, one of the massive portraits on the wall shows something else, like a vampire with their three-inch-long barred fangs sunk into the neck of a wolf. Those are even more disturbing than the portrayals of humans, which could've been us in our two-legged form. We know for a fact that these vampires won't think twice about ripping our throats open.

One painting in particular catches my eye, perhaps because the woman looks so very much like me. Long red hair flowing down her back in soft curls, her emerald eyes looking directly at the painter, her face pristine and unmoving as a man with black hair almost as long as hers prepares to sink his fangs into her neck.

She is nude, holding a blanket up to cover her breasts as the rest of the fabric falls between her legs so that her thighs are exposed. He is shirtless but wearing black pants. It is clear they are in a bedroom, and I have to wonder if perhaps she isn't afraid because she knows he will not kill her—not on purpose anyway. Maybe they have an understanding, and she's come to trust him over the many times he has swallowed down her sacred waters of life.

Maybe this woman is a feeder.

"Emory?"

It isn't Lola speaking my name this time; it is my father. We are coming to a stop in front of a large set of doors, and he wants to make sure that I am paying attention. I lock eyes with him and nod. If this goes badly, my warrior training will have to help us to escape. Perhaps I haven't met my wolf yet, but that doesn't make me incapable of fighting.

A sharp nod is my response to my father, and he turns back to face the double doors.

We wait for a moment with the vampire guards on either side of the barricade only staring straight ahead, their light blue eyes focused on the wall across from them, as if they are also paintings, works of art incapable of moving or feeling.

When they finally move, it is at the exact same time, and I suppose it has to have been in response to a telepathic message from someone on the other side of the doors. We have the mind-link that allows us to communicate mentally with family members and other members of our own pack, but vampires can all communicate with one another via their telepathy, whether they are related or not. After all, most vampires are not born this way; they are created, so it isn't as if they are actually related to one another—not in the same way we are.

They give the phrase "related by blood" a whole new meaning.

As the heavy wooden doors creak open, and we enter the throne room, I am reminded that part of the reason the king that sits on the throne now was given such immense power is because he has never been a human. He comes from a long line of blood-born vampires as they refer to themselves, the offspring of other rare vampires who are able to procreate. It is a phenomenon I don't understand.

My mother calls it witchcraft, but since I've never actually met a witch, I am not sure how that can be.

This room is even more elaborately decorated than the hallway. It seems that half of the walls are covered with gold leaf as intricate trim divides every surface into large twelve by twelve blocks that are filled with hand painted portraits of various former rulers and their clan members.

Most of them strike regal poses, their physical features similar to the man in the painting I'd noted before—pale skin, light colored eyes, and dark flowing hair. The women are a bit different. Some have red eyes and blonde hair. Many of them wear outfits from hundreds of years ago, but then vampires even today tend to wear old-fashioned clothing. Even their military uniforms are dated—tight black pants and fitted red jackets. Not that it matters. When warriors can move as quickly and powerfully as vampires do on the battlefield, they can be wearing anything, and it becomes difficult for us to keep up.

Not that wolf shifters aren't fast—we are. And we are huge when we shift. Some of us are over six feet tall at the shoulder, but we are not as fast as vampires and often not as strong.

Which is ultimately what has led us to be standing here now.

The throne is empty as we approach it, which is puzzling to me. Where is the Vampire King? He must've known we were coming.... Father said he planned this the night before.

Lola shifts on her feet, looking around, and I adjust my grip on her hand. I know she is terrified. I want to hold her and tell her it will all be okay, but I can't promise her that yet.

I have been the only mother she's ever known, and I will protect her to the ends of the earth, but I am only one person, and the room is full of dozens of vampire guards.

The curtains behind the throne stir, and the man who walks out looks so much like the one from the painting with the woman, a chill shoots down my spine. A few others accompany him, but my eyes are locked on his blue eyes, the same shade as the patches of sky that peeked through the rain clouds as we'd entered his home.

His dark hair is pulled back in a ponytail that flows down his back, and he is dressed in a traditional white button-down with puffy sleeves, black pants, and a regal gold and white checked vest. His expression is difficult to read. If I didn't know better, I'd say he was bored.

"Well?" he says as he stands before the throne. "Bernard, I'm glad you've come and we can be done with this. You have it then? The final payment? The five million drakes?"

My heart leaps into my throat. Five million? My father doesn't have that kind of money. In fact, as far as I can tell, he hasn't brought any amount of money at all.

"King Kane," Father says, bowing his head. The rest of us follow suit, realizing we'd been rude before, but in fairness, he hadn't given us much of a chance to show proper etiquette since he'd begun to speak almost the moment he appeared. "I'm sorry, Your Majesty," my father begins. "I do not have the money."

King Kane Alexander's face doesn't waver one bit as he stares at my father. It's almost as if he has expected this to be the case. "Then why have you come?" His voice is smooth and immediately makes me feel at ease, which is one of his weapons.

Father clears his throat. "Because… I am hoping you will settle for something else, something better."

"Something better than five million drakes?" King Kane repeats. "What could possibly be better than the remaining money you owe me, Alpha Bernard?" A bit of amusement seems to play around his perfect pink lips, and one blue eye narrows almost into a wink.

My father's voice cracks as he says, "M-my daughter."

I feel my heart leap into my throat as my father's words register in my mind. What? Could he have actually said what I think he said?

"Your daughter?" King Kane repeats, just as taken aback as I am. "Whatever do you mean?"

"Yes, my daughter." My father sounds more confident now as he says, "I want to sell her to you for the remaining debt. I want you to take my daughter… to be a feeder."

2

TAKE MY DAUGHTER

Emory

"TAKE MY DAUGHTER... TO BE A FEEDER."

My father's words echo around the throne room as I stand behind him with my throat so constricted, I can hardly breathe, let alone speak. I can't believe the words that have come from his mouth, and by the look on Vampire King Kane's face, neither can he.

"What in the hell are you talking about?" the king asks. "You want me to take your daughter? To replace the debt you still owe me for waging war against my lands for all of these years?" He is standing on a dais, but as he speaks, he descends one step. He's still a good ten feet away from us and probably three feet taller than my father in this position, who is six foot one. I'm sure that King Kane is taller than my father anyway, but from this angle, he looks like a giant bearing down on my father, an angry giant.

I am more than a little angry myself as I try to process what is happening. Lola begin to whimper, and with her cries, my father flinches. I've also heard a startled gasp from either Darius behind me or his mother, Margaret, or maybe both of them. I still don't know

9

what to say. All I can think is that I'm missing something. Surely, my parents must be using this opening as some way of getting the upper hand on the vampires. It must be part of some nefarious plan I am unaware of.

They can't really mean to sell me—can they? I can't even process what that would mean. I'm meant to be the next Alpha, after all. It doesn't matter that I am female. My father has been training me to take over the pack since I was a little girl. No, something isn't right.

"Please explain yourself, Bernard," Kane says, resting his elbow on a folded arm as his long, slender fingers stroke his cheek in contemplation. "Explain to me how your daughter, whichever of these females that happens to be, is of more use to me than the money you agreed to pay me."

When he says the words "these females" his eyes briefly passed over all of us, and for a moment our eyes lock, as if he is saying he knows that my father has to be referring to me. I am the only woman here who is young enough to be his daughter, other than Lola, and she's just a child. None of the warriors we brought along with us are women, so that only leaves my mother and Darius's mom beside me. Clearly, they are not his daughter.

Reasoning through this sends another bolt of fear passing through my body. What would it mean to stay here and become a feeder for the Vampire King? I can't even let my mind ponder it. All of the feeder stories I have heard are worse than even death on the battlefield.

Again, my father must clear his throat before he speaks, which at least indicates that he isn't particularly pleased with this plan, but the betrayal that settles in my heart is unreal as I consider what he is doing right now.

My mind flutters over the various images I have of my father and I as I grew up and he taught me so very much about so many things. Special memories stick out to me—the first time he gave me a ride on his wolf's back through the forest, watching the Northern Lights at solstice when I was younger, how he'd taught me to catch a fish with my bare hands.

No, it can't be that my father, the man I used to call daddy, is now selling me to this monster, our enemy. He may look like the perfect man, with his handsome face and tight, muscular form, but he doesn't fool me. He is the devil himself.

So what the hell is happening?

"Well," my father begins, gulping for air. "I think you shall find that she will be the perfect feeder for you. She comes from good stock, obviously, since I am her father. She's intelligent, obedient, and may even be an asset to you at court one day, if she li—if you allow her to be."

If she lives that long… that's what my father was going to say. I have to swallow back my own outburst as I want to ask him how he can do this.

My eyes flicker to my mother, and it appears as if she's wearing a bit of a grin around her red lips. I am puzzled. My mother and I have always been close. Just like my father, I have learned so much from her. She taught me how to be a lady, how to dance, sew, entertain. Now, is she truly going to stand there with that smirk on her face as her only daughter is sold away?

I don't understand it. I think of how devastated she was when Lola was born, how betrayed she'd felt that my father could do that to her, have a child with another woman, and how it had been me to comfort her and assure her that everything would be all right.

Now, she is just going to let my father trade me to our enemy for a war debt? It doesn't matter to me that the debt is so high, that some might think it an honor to be priced at such a rate. I can't imagine selling my child. I look down at Lola, the closest thing I've ever had to a child at my young age, and I see the tears streaming down her cheeks. No, I could never, ever give her up.

I mouth to my sister, "It's okay," but that doesn't keep her from crying. She knows we are about to be torn away from one another, and then she will have no one, and I cannot trust my father to take care of her.

I want to turn to Darius, to beg him to watch over Lola, but I can't find the will to look at him right now. Will he speak up for me? And if I am not to be the next leader of the pack, then who will be?

My head swivels to my brother, and on Colt's face, I see the same hint of a smile our mother wears. So he is happy to see me go so that he can become the Alpha after all.

"I'm afraid I simply don't understand." King Kane turns around and goes back up the steps, walking to his throne, and drops down into it. The men on either side of it adjust their postures slightly. My eyes flicker to them, but they don't stay there long. With the king in the room, no one else is worthy of much more than a fleeting glance.

Right now, I'm not staring at him because of his visual appeal, though. I'm staring at him because I'm awaiting his verdict. Clearly, he doesn't know why one feeder is worth so much, and neither do I.

"Please, Your Highness." My father literally drops to his knees, dragging my mother down with him. "The war… it's taken everything from my people. We just shipped out our stock piles of natural resources to you. As it is, we may not make it through the winter. We have nothing left to trade or sell…. My people are starving. I don't have enough money left in the accounts to pay you even a third of what I owe you, but I promise you, she is worth it."

King Kane is shaking his head. "If you didn't have the money to pay me back, you should've never borrowed it to begin with. Didn't we have this same discussion fifteen years ago, Bernard? Back when you told me if I loaned you ten million drakes you would be able to use that money to conquer the packs around you, in which case you would easily pay me back twenty million? I told you then I didn't think it was a good idea, but you insisted, and because of your father's relationship with my father, I decided to allow it. Now, here we are, ten years after repayment was due, and you are still falling short on your end of the bargain."

I listen to King Kane's words, and my mouth wants to fall open. So that's what the war has been about? Because my father wasn't able to repay a debt? I do remember, vaguely, the wars with the other packs from when I was a little girl, but I had been told—as had all of the children who were school-aged at the time—that the other packs had attacked us.

My father is quickly becoming a stranger to me.

"It was a fool's errand!" My father releases Mom's hand to lay prostrate on the floor, sobbing. "I cannot blame your anger, Sir. I cannot. I meant to make a name for myself independent of my father, and I failed. Please, have mercy on me."

"I did have mercy on you!" King Kane doesn't seem nearly as agitated as he should be. "I wrote off over half of the debt before we even began to fight. And then, you still refused to give me even that, so I had to take your eastern lands as payment. I know you lost tens of thousands of warriors in the battle, but it wasn't without a price for me either, you know? If I were to add the toll of the war onto what you owed me, you wouldn't be able to repay it in ten of my lifetimes."

His comment makes the man on his left chuckle under his breath, and I suppose it might be a funny remark for a vampire who would live forever if he was never murdered to say he had ten lifetimes.

But no one else is laughing, least of all me.

I understand now that this situation is much different than I ever thought it was. All along, I've believed that the vampires, like the other packs, attacked us, that they simply wanted what was ours, that they even wanted us to feed on. Unlike humans, feeding on wolf shifters doesn't run the risk of creating another vampire, something it is my understanding is against the law for their kind without specific permission from the king for population control issues. We cannot become like them because our bodies naturally know how to combat the venom that turns humans into the undead.

But we can die.

If greedy vampires take too much, we can be drained and killed. While it's not illegal for a vampire to kill a wolf shifter by draining them, it is frowned upon. Most of them prefer our blood or human blood to animals, so it is easier to simply keep a supply of wolf shifters on hand to feed from. Humans can't be kept that way because they must be completely drained and killed with one feeding so as not to break the law about creating more vampires.

Thus, many of our warriors carry tablets containing poison to prevent themselves from being captured and living the miserable life of a feeder.

I have no idea what will happen if the Vampire King refuses my father's offer, but I know we can never repay a sum of that size.

My bottom lip trembles as I begin to formulate a sentence. I need to try and convince King Kane to take me, that I am worth that amount of money, that I will somehow make it worth his while to keep me as a feeder, but before I can open my mouth, my father is standing again.

"I promise you, she's worth it. Look at her. See how beautiful she is?" He turns and beckons in my direction, but his next statement has bile rising up the back of my throat.

"Come here, darling. Come and meet the king… Lola."

3

NOT LOLA

Emory

Lola?

Lola!

The word my father has just spoken fills my head with shock as I try to process what is happening. For the second time in only a few minutes, I cannot believe what my father is saying.

My eyes immediately go to the Vampire King who is clearly surprised by what my father just said, too, because he is sitting bolt upright in his chair.

For a brief second, my eyes meet the king's, and we are looking at one another intensely, sharing a moment of disbelief, sharing a moment of surprise. And in my mind, I am also wondering if I see a hint of disappointment in his eyes as he realizes it is not me that my father is beckoning.

As far as I know, the king should've had no idea which of us was Lola, but with that reaction, I am thinking he must have. But then, he is an intelligent leader who has been the king of Crimson Peak for decades. His youthful looks are a common deception amongst vampires; he is old and wise. He must know his enemies well.

He must know that Lola is my little sister's name, but for a moment, I am wondering if my father knows that. Has he accidentally called out the wrong name?

I look to my mother and see that her smile has widened.

Suddenly, it all becomes clear. Yes, my father did mean to say my little sister's name. His motherless child, the one who was born to him from a scullery maid, who allegedly died in childbirth, though now that I am questioning everything, I have to wonder if that is the truth.

As Lola's sweaty palm starts to leave mine, I am too terrified to let her go. I can see on the king's face that he is unimpressed with my father's offer. Lola is a child. What in the world would a vampire want with a child?

But as Lola steps forward on shaking legs and goes to my father, the Alpha of Moonraker pack begins to explain.

"I know she's young, but she's a good girl." Father puts his arm around Lola's shoulders, and she begins to cry loudly. I step forward, wanting to go to her, but Colt reaches out and latches onto my arm. I feel Darius's presence right behind me as well. They don't want me to interfere.

Father continues. "She's intelligent and strong. She's a hard worker. You'll see. Really. And… if at some point you move your designs past simply feeding, well—"

"That's enough." King Kane cuts my father off before he tries to prostitute my underage sister to him, and I am at least thankful that the bloodsucker seems to have some moral scruples. More than my father, anyway.

"You want me to take this little girl from you in exchange for the money you owe me?" Apparently, I am not the only one still in shock.

"That's right." My father is stepping forward now. He attempts to remove his arm from Lola, but she clings to him. While I can only imagine what she is thinking, who else can she turn to for help, for mercy?

That Vampire King, apparently. "You have two other children, don't you? Why did you choose this one to bargain with?"

My father is back to clearing his throat. "Well, uh... you see... I only have one son. And he will be Alpha one day, so I couldn't possibly offer him. And my older daughter, well, she is a strong warrior. Intelligent, a vital part of our pack."

I feel the weight of that icy blue stare on me again, but I am having trouble processing. My father's words continue to shock me. My brother will be the Alpha one day? But... I have always been told I would lead the pack.

My head turns toward Colt, and I see that his grin has widened as well. It's not quite as broad as our mother's, but he is happy to hear our father proclaim him the next leader in front of our sworn enemy.

'What is he saying?' Darius's voice fills my head via the mind-link 'I thought you were meant to be Alpha.'

I can't answer him. All I can do is shake my head.

Lies. Everything my father has ever told me has been a lie. From my place in the pack, to who started the war, to why we have been fighting for so long. Is there a single word he's ever told me that is true?

"She's worth the money, I promise you." My father frees himself from Lola's grip and gives her a little shove forward.

The moment I've been expecting and dreading unfolds before me as Lola completely loses it. Her soft cries turn into shrieks as she throws herself back at my father. "Daddy, no!" she begs, latching onto his arm. "Please, Daddy! Don't make me go with him. I love you, Daddy! Luna Vivian, please!"

"Lola, stop that this instant!" my father barks pushing her off again. "Lola! I command you as your father and your Alpha to stop this blubbering right now! Show the king that you're an obedient child!"

"She is a child!"

The words leave my mouth before I can stop them as I yank my arm free from my brother and step forward against my father's orders. He had told us before we even left that no matter what happens, we had to remain together. Solidified.

But he is the one who threw that out the door when he offered to leave one of us behind.

I go to Lola, and she turns and runs to me, throwing her arms around me. "Please, please, Emory! Please, save me!"

I keep my eyes locked on the man on the dais as I hold her against me. "It's okay, baby. It's okay. I won't let this happen. I will never let anyone hurt you." I mean every word I say. I have no idea how I can be successful against a room full of vampires and my own traitorous parents and pack members, but I will not let my father do this.

"Emory!" my father scolds. "Get back in line." He is looking at me, his eyes turned from the king. In my head, I hear his voice. 'Don't fuck this up!'

I shake my head. "I'm sorry, Father, but if you want to leave Lola here, you will have to kill me first. It was one thing for me to stand here and listen to you barter for what I could only assumed was my own hand in all of this, but now, to hear you say you will leave your twelve-year-old here, alone, in the castle of your greatest enemy? I am beginning to question everything I've ever known about you!"

"How dare you say such things to your Alpha!" The voice booming comes from my left—my brother. "Show some respect, sister! As the next Alpha, I command it."

"You have no authority over me, little brother." I narrow my gaze at Colt, knowing I could beat his ass without ever even letting go of Lola. He knows it, too. That's why he doesn't move. He is only trying to show Father he's made the right choice for the next Alpha.

With Colt back in his place, I turn my venomous gaze to my mother. "I can't believe you'd approve of this."

She lowers her eyes, knowing I'm right. I can't even look behind me at Darius and his family. If Darius were truly to be my mate one day, wouldn't he stand up for me? But he's not saying a word. He doesn't want to ruin his chances of being Beta one day—Colt's Beta.

"You are Emory." The words leaving King Kane's mouth are not a question.

I nod. "I am Emory Moonraker, first born of Alpha Bernard Moonraker, leader of the Moonraker pack." I keep my chin held high as I speak. "I'm sorry to cause a disturbance in your throne room, King Kane, but I'm afraid I can't stand idly by and let you take a child as repayment for the debt owed to you."

He arches an eyebrow at me. "I don't believe I ever said I accepted the girl as payment."

I swallow hard but try not to show him any fear. He can sense it, though. Like wolf shifters, vampires have incredible capabilities when it comes to all of their senses. He can likely see the fine hairs on my skin, not to mention smelling the change in pheromones when I began to realize what my father was doing and terror filled me from head to toe.

"Miss Emory," he says, his gaze unwavering. "What do you propose I do in order to clear up this debt? Your father says that you are intelligent and an asset to the pack. Surely, you must know quite a bit about the financial state of Moonraker pack."

I take a deep breath before I decide it is best to work with the only possible ally I have in the room, and right now, that's him. "I must say a great deal of information is being revealed to me for the first time today, Your Highness."

A rich chuckle escapes his lips, and while I don't find what I said funny in the least because it's true, I am glad he is at least at ease.

"I do know of our financial struggles, and I am unfortunately able to confirm that we cannot possibly pay you such a steep debt, not any time soon. I would be more than willing to do whatever I can to earn the money for you."

Before he can comment, my father asks me, "Doing what? No one in our pack has that sort of money. We have no allied packs anymore. You'd never be able to pay off that debt if you live to be two hundred years old."

"A short life," I hear the man to King Kane's left say, and they both snicker. My eyes go to him only briefly. He is not quite as tall as the king but his build is much broader, with muscular shoulders and powerful arms. He has a mop of curly black hair that is different than most of the other vampires I've seen.

The man on the king's right is older in appearance, shorter and not as muscled, with spectacles which must be left over from his human life because vampires do not need eyeglasses. He is a vampire, though. I can tell by his skin tone and eyes.

The king is still staring at me, and I can't tell if I'm meant to say something else or if he's only thinking.

"What about you?" King Kane asks me, standing. He takes a few casual steps in my direction, descending to the second step of the dais. "Emory Moonraker, are you worth five million drakes?"

My heart stops beating for a moment as I contemplate what he is asking me. Am I worth the money—am I willing to say that I believe a trade for me would be worth forgiving my father's debt?

For a moment, I let my mind wander over what will happen when we leave here. If King Kane accepts Lola, I will fight. I will lose. Either the vampires will kill me, or my own family will. And Lola will have to stay behind. I'll be dead. I'll never be able to help her break free.

If he doesn't accept her, he will likely kill my father. Colt will become Alpha, and I will be forced to help my cocky, untrained, ill-prepared brother rule the pack. But if my father does live, he will never forgive me for speaking out against him.

So... I can never go home again.... Not to the home I knew a few hours ago before this disaster began to unfold.

I don't want to stay here. Images of pale, thin, dying feeders come to mind, their lips dry and cracked, their eyes sunken. I've heard the horror stories. They live in squalor and pray for death.

Lola's crying isn't as loud now. I know the answer I give will cause her to begin to cry again, and there's no one to protect her but me.

And... now, there won't be me.

I nod. "I will make myself worth it. Take me instead." That's all I can say. He can interpret it however he wants. Am I truly worth five million drakes. No. But... if he takes me and lets my sister go, I will find a way to convince him I am.

I hope my blood is sweet like honey to the king or whoever else feeds from me.

King Kane's eyes stay locked on mine for another beat before his lips are moving and he says, "Take her away."

4

I'LL SEE YOU AGAIN--SOMEDAY

Emory

"Take her away."

The Vampire King's declaration echoes off the walls of the throne room as he turns around to walk away. The two men who had been flanking him for the entire duration of the meeting move forward, toward me.

"Does this mean we have a deal?" my father calls after King Kane, and obviously, my father has decided in the span of a few moments that he is no longer concerned about the fact that he said he didn't want to let me take my little sister's place. Apparently, if it means the debt is paid, he's willing to give up any of his children.

Well, the female ones anyway.

The Vampire King turns around and looks at my father for a few seconds before he simply says, "Fuck off, Bernard," and then turns around to go.

I believe that probably does mean that the debt is forgiven and the king is too busy presently to take care of filing whatever paperwork needs to be handled in order to make sure that is the case, but I don't know.

And at the moment, I have more important matters to attend to.

"No! No! Not my Emory!" Lola is screeching, digging her nails into me, trying to hang on to me as I do my best to separate from her just a little bit. The two male vampires are hovering just in front of us, giving us a moment, but I can tell neither one of them wants to put up with what they probably see as a display of bullshit.

"Lola! Lola!" I say, prying her hands away from me but keeping hold of her fingers so she can't latch on to me again. I drop to one knee and look into her eyes. "Lola, baby, it's okay," I tell her, forgetting my own fears and sorrows at the moment. "It'll be all right."

She is crying so hard that her tears are mingling with the snot streaming out of her nose, and the normally poised young woman who cares so much about her appearance, who is always asking to go shopping or get her hair and nails done, looks like the child she truly is. I want to squeeze her tight and never let her go, but I have to convince her that she will be all right.

I have to try to tell her that she can trust these people, go home with them, the father that tried to sell her and the stepmother who has always hated her. The brother who is so focused on the fact that he is set to be the next Alpha that he appears oblivious to the chaos around him. I have to look this person that I love more than all others in the face and tell her she will be fine, even though I have no way of knowing for sure that she will be.

"Go home, sweet child." I let go of one hand enough to smooth her hair back. "I'll talk to you soon." I don't know if that is the truth because I have no idea what the rules are for feeders calling home, but if everything I've heard is true, I will never see anyone I've ever met before today again for the rest of my life, which could consist of years of agony or a few minutes of torture before I am completely drained and lying dead somewhere in the castle.

"No," she says again, but this time all of the fight is out of her.

From behind me, I hear Darius's mother, Margaret, say, "I will see to her, Emory." Her hand comes down on my shoulder, and I can hear in the kind woman's voice that she is also crying. "Don't worry about Lola. I will look after her."

I look up now, unable to keep my tears back any longer, and I know that I might not be able to count on my own family or even Darius, the man I imagined I'd be mated to and spend the rest of my life with, but I can count on Margaret. Darius is behind her, looking away from me, and it's not a face that lets me know he's just sad that I am not going to be his mate. He is indifferent.

I give her a smile of gratitude through the tears that are beginning to slide down my cheeks and then turn back to Lola. "See?" I ask her. "Everything is going to be okay. You know that Margaret will keep you safe and happy."

"But… I… w-want… you," she manages to get out on the verge of hyperventilating.

One of the men behind her, the towering brute of a vampire with messy curls clears his throat. He is trying to politely tell me that I am preventing him from following King Kane's order, and he doesn't appreciate it.

"I'll see you soon," I promise her. It is an empty promise, and we both know it.

"But… how?" she squeaks out.

I force a smile to my lips. "One way or another."

The other man, the older looking one, reaches for my arm. He is not as patient as the younger looking one.

"One moment." I use my authoritative voice with him. He doesn't withdraw his hand, but he doesn't keep reaching either.

Leaning forward, I kiss Lola's cheek, and squeeze her tight. "I love you so much," I tell her. "More than anything in the whole world. I will see you again. One way or another." I don't mention that it might not be until we are reunited by the Moon Goddess on the other side.

"I love you, too, sister," she says, and I can tell that she's resigned herself to the fact that she cannot save me. She cannot interject herself into the situation and be the one who is taken instead of me as I have, and she cannot beg to come along with me.

As tempting as it is for me to throw myself at the mercy of the

Vampire King and beg him to let her stay with me, I would never subject my Lola to the life of a feeder, a life spent living or dying among our enemies. No, I love her too much for that. Even if it means I never lay eyes on her sweet face again, I do believe she is better off with the pack. Perhaps my parents have failed her miserably, but my pack will care for her. I have to believe that.

As the younger vampire gently guides Lola away from me and to Margaret's open arms, I stand and take a deep breath. The older vampire is glaring at me already, and we haven't even left the throne room.

I turn to my parents. My mother has her face covered as she cries silent tears. I can imagine she didn't mean for this to happen. She obviously wouldn't hesitate for a moment to see Lola go, but me? She actually cares about me—or so I've always thought.

My father's eyes are locked on my face, and though he hasn't shed a tear because he is in the home of his enemy, I can see that he is on the verge of losing control of his emotions.

"Emory," he says, shaking his head slowly. "I never—"

I cut him off. "I will never forgive you for this, Father. Never." I look him straight in the eyes and watch his face crumble. "You are not the man I always thought you were." The older vampire's hands clamp onto my arms. Long, yellowing nails, wrinkled fingers, I am disgusted by his cold touch, but I don't pull away.

Instead, I continue to address my father. "One day, you will realize how despicable you truly are, to have waged war and lied about it, to have betrayed your pack by spending money you did not have to acquire territory you did not need, and then sacrificing your own children to attempt to make amends. May the Moon Goddess scorn you, and may your enemies receive the justice they deserve."

That is all I have to say, so when the vampires begin to take me away, I walk with them, not needing to be dragged.

I hear my father barking my name, not out of concern anymore but out of anger. Lola is crying again, screaming for me, and I hear a thunk on the floor that tells me what has happened before I glance over my shoulder to see my mother lying in a heap. My brother runs to her while my father continues to swear at me. Margaret has Lola buried in her skirts.

I look at Darius, and the expression on his face is unreadable. I can't tell if he's complacent, irate, or… shocked.

We reach the dais and I nearly stumble over the bottom step because I'm not looking where I'm going. The vampire's claws sink into my arm, and I smell a spurt of my own blood as it trickles down my arm. I look up at him, wondering if the scent will entice him to begin feeding on me right away, but he only shouts. "Watch where you're fucking going!" and hauls me up the rest of the stairs.

"Hey, Clark," the other vampire says coming up on my right and getting in front of us. "Be nice. She's had a rough day."

Clark, the old guy, says nothing, only growls at me, and leads me through the curtain that the other one, the one who actually looks like he might be mean but clearly isn't, is holding open for us.

Beyond the curtain is a door, and when it is opened for me, I fully expect to see an empty hallway or several guards.

What I don't expect to see is familiar blue eyes staring at me.

The Vampire King has waited on the other side of the door? For me?

But it isn't me he is addressing. His eyes leave my face without a word as he says to the younger vampire, "Rainer, I've got to go out to the garden." He sighs loudly and drags a hand down his chin. "Will you accompany me please?"

Rainer—the younger vampire—laughs that rich chuckle again before he says, "Sure. I love a show."

I have no idea what they are talking about, but it doesn't concern me.

King Kane mutters, "I did not need all of this fucking drama today," and shakes his head. Then, turning to Clark, who is still gripping me tightly, he says, "She volunteered. You can probably loosen your grip. You cut her arm. Be more careful."

The man only grumbles a bit, and I think I might've heard an apology to his king, not me, in there.

King Kane tells him. "Find our guest a... room. Then, go check on the situation with the unhappy maids."

"Yes, Your Majesty," Clark says and I can hear he's not happy with one or both of those assignments.

King Kane's eyes land on me one more time before he turns to walk away. Right before his head swivels around, he makes the quiet remark, "You're very brave."

I have no time to respond to that, even if I knew what to say. He is gone, down the hallway in a blur, Rainer with him, leaving me alone with Clark.

"All right, missy," he growls. "You're coming with me. And if you don't want me to drag you, you'd best keep up. I've got lots of fucking things to do today."

He gives me a little shove to get my feet going, and I momentarily wonder what would happen if I tried to take off back the way I've come, to throw open the door, make my way through the curtain, and out through the throne room, back down the hall filled with bloody paintings.

I'd never make it. I know that. And even if I did, where would I go? Not to be with my parents, that's for certain.

So... once again, I resolve myself to my fate and following along behind him as he quickly navigates the hallways, taking more twists and turns than I am able to keep track of.

Eventually, we stop at a door that is guarded by two male vampires, their eyes staring dead ahead like the ones that guarded the throne room.

Clark produces a key and opens the door, a waft of mold, mildew, blood, and urine hitting me fully in the face as it swings ajar.

In front of me is a staircase leading down, and I know where we are going now. To the cells, the dungeon, the place where the feeders are kept, and most likely....

The place where I am going to die.

5

MOVE THE MOON

Kane

A MILLION THOUGHTS are flying through my head as I make my way down the hallway toward the rose garden, Rainer, my best friend and second, at my side. I can tell he is dying to say something, but even he has to be careful at a time like this not to say something to piss me off, and he knows it.

As we approach the door that leads out to the rose garden, located on the south lawn, about fifty yards from the castle, Rainer says, "Well… that was unexpected."

All I can do at first is grunt as my mind goes back over what has just happened. While I had known better than to expect Alpha Bernard to show up here with the money he owed me—in its entirety, anyway—I had no idea that he was going to try to convince me to take one of his children instead.

And then… when he'd told me it was the younger girl, the one that's barely out of diapers compared to me at a hundred and forty-seven, well… I wanted to just kill him and be done with it.

But… then a remarkable thing had happened. With absolutely no concern for her own well-being, his other daughter, the one with the long red locks and the stunning jade eyes, had interjected herself between the insane proposition her father had offered me and what she likely sees as a miserable future living with the enemies of her pack.

The devil only knows what sorts of lies she's been fed over the years about me and my kind.

Her bravery is remarkable to me. I still can't believe anyone would be willing to subject themselves to that sort of an uncertain future. What I'm going to do with her, I don't know, but she can be of value to me in more ways than I am currently aware, I'm sure.

"You didn't tell Clark which room to take her to," Rainer reminds me.

He's right. I should've been more specific. I think perhaps I should send him a quick mind message to tell him which room I had been thinking of when Rainer pushes the exterior door open, and even though she's far away, on the other side of the rose garden, I hear the screeches of Opal's voice, and my stomach tightens.

"No! You never fucking listen to me!" I hear her shouting. "What the actual fuck is the matter with you, anyway? Are you some sort of a fucking moron?"

I stop in my tracks, not wanting to move forward, not wanting to deal with this after what's already transpired this morning. Rainer stops too, and I can't fault him when he hooks a thumb over his shoulder and says, "I've gotta go. There's a… former governess with a skewer waiting for me in the library who wants to shove the sharp wood right through one of my ears and out the other, and I kinda think that would be more fun than listening to Opal scream at the poor wedding coordinator."

I narrow my gaze at him, and we both know he's not going anywhere. "You always have had the strangest fetishes," I say to him.

He shrugs, "The heart wants what the heart wants."

"Come on," I say, stepping forward. I take a deep breath because that's what one is supposed to do, not because oxygen has any usefulness in my body.

I see that the overcast skies from earlier today have dissipated while I was inside dealing with the likes of Alpha Bernard. I would say that's a good thing, but the sun always makes me a bit nauseated. At least it doesn't burn my flesh and turn me into a pile of ashes as is rumored of my kind.

It really is silly what humans will write in books.

The closer I get to where Opal is standing with her friends and the poor wedding coordinator, Blanca, the best in the kingdom, one who came with thousands of excellent reviews, the more irritated I become until I'm ready to claw my ears off just so I don't have to listen to her. A curse on the asshole servant who came to fetch me while I was awaiting the removal of the Alpha's daughter from the throne room. Though, in fairness, the servant was just doing his job.

"Do these look like the queen consorts fucking prized red roses?" Opal is shouting as Rainer and I step around a large hedge of pink flowers. "Well, do they?"

Opal is perfectly named. Her alabaster skin is nearly opaque in the glints of sunlight that reach her beneath the parasol one of her maidens is holding above her head. There are three other girls with her, and while they are pretty enough, none of them can hold a candle to Opal. Her raven hair is pulled up in a perfect bun on top of her head, with little curls framing her beautiful face. Her blood red lips give a sort of glowing quality to her sapphire blue eyes. Her eyes are by far the brightest of any vampire I've ever seen.

There's no question that Opal Maxwell is a beauty. It was one of the selling points her family had made when they came to visit last year, speaking to my mother and I about how an alliance would do both of our kingdoms well. Not only could we work together against our enemies, there was a good chance offspring could also be born from this union since Opal was also a vampire since birth, like myself. We are a rarity, and our kind is said to be a gift from the powers that be....

Whatever powers those are. At the moment, the only being I'm certain exists beyond vampires, humans, and wolf shifters is the devil himself....

Especially as she continues to scream at the wedding planner.

Blanca stands with her shoulders back and her head held high, her usual stance from what I can tell. But even she has a tipping point, and I can see her on the cusp of breaking.

"Are you even listening to me, you stupid bitch?" Opal shouts at the woman.

"I hear everything you are saying, Princess," Blanca says. "There's really no need to yell."

"I guess there is since you've not done a fucking thing to fix this since you first told me about it ten minutes ago!" Opal is flinging her hands around, causing her long, layered red skirts to bustle about, and the more she does so, the more she looks like a bloody tornado.

"Seriously, my mom is calling for me," Rainer tries again. I elbow him in the side, and he continues along with me.

"Your mom died decades ago," I mutter, and the two of us arrive at the scene of the battle, ready to figure out what is going on. "Opal?" I say, causing her to jump a little at the sound of my voice. The whirling dervish has been too busy with her chastising to notice my approach.

"Oh! Kane, darling!" she says, putting on her best "good girl" face and blinking her long eyelashes in my direction. "How are you, dear? How was your meeting with the werewolf?"

I grimace at the use of the derogatory term. I've told her we shouldn't use that word. There are some wolf shifters in the castle that are quite useful and good people, but she likes to think of them all as unhinged beasts. In Bernard's case, that probably fits.

I see Blanca relax only a margin as I take the focus off her. "It was fine," I tell Opal. "But… I don't understand what's happening here."

"Oh, well, you're not going to believe it!" Opal says, releasing my arm so that she can gesture wildly again. "I told this idiotic bit—"

"Opal?" I say, giving her a stern look. She takes a deep breath and tries again. We've talked about how she needs to behave like a polished princess all of the time, not just when she thinks "important people" are listening.

"This Blanca," she modifies, "that I wish for the ceremony to be held in the middle of your mother's antique roses, beneath the light of the full moon, but she insists on trying to make me choose! And I won't hear of it!"

The three girls behind Opal, two blondes, one whose color is probably out of a bottle, and one with orangish-red hair that isn't nearly as stunning as the locks on the head of that shifter girl, all humph in agreement.

I look to Blanca, knowing there has to be a good reason for her dying on this sword. "Blanca, what's the problem?" I ask in a calm voice.

She clears her throat, something most people must do while gathering the courage to speak to me, even when I'm not trying to be intimidating. "Your Majesty, the princess would like for me to somehow change the course of the bodies that navigate the heavens."

Biting back a chuckle, I nod, getting the gist of the problem. "She wants the moon to be in a specific spot over the rose garden at an exact moment in time when it will not be?" I ask.

Blanca's head rocks back and forth, her light eyes blinking in relief as she sees that I understand.

Turning to Opal, I say, "It can't happen, Princess. The moon won't be in this location, right over head at the time you want to get married. You can change the time. You can change the location. Perhaps you can even change the date. But you can't move the moon." The third option, the one where she changes the date... that's the one I'm hoping for. I have rushed into this marriage of convenience for my clan's sake not realizing it is actually quite inconvenient, and even though Opal and I both know this is a marriage only for the sake of such a thing—she certainly takes many lovers into her room—I have been second guessing my decision a lot lately.

"No!" she shouts, pulling down on my arm. "I can't change any of those things! It must be at three in the morning, during the fall equinox, here, in the rose garden, and I want it over there!" She points about seventy yards to the north. "That's where the prettiest flowers are!"

I am not going to run the risk of transplanting my mother's

favorite flowers for this immature woman-child. "Well, there's nothing else that can be done. Why can't the moon be slightly to the south of the ceremony? It'll be like… backlighting. You can use it to show off your best features."

She mulls that over for a moment before she leans close to me and whispers, "You mean my breasts?" and winks at me.

I did not mean her breasts. I actually had nothing in mind at all. But if that is what she needs to hear, I lean over and give her a quick peck on her cheek. "I have business to attend to, Opal. You handle this, and no more shouting. I don't want to have to come back out here."

"Yes, my darling," she says as if there's actually any affection between us. Perhaps she thinks there is. I am being polite. I am going through the motions. I am about to tear two thorns from the rose bushes and gash my own eyes out….

As I head back into the castle, I see a familiar form leaning against the wall, waiting….

Waiting for me.

A crooked grin on his face, I can tell he has something to tell me that he thinks is amusing that I am sure to think is anything but.

"What the fuck does he want?" Rainer says, as much contempt in his voice as I feel inside of me.

"I have no fucking idea," I admit as I address him. "Lex?"

His grin widens as he says, "Hello, brother."

6

IT'S BEST NOT TO RESIST

Emory

I FOLLOW Clark down the stairs, deeper into the darkness, as they wind and twist. When we get to the dungeon, I take a deep breath, seeing dirty people in rags sitting in cages that are barely six feet by six feet. It's no wonder that no one wants to be a feeder.

"These are the regular prisoners," Clark explains, and I feel a lot better. I realize as he is speaking that most of these people are actually vampires, so they can't be feeders.

Feeders like me....

I follow him as he goes to another door down a narrow hallway. This one takes a key, too, and from the looks of it, it's a different key than the one he used to get us down here. More soldiers with death stares stand guard. The Vampire King uses a lot of security precautions when it comes to his feeders.

I wonder why....

We head down another flight of stairs, and as we walk, Clark answers my unspoken question. "Most of the members of court can be trusted to feed without killing when it comes to wolf shifters. They know their limits. The staff, however, that is a different story. Sometimes, they over indulge. For that reason, King Kane has established a system for draining blood from humans via a needle and tube that he uses to keep the staff fed. But just in case some of them, particularly the younger vampires, get a bit hangry, he keeps the feeders locked up for only those who can be trusted."

I don't ask the myriad of questions that fill my head. How young is young when you it's so difficult to make any new vampires? Are their vampires here that have been made illegally? What happens if a feeder feels themselves slipping away and tries to fight back or beg for their life?

All of those questions fill my mind, but I don't ask them.

I hope to make a confidant here. I think it's too much to think of making a friend, but someone I can confide in, someone I can ask questions of, that would be nice. I was easily able to make friends with staff members back home, and because of it, Lola and I were always treated differently than the others. We were treated better—given little gifts, like extra meat pies from the cook, flowers from the gardener, having our beds made extra tidily, etc. Maybe I can find a way to make the workers here like me, too. Although, if they are the most dangerous, maybe not. I have to wonder about the guards. Surely, the Vampire King would only put the most trustworthy people as guards.

Maybe whomever feeds on me will like me and talk to me about what's going on. I have no hope of escaping any time soon now that I'm down in the bowels of Castle Graystone, but I haven't lost hope of getting out one day. I have to see Lola again. Her image flashes before my eyes, and I start to tear up, but I snuffle my tears back because I can't let Clark or the guards see me cry—they'll think I'm weak.

When we step out through another locked, guarded door that takes yet a different key, I gasp, and it takes a moment for me to will my feet to move.

This is… not as awful as what I'd witnessed above me, but it is not at all what I was hoping for either.

It's the smell that hits me first. It's hard to put one's finger on exactly what it is. Being a wolf shifter, I have a more sensitive nose than most creatures. I can distinguish thousands of different aromas from one another and smell as much as a drop of blood from over twenty miles away.

But this? This is the first time I've been in a situation where I can't distinguish exactly what I'm smelling. It's... blood, urine, human sweat, some form of deteriorating tissue, mildew, damp concrete, dirty bedding, bed bugs, roaches, rats, rat droppings, and something else very distinct that I don't think I've ever smelled before all mingling together into some sort of funky potpourri. It's the most horrid scent that's ever coated my lungs.

"That smell?" Clark says, turning to look at me through his useless, wire-rimmed glasses, "That's the smell of death."

I stare at him, blinking for a moment, as he begins to laugh and then walks forward.

The people here don't look like people at all. They're mostly wolf shifters, like me, though some are the humans he was referring to that can be drained by a needle, and at a glance, I'd say I can see at least fifty figures, but all of them look like zombies or ghosts. They wear white gowns that fall to their knees, stained, dirty, smelly clothes that others have probably worn before them, probably without a proper wash.

They sit in cells or in a public area where it looks like they are allowed to play chess or checkers, or participate in some other activities. I see a bookshelf with a bunch of old paperbacks that look to be falling apart. The sun doesn't reach down here, and the bulbs that hang above our heads are dim, some of them flickering.

Their skin is nearly as translucent as the vampires' They are dirty, with greasy hair and sallow cheekbones. None of them are at a healthy weight. All of them have bags beneath their eyes. When my eyes meet those of another girl who looks to be about my age, it's like there's no life there. She stares at me, unblinking, not speaking, not reacting at all, as I follow Clark down another hallway lined with cells.

"Since you're new, I'm sure you'll be chosen by a nobleman or noblewoman soon enough. It doesn't take long for new feeders to get used up. Expect it. But at least you'll have some free time down here, unlike the other dungeon.

I don't know what to say to that. I'm supposed to be thankful to be here?

He pauses at a guards' station and asks, "What cell's available?"

"Uh, fifteen," the guy barks back, glancing down at a list on a clip-board. "Died this morning."

"Perfect," Clark says, tapping the wooden stand at the station a couple of times in thanks before he leads me forward.

I want to ask if fifteen has been cleaned since someone died in it, but I probably already know the answer to that and can't bring myself to ask. Nothing will change whether it has been or not.

As we walk, Clark says, "You'll get three meals a day here. Mostly protein mixture. I hear it doesn't taste good, but you're required to eat it and drink all of the necessary ounces of water to make sure you can continue to produce blood. You'll probably get light headed when you've fed a lot of us over a short period of time, but when someone chooses you, you can't say no. If you start to feel too sick, let the guards know, and they'll see about getting a medic down here. Some-times they do, sometimes they don't."

I want to ask him, if he knows all of this, why does he allow it to happen? Does the king know about this? I have to imagine that he does. He seems to know everything.

We arrive at a cell that's probably ten by twelve if that. It has a cot in one corner covered in a sheet and blanket. It's not made, and I assume that's because it's not clean. In the corner is a toilet and a small sink.

That's it. That's all there is.

While it does have walls and a door and isn't just bars, the door is made out of see-through material, something thicker than glass. Still, if I pee, everyone is gonna see it who walks by.

"We'll get you a uniform. You're allowed to shower once a week. They'll tell you which day. You can go out to the common area any time between seven in the morning and six in the evening. And remember, if you shift, you'll be killed immediately. In a day or two, you'll be too weak to do so, but before that happens, don't try it. Down here, the only people you'll be able to reach via your mind-link are the other prisoners, and most of them are too weak to respond, so don't bother to try to reach someone to break you out. And as you saw, we have a lot of security they'd have to get through in order to get to you. It'd take the king ten, fifteen minutes to get down here and that's with everyone reacting to his presence and letting him in." For some reason he chuckles when he says that, but I don't get the joke.

I have nothing to say, so I say nothing.

"I know you're brave. Probably think you're smart. Don't worry. This place will break you."

I turn and look at him as a cocky smirk spreads across his face. I don't know this man, and I don't know the king, but I have to wonder... does King Kane know who he's trusting with such important tasks? I have to think that the other guy... Rainer... wouldn't have treated me this way. I may be the daughter of their primary enemy, but I am still a person.

As he turns to walk out the door, he says, "Oh, and if the guards come calling, well, it's best to just let them do what they're going to do."

That gets my attention. "Excuse me?" I ask, my body whipping around to face him as I feel myself being threatened.

His laughter fills my cell, and a tingling races down my spine. "Oh, I saw the way you and that other wolf were looking at one another. It's not like you're a virgin."

My mouth drops open as I try to figure out how to respond to that. It's none of his business, but I am a virgin.

"That's it," he says. "That'll do."

I close my mouth with a snap, wishing I could shift and teach him a lesson, but I'm not even old enough to have met my wolf yet, so I can't shift to protect myself if I want to. He doesn't need to know that.

I have other ways of protecting myself that don't require me to have a wolf, and regardless of his advice, I know, if a guard comes looking for anything, even to feed off of me, he's going to encounter some resistance.

When Clark leaves, I toss myself down onto my bed, pulling my knees up and leaning against the wall. I refuse to cry. I absolutely refuse. Crying will just cloud my judgment, and I've got to keep my head on straight.

Some time passes—I don't know how much—and then, I hear footsteps approaching, and even though there are a lot of cells through here, I know they are coming to mine.

The snickers I hear tell me there's more than one of them. And when shadows fill my doorway, I am ready to defend myself.

I'd rather die than let some nasty guard put his hands on my body. I wasn't sold as a breeder or a whore. I was sold as a feeder to the king —and I'm not baring my body for anyone. Not even him.

7

SHE'S NOT IN A ROOM

Kane

"WHAT DO YOU WANT, BROTHER?" I ask as I take in my younger brother's cocky grin. He clearly has something up his ass or else he wouldn't be over here bothering with me at all. Most of the time, he is out chasing women or feeding on whores in the human village nearby, which means, of course, that he's killing. He does so with absolutely no moral reservations.

"Just came to check on the wedding planning," Lex says with a smooth chuckle. His blond locks dance around his pretty face as he does so. He's slender, with delicate features that used to make others mistake him for a girl when he was younger. If he wasn't such a womanizer, it would be easy to see him liking men, not just because of the way he looks but because he often acts effeminate, as well as... emotional.

But he'll be the first one to tell you he only swings one way, and I don't think it's a matter of him protesting too much.

"She's on the warpath, as usual," I reply with a sigh.

"I know. I could hear her screaming from my room on the top floor," he replies. "I had my window open, but still…."

"I've taken care of it," I tell him, but he doesn't look like he believes me. He's probably right. It's just a matter of time before she starts screaming again.

He adjusts his weight and says, "I bet you're super glad you made the decision you did, brother. Marrying her is definitely going to help the clan out, and ultimately, it will be worth it. That way, when you decide to retire in a couple of hundred years, you'll have a child to take your place and won't have to worry about leaving the kingdom to a shithead like me."

A chuckle catches in my throat. I know what he's getting at. He's jealous. He wanted me to let him be king at some point, the way our father's older brother abdicated the throne to him before the Great Vampire War, which started before either of us was even born and ended when I was about thirty, which is when our father was killed. I took over then, won the war, and established Crimson Peak as the kind of kingdom people know not to fuck with.

Still… that could all be ruined if the right asshole was left in charge, and I'm pretty sure the asshole standing right in front of me could undo all of my hard work in a matter of minutes if he wanted to.

"You? As king, Lex?" Rainer asks, his chuckle flying freely. "That sounds like a horror story yet to be written."

"Fuck you, Rainer." Lex pushes up off of the wall, clearly ready to fight. The two of them have never gotten along.

I'm not in the mood for any fighting today, though. "All right. That's enough," I say, and they both back down immediately. Rainer because he knows the mood I'm in; Lex because he knows Rainer could rip his head off with one hand if he really wanted to. "I need to go check on our guest."

"Guest?" Lex repeats, perking up. "Who's that now?"

"She's off limits," I tell him, using my most authoritative tone. "That prick Alpha Bernard brought me his daughter instead of the money he owes me."

"What?" Lex's eyes widen. "Seriously? I mean, I know it was only, like, five million drakes, which is pocket change to you, but still. What the fuck would you want with his daughter?"

"He thought she'd make a good feeder." I don't even want to get into how he'd meant the other daughter. Lex doesn't need to know all of that bullshit. "I need to find Clark and see what room he put her in."

"Clark?" Lex echoes. Apparently, listening is not his strong suit today. "Oh, I ran into him a few seconds ago. He said he was on an errand for you, but he wasn't coming from the guest suits."

My heart wants to race at just the mention of Clark potentially doing something different than what I told him to do. The old cuss was my father's advisor first, and I'm not always sure I can trust him. Still, my instructions were pretty simple—find her a room. "Where was he coming from?" I ask.

Thoughts of something happening to Emory Moonraker when she just got here flood my mind, but I remind myself I'm overreacting. She's a strong, brave woman, and I'm sure she's fine. Perhaps he just found her a room in a different wing of the house, away from the vampire guests we have staying in the usual wing—like Opal.

What Opal would do to Emory, given the chance, I didn't even want to know....

"He was coming up the stairs when I met him," Lex says, running his fingernails along the shoulder of his yellow velvet jacket.

"The stairs?" Rainer repeats for me. "What stairs?"

Lex takes a deep breath and slowly lets it out, clearly looking for a dramatic effect, before he says, "The dungeon."

"The... dungeon?" I repeat, wanting to shout every swear word I've ever heard in my life.

"He's just fucking with you," Rainer says, but I'm already moving down the hallway. I don't know if Lex is just trying to get a rise out of me or if it's true, but I did not intend for Emory to be taken to the dungeon.

I hurry toward the door, thinking about all of the awful things that can happen to a new girl in the feeder's dungeon. The wolf shifters down there are usually prisoners of war, criminals, or people who have decided they'd rather come here than try to repay their debts. A large swath of Moonraker pack's lands have become mine lately, and while I try to make sure those people can remain free, collecting taxes is an important part of any kingdom's functionality.

I don't typically allow people to sell their offspring to pay for their debts, so most of the people that are there for that reason have decided it would be best to be a feeder for a few years and then be released—debt free. If they survive.

Ahead of me, I see the door to the main dungeon and order the guards to open it as I dart forward. They do so, and I fly down the stairs, headed for the next door, the next set of stairs, and the next level down.

I haven't been in either dungeon for years, especially not the feeder one. Most of the time, the blood I consume is drained via needle, cleaned, flavored, and served to me in a goblet. It's not that I don't like biting people, but it seems a little undignified to me. I like to have my blood as a meal with rare meat and fruit. Contrary to what most humans believe, vampires can eat other food, but we need blood to function. If we go too long without it, we will shut down. We can't die without it. Only a beheading or a stake to the heart can do that, but we can feel the effects of a human death over and over again until we are able to get the liquid that sustains our ability to function.

I will have to explain to Rainer and Lex later why I am in such a hurry. They will not understand my need to make sure that Emory is okay. But after the courage I saw her display earlier in the day, I am worried for her. She doesn't deserve to be tormented by the guards or chastised by the other feeders. I only hope she hasn't been down here too long, and when I find her, she's safe.

Rainer is behind me, but he's not in such a hurry. I can hear his boots echoing off of the steps at the top of the stairs when I demand that the guards open the door at the bottom. I have my keys, but they should be ready for this.

They're not. They fumble with the keys, and I want to tear both of their heads off.

Finally, the door opens, and a pungent smell hits my nostrils. I recoil, knowing exactly what it is and praying I'm not too late.

It's the smell of death.

I step into the main room and have a quick look around. I see dozens of feeders dressed in white gowns, mulling around, the vacant looks in their eyes alarming. My eyes flash over their sullen face. They look like shit. They look like they are mostly dead already.

A million questions flash through my mind. Clark is in charge of the conditions down here. How the fuck did he let it get this bad? The last time I was down here, it was well-lit, with lots of activities, games, laughter. The feeders were well cared for, dressed in their regular clothes, clean, and fairly happy. But these people look like they would rather just have it all ended for them, and the thought of it makes me disgusted—not to mention the smell.

It smells like piss, shit, vomit, old rotten blood, sweat, and dead bodies, not to mention the dampness of the dungeon.

I don't have time to stop and try to fix all of these problems at the moment, though, as I rush to the guard at the station that leads to most of the cells. "Where's the new girl?" I demand, wanting to grab him and shake him.

"Your Majesty!" he declares, dropping into a bow at the waist. "It is an honor—"

"I don't have time for that, goddamn it. Where is she?" I was alarmed before just at the idea that something might happen to Emory, but now that I'm standing down here, I know I was right to follow my instincts.

This is bad… really bad.

"I'm sorry, Sir," he says, looking at his clipboard. "I just came on for my shift, and I am not aware of a new girl. What's her name, please?"

"Fuck," I mutter. "Emory Moonraker."

He looks down at the paper, still taking his time. "Emory… Emory… Emory…."

"For the love of all things holy!" I shout, abandoning him. "I'll find her myself!"

I take off down the hall, looking in every cell, praying I get to her in time before anything bad happens.

When I hear a commotion in the distance, my instincts tell me that's her. I pick up speed, hoping that I don't get there too late.

If something happens to Emory Moonraker before I even get the opportunity to figure out what it is about her I find so intriguing, heads will roll—and Clark's will be first, regardless of how he served my father.

And that's a promise.

8

THE GUARDS MOVE IN

Emory

"WELL, WHAT DO WE HAVE HERE?"

The snarl from the squatty guard filling the majority of my doorway is enough to set my teeth on edge as my shifter body longs to call forth my wolf to defend myself.

Unfortunately, I'm not quite old enough for that yet and will have to rely upon my other fighting skills to protect myself.

As my eyes meet his, I can't help but pull myself to standing, my hands fisted at my sides. He is short, a bit overweight, it appears, with dark hair, a beard, and those light eyes that look like they're almost sightless. He can see me, though. I feel his eyes roaming all over me.

He's not alone either. Two other guards flank him, one tall and the other with a medium build and a bit of muscle. They all wear the same gray uniforms I've seen on the other guards who work in this part of the castle. It fits the overall ambiance of a dismal, lifeless existence the prisoners here have come to know.

I can't think about any of them right now, though. None of them are going to be able to come and help me. They are all too weak and have their own concerns to occupy what's left of their minds.

"Well, look at that," the first guard says as he enters the room, the others following him. "She thinks she's gonna fight us. Ain't that cute?"

"She best know it's illegal for her to shift down here," the tall one says. "If she does, we'll have no choice but to kill her—after we have our way with her."

His words make my skin crawl. It's fairly clear to me now that they intend to do more than just feed off me.

"I've got the injection right here," the other guy says, patting his pocket. I know they carry shots of wolfsbane and silver nitrate with them that are meant to incapacitate or kill us. I don't want to find out which, but if that's what happens, so be it.

"I got her injection right here," the short guy says, only it's not his pocket he's patting. He grabs his balls and shakes them at me, making a lewd face, and they all three laugh. "Grab 'er for me, fellas."

"Ah, how come you always get to go first?" the tall one asks, giving me a moment to consider my strategy. "I'm tired of your sloppy seconds."

"Or thirds," the other one says.

It's clear that the short one is the leader here, though. He must've been made fun of for his height as a child. Perhaps that's why he is so evil now. That, or maybe he's just an asshole.

"Stop your whining, jackasses," he says. "Now get her."

They move toward me, and I am ready. I kick the tall guy in the stomach while I lash out with my hand and catch the other one in the throat. They both sputter, but they're not completely caught off guard, which makes me think I'm not the first woman to try and fight against them. They manage to grab me by my arms as the third one keeps me from trying to run out the door.

"Nice try, bitch," he says. "But you're not getting away from us." He laughs again, sticking his tongue out at me and licking his lips as he unfastens his pants and pulls them down in the front to expose himself.

This is the first manhood I've ever seen, and while I am disgusted and terrified, part of me also wants to laugh because he is so tiny. I can't help but say, "I guess it's more than just your stature that is short."

The other two guys break into fierce laughter as shorty fumes, his face turning a hue of pink I didn't think a vampire capable of. "What the fuck did you say, little bitch?" he asks me. "You fucked up now, you cunt!" He comes at me as the other two strengthen their grips on my arms, and it is honestly just what I need to perform one of the moves I've perfected in training.

As he comes toward me, I use his torso as a stepladder, twisting my body so that my feet go over the top of my head at the same time as I bring my arms together. It burns in the places where they have their grips on my skin, and in my shoulder blades, but when I hear their skulls whack into one another, it's worth it, especially when they let go.

While the one with his dick out is still stunned, I slam my boot into the crotch of the taller one who is lying on the floor to my right and into the gut of the other one who is lying on my left. Then, as quickly as I can, I advance on the dick, kicking him hard in the abdomen and driving him back against the wall near the bed. He is struggling to recover as I grab hold of his tiny penis and his balls with one hand and twist and pull. He lets out an earsplitting scream, so high pitched, he sounds like a woman in labor, a sound I have heard from all of the births I've attended with my mother over the years, one of her duties as Luna, and while it hurts my ears, I don't let go, not even when the other two get up off the floor and come at me.

I kick out behind me, connecting with the taller one in the face, knocking him against the wall, and hitting the other one with a second kick right in the throat. They both tumble down onto the ground as I turn to the asshole in front of me and head butt him as hard as I can in the nose.

A crack is followed by a spurt of blood which tells me he must've eaten recently. I let go of his privates and am about to toss him across the room when I hear hurried footsteps at the open door and know my battle is just beginning.

Of course, they've likely used their telepathic powers to call for help. I keep one hand on the dick as I turn to the door ready to kick who ever walks in first, but just as my foot goes up, I see a flash of familiar black hair and pull my boot back. He wraps his hand around my foot to protect himself, and the two of us move in a sort of semicircle that leaves me off balance and falling toward the bed.

As quick as a bolt of lightning, King Kane lets go of my foot and thrusts his hand out to catch me. He loops it around my waist and stares down at me, his blue eyes wide with confusion as he grapples with the situation.

All I can mumble is, "Oh, fuck." I'm screwed now. The king just walked in to find me beating the living shit out of three of his guards. He won't care that they were trying to rape me.

But then, what the hell is he doing here?

He doesn't respond to my muttered curse as he lets me drop onto the bed and looks at the three mangled guards.

"What the actual hell is going on here?" he asks.

The two that I knocked across the room manage to pull themselves to their feet first, looking like shit. They are bleeding, their clothes torn, and they certainly have some broken bones. They both bow low at the waist, but neither of them is answering his question.

By the time the third one scrambles to standing, he has recovered slightly. Blood still drips down his face. "She… attacked us, Your Majesty," he says.

I open my mouth to protest, but it isn't necessary as King Kane quickly asks, "Then why the fuck are your trousers down around your ankles?"

His mouth opens and closes several times like a fish out of water, but there's no answer he can give short of the truth, and it seems clear to me that if he tells the king he was trying to rape me, he will most certainly be in trouble, which actually makes me quite glad to hear. I was afraid the king might condone, or at the very least, turn a blind eye to such behaviors. I can tell by his tone that I was mistaken. He isn't happy at all.

I feel his gaze on me before I turn to see him looking at me. "Did they harm you?" he asks me.

I know I have some bruises on my arms and maybe a few scratches, but I am confident when I shake my head. "No, Sir."

He stares at me for a long moment, and I feel a chill pass down my spine, something I can't quite explain. His eyes seem to penetrate far deeper than anyone's I've ever gazed into before, but I can't pull mine away.

A moment later, Rainer is in the doorway, sliding to halt. "Holy fuck," he mumbles, looking at the three of them before he looks at me. "Emory! Are you okay?"

I can hear true concern in his voice. "I'm fine," I assure him.

A low rumble escapes King Kane's throat, and at first I am confused as to why his friend asking me if I'm okay would bother him, but then I realize he's just angry in general. "Rainer, take these three assholes to lockdown. I want them castrated or killed. Their choice. I don't care. They either lose their dicks or their heads."

"Yes, Sir," Rainer says, then adds, "although I think castration means they lose their balls."

King Kane growls again. "I am aware. Do it now." Then, turning to me, he says, "You—come with me."

I feel my heart lurch into my throat as I realize he is probably angry at me for causing such a fuss in his dungeon. I say nothing as I climb to my feet and follow him out the door.

As I pass him, Rainer says, "I'm so glad you're all right and Kane got there in time to protect you."

I almost laugh. He thinks the king did that? Instead, I just say, "Thank you."

It's the king who corrects him. "She's the one who beat the hell out of them, dumbass." He says the last word like it's a term of endearment. I see Rainer's eyes widen as I shrug and turn to follow the king.

I have no idea where we are going, but I imagine it's just another cell. We pass all of them in this section, and he stops at the same guard station that Clark stopped at to ask what cell to take me to. The man standing there is different but looks equally disinterested in life in general until he sees the king and bows his head.

"Never in my life have I seen such deplorable conditions," he begins, keeping his tone even, though he's clearly mad. "This is not at all what this place is supposed to be like! These people are PEOPLE, and they deserve to be treated as such."

"Yes, Your Majesty. I'm just—"

Now, King Kane is mad. "I don't give a fuck what your station is, soldier! You work here, it's your responsibility to take care of them!" He slams his fist down into the podium and it splinters, breaking into several pieces. "I want this place cleaned up immediately! These people need to be allowed to shower whenever they'd like. They need proper nutrition, proper lighting, proper activities! I will send someone to oversee this, but as for now, I want all of you working on this nonstop until it's better, do you hear me?"

His shouting has drawn a crowd, and as I look around, I see that there are at least ten other guards listening in, all of them looking embarrassed and afraid.

"Yes, Your Majesty," the first guard says, and then so do the others.

He gives a nod, his breathing still uneven and moves toward the exit again. This time, he reaches behind him to grab my arm and pulls me along. "Come on, Emory."

I have no choice but to go—but I'm glad when we begin to ascend the stairs. I have no idea where we are going—but it can't be worse than this place.

Can it?

9

IN THE BEDROOM

Emory

KING KANE IS FLYING up the stairs, and I am going as quickly as I can
to keep up with him. Normally, I think of myself as pretty fast, but
clearly I am either too tired after the adrenaline rush has worn off, or
he is even faster than me.

Not that it would surprise me that a vampire is faster than a wolf
shifter who has yet to find her wolf, but I don't know why he is
moving so quickly. It's clear to me that he is still angry. He has been
furious since the moment he came into my cell in the feeder's
dungeon and I almost kicked him, but I would've thought he'd settle
down by now.

I guess I was wrong.

We make it to the top of the first staircase and then he goes right
past the guards and up the next flight of stairs. I am a little confused. I
thought perhaps he was moving me to the other dungeon, one where
the guards are more responsible or something, but that's not where
we are headed either, obviously, so I follow along, and as we reach the

top of the second stairwell, he seems to have cooled off enough that he is no longer running at full pace.

If that was even his fastest speed….

The guards open the door for us, and he proceeds down the hallway, walking at a normal quick pace but not so fast that I can't keep up. A million questions come to my mind as we are walking along, but I don't dare to ask them because I know that he won't want to answer them. He doesn't seem like much of a talker.

All I can keep thinking about it is what almost happened back there. What would I have done if it would've been more guards come to attack me? Would I have been able to keep holding them off?

That... and I really want to wash my hand. Thoughts of what I was squeezing make me want to vomit. I can taste bile in the back of my throat.

He is quite a bit ahead of me now, and I realize the more lost in my head I become, the harder it is for me to keep up. I pick up the pace and catch up with him.

The hallways are a maze, as I recall from earlier when I was walking with Clark. I absently wonder what is going to happen to him. He seems important. After all, only two people accompanied the king into the throne room to meet with my family, and Clark was one of them. Surely, he won't be in too much trouble over what happened. He must not have realized he put me in the wrong place. He must not know that the dungeon is such an awful hellhole.

But then... he didn't seem surprised when we went down there together—which makes me think he knows.

King Kane comes to a halt in front of me, his head tipped back so that he is looking at the ceiling, and I have to pull up abruptly to keep from crashing into him. I stop just short of him and find myself slightly disappointed not to have an excuse to touch him, which makes no sense to me.

After all, his cold body can't possibly feel that good beneath my hands. He probably feels like a marble statue. When he'd grabbed my hand earlier, it had been warmer than expected, but still... he's a vampire, not a cozy blanket designed to snuggle up with on warm nights.

He lowers his head from the ceiling and turns to look at me. "Am I walking too fast?" he asks, and I hear tones of frustration in his voice.

I don't want to tell him that he is, so I say, "No, Sir."

"Then… why are you so far behind me?" he asks, arching an eyebrow over a blue eye that suddenly has me lost in an ocean. It's as if I'm drifting out to sea, and the further into those blue orbs I wade, the less likely I am to ever return to shore. "Emory?"

I shake my head, returning to the hallway. "Oh, uh… because… you're the king," I stammer. "It's not polite to walk next to you."

He snickers and shakes his head. "How about right behind me instead of so far away I have to keep pausing to make sure you haven't gotten lost? Or stolen?"

His voice is gentler now than before, and I have to wonder why he would think I might get stolen, but then, after the scene he walked in on, perhaps he knows there are more reasons for me to be leery in this castle than I previously thought.

"Yes, Sir," I say with a nod.

He starts walking again, but this time, his pace isn't as quick, and after a few more turns, I find that we are in a fancy part of the castle where the marble floors are particularly polished, and the wooden carvings that make up the trim, doors, and doorways is even more elaborate than normal.

Wherever we are, important people must stay here….

Back home, we live in a castle, but it's nothing like this one. It's not nearly as large, and most of our finer items were sold many years ago to finance the war. I have always wondered what became of them, and now I wonder if Father might've traded some of them to King Kane to help pay back some of his debt. Will I see some of our belongings here if I look long enough?

We didn't have anyone else living in our house, other than my family and the servants, but here, it seems that there are a whole host of people who live and work in the castle, people like Rainer and Clark who consult the king, and who knows who else? I haven't even seen the queen consort yet, King Kane's mother, or his brother, Prince Lex, who has quite the reputation as a womanizer.

Who else is hiding in these hallways?

We reach a door with butterflies and flowers carved into the door-frame and the door itself. It's quite beautiful, and I can't help but stare at it for a moment as King Kane opens it. The door opens silently, and we step inside of a suite.

I am confused. The room is much more elaborate than any of our bedrooms back home. Even my father and mother didn't have this sort of luxury. The carpet beneath my feet is plush, a nice beige color, with plenty of handwoven throw rugs in reds and deep blues around the large space as accents. There's a sitting area with a comfortable, yet formal looking, blue sofa and chairs. The bed is a four-poster big enough for three or four people, I am guessing. It has a canopy, and all of the linens are the same deep blues as the couch and rugs. The bed itself has butterflies and flowers carved into it. In the distance, I see an en suite bathroom, though I can't see inside of it from this angle.

All of the furniture is heavy wood, cherry, I believe, and it smells clean and fresh. Flowers on the round table in the dining area near a small kitchenette make it smell even nicer.

This is by far the most beautiful room I've ever been in before, and despite the feminine touches, I can't help but jump to one conclusion as to where we are.

"Here we are," King Kane says, lifting his arm just slightly.

My eyes flutter back to his face as I ask, "Your room?" A small quiver gives away my nervousness as I wonder what he would've brought me to his room for. Is he ready to feed from me?

Or… is it something else?

His eyebrows knit together as a crooked grin slips into place for a moment before it fades away. "No," he says, shaking his head slightly. "Not my room—your room, Emory. Do I look like the sort of vampire who likes butterflies?"

I can't help but giggle slightly. He most definitely does not. But I am still at a loss. "This room is for me?" I ask him. "I mean, I'm a feeder. Not a guest."

"You are the daughter of an Alpha," he reminds me. "A princess for all intents and purposes, and it won't do for someone of your stature to stay in a filthy dungeon."

I honestly don't know what to say to him. I feel tears threatening to slip from my eyes, but I don't want to cry. It's been such a long, emotional day, and all I want to do is curl myself into a ball and go to sleep—right after I wash my hands.

A noise at the door behind us has me looking past him. Two maids stand there with what looks like arms full of clothing. He waves them in, and they move toward a closet on the other side of the room near the bathroom.

"This is Helga and Nellie," he explains, gesturing first at an older looking woman with broad shoulders and a bit of a severe look about her. Nellie is younger, about my age, I'm guessing, with a broad smile and cheerful eyes. They are both vampires so who knows how old they really are. "They'll be taking care of you."

It almost seemed like he was going to say for as long as I stay here, but, that will likely be forever—or until I die. I never would've imagined I'd have servants. I didn't even have my own designated servant back home anymore. I hadn't since I was a little girl. "Thank you," is all I can manage. They hang up the clothing and come back out of the closet, tipping their heads.

"They'll be bringing you some more clothing and other items you'll need since you didn't have the opportunity to pack before you came."

I can't help but scoff at the statement, not at the king but at the fact that I'd had no idea that I was about to leave my home forever.

"If there are items you want from your former home, I'll be happy to retrieve them for you," he assures me.

Again, I am shocked. I want to ask him why he's being so nice, but I figure there's something I'm missing. I wonder if maybe he thinks he can make some of his money back by reselling me. Could some of his vampire friends be willing to pay for me? I can't think about that right now. It isn't right to question his kindness, though I will never let anyone catch me off guard again.

As if he was reading my mind, he asks, "You didn't know, did you?"

I turn and look at him, trying to avoid his eyes, but I can't. I stare into them again for a moment before I finally say, "No."

He nods. "Well, it's all very unfortunate, but you are here now. So… get some rest. Take a bath if you'd like. Dinner is at 7:00 sharp. I'll send someone for you." He turns back toward the door, like he is leaving, and I'm not surprised. I'm sure he has a million things to do, and I have already been a big enough nuisance.

But I can't help the final question that comes out of my mouth just before he leaves. "King Kane?"

He looks at me, his eyebrows raised, waiting.

I take a deep breath and ask, "Dinner?" He nods, beckoning me to continue. "Am I going to dinner… because I am dinner?"

A chuckle escapes his lips, and he says, "I'll see you later, Emory."

1 0

THE KING HAS A FIANCÉE?

Emory

I TAKE A BATH, soaking in notes of rose and lavender, letting my muscles relax as much as they will after the hellacious day I've had. King Kane had suggested taking a nap, and that does seem like a good idea, but I know I won't be able to sleep. My mind keeps puzzling over everything that's happened. How, exactly, did I come to be here? At what point did my father reach such desperation that he was willing to trade his own child to his enemy to pay off his debts?

I can't say, and by the time the water has cooled, I have decided it's futile to keep going over such questions in my head. What's done is done. Now, I need to figure out the rest of my life anew.

I get out of the tub and dry off with the most luxurious towel I've ever felt in my life. The maids have brought in all kinds of lotions and creams, as well as all sorts of makeup and hair accessories. I've never been one to spend too much time on my appearance, but Nellie already told me she'd be happy to help me get ready for dinner and that I would be expected to look, "presentable."

As the two maids help me dress, put my makeup on, and fix my hair, I can't help but wonder what will happen at dinner. King Kane didn't answer me as to whether or not I am a guest at dinner or the meal, and I can't help but feel nervous. I might be able to handle one or two vampires feeding on me for a bit, but if there are a lot of them there... they might drain me completely.

At least then I wouldn't have to worry about what the future holds....

"Are you all right, Princess?" Nellie asks in her sweet voice. "You look worried."

"Oh, uh, I was just thinking about... dinner," I reply, pressing a smile to my face.

"You should be," Helga says in a thick accent that makes her difficult to understand. She always sounds mad. Maybe she is always mad. "One wolf, lots of vampires."

"Well, I don't know about that," Nellie says. "King Kane sent out a decree earlier today that no one is to bother you. No one is to approach you or attempt to feed off you, so that should make you feel better."

My eyebrows raise in surprise at that statement. It does make me feel better, but I wonder why he would feel it necessary to make such a statement.

I clear my throat. "Do either of you know how many... others... I should expect at dinner?"

"Presently, there are about fifteen guests in the castle," Nellie says. "Plus the king and his family, and his four consultants."

"As well as the other princess," Helga adds, and I immediately feel a tightening in my gut. "Her brother is also here."

"That's right," Nellie says, her smile fading as a dismal look takes over her pretty face. "How could I forget about her?"

"I have no idea," Helga replies.

"So... maybe twenty-five vampires?" I ask.

They both nod. "Something like that," Nellie agrees. "It'll be fine. The king will keep you safe."

I manage a small smile, but I have no idea whether or not she's right. He hadn't been so quick to assure me I wasn't the meal.

A half hour later, at 6:45, I am ready to go. I am looking in a mirror, but I don't recognize myself. My hair is piled on top of my head with curls framing my face. My eyes look so bright thanks to the makeup colors the girls used, and my lips look luscious and full.

The dress I am wearing is almost the same shade as my eyes. It hugs me tight at the top before settling over my hips and swinging out near my ankles. A slit runs up so high on my right side, it seems almost scandalous to me, but the girls assured me I look like a high-fashion diva. I'm not sure that's what I want to look like, but it beats looking like an entrée. I also have on diamond earrings and a necklace that probably could be sold to repay my father's debt—if it were mine to sell.

I'm not used to walking in heels, so I try the black pumps out a bit before I decide I've got enough balance and coordination to fake it. If I take a wrong step, I'll go tumbling down, though. I am not overly confident.

With a final spritz of rosewater, I am ready to go, just as there's a resounding knock on the door, and my heart lurches into my throat.

I can't help but wonder if it might be the king himself come to fetch me, but I remember him saying that he would send someone for me, and I get the feeling that it isn't him behind the door.

Helga goes to throw it open, and I stand behind her, only slightly disappointed to see Rainer standing there with a big grin on his face.

My own smile widens as I see how happy and carefree he looks. It must be nice to be so good natured all of the time. "Holy wowza," he says, stepping into the room. I don't know that I've ever heard anyone use that expression before, but I think it must be a good thing. "Look at you!"

I do as he says and stare down at my dress. "Does it look okay?" I ask him.

"You look… stunning," he says, finally dropping his outstretch arms. "I mean, you always look beautiful, but this is… damn. That's all I can say."

I feel my cheeks pinking as he offers me his arm, and I take it. "Thank you, ladies," I tell them.

"Have a good time!" Nellie says. Helga says nothing, doesn't even wave, but I think she will soften up eventually. At least she was speaking freely by the time they were done getting me ready to go.

As we walk along, Rainer points out where we are in the castle, based on the important rooms, like the library and the exit to the rose garden. I try to keep everything in mind, but I probably won't remember. After a little while, he grows quiet and asks, "Is everything okay?"

"Yes," I say quickly, though I'm not telling the truth. "It's just... can I ask you something?"

"Of course," he says in the same good natured tone he always uses. "Just don't ask what I really think about the salmon." He makes a face that has us both giggling.

"Actually," I tell him, keeping my voice low. I am a bit embarrassed to be asking him this because I'm not sure it's fair for him to have to answer me. "It is about dinner."

"What do you want to know?" He is more serious now than he was before.

"Well, uh...." I look around and see two large doors in front of me and imagine that's probably the dining room. I'm about to find out whether I ask or not. "I'm, uh... not... the main course, am I?"

Rainer stops walking and turns to look at me, his face frozen in an expression I cannot read, and for a moment, I think he's trying to decide how to tell me that I am, but then he says, "Why would you— no! No, of course, not, Emory."

I let out a deep breath, so glad to hear that. He seems so certain of himself, I can believe him.

"Sweetie, I'm so sorry you thought that was a possibility." He pulls me into a hug, and I suddenly feel so much better about the entire situation. The scent of pine fills my nostrils as my face is crushed against his shoulder, his black vest soft against my cheek. He has an extremely manly scent, and for a moment, I forget he's a vampire. He's not stone-like at all, despite his large muscles.

When he releases me, he says., "Don't worry. You are a guest at the dining table, just as you are now considered a guest in the castle." He offers me his arm, and I take it again.

It's nice of him to say that, but I'm not convinced.

We walk into the dining room to see several people milling about. They all turn and look at me, and I feel like I have two heads. I've never seen any of them before, and I have no idea who any of them are, except for perhaps the strikingly beautiful woman who is standing near the chair at one end of the table. She has long black hair that is pulled up into an opulent braid and wrapped up in a bun, with hints of silver streaking through it, though she doesn't look old at all.

"That's Queen Agatha," Rainer whispers. "None of the rest of these people are important." He bows to the queen, and I do the same. She nods in response, but he doesn't take me over to meet her, and I'm glad.

Instead, he leads me to the other end of the table, and I suddenly realize I'm about to cause a problem. "Whose seat am I taking?" I whisper to him. I have been at enough of these fancy dinners to know everyone wants to sit next to one head of the table or the other, and the closer to the middle of the table one gets, the less important one becomes. So unless they've pulled up another chair for me smack dab in the middle, someone is going to hate me.

"Oh, uh… Clark's," he says with a shrug as he releases my arm and shoves his hands into the pockets of his slacks. "He couldn't make it."

"Oh. Why is that?" I ask.

"Because he's on house arrest."

Rainer is serious. I can tell. He's rarely serious, so when he is, I have already learned to spot it. "He is?"

"Yes, he's in charge of the feeders, and Kane was not at all happy with the way that they've been treated. Especially you, but everyone else as well." He nods his head and adds, "It's been a long time coming. I never liked that guy."

I don't know what to say. I remember how angry King Kane had been when he spoke to that guard in the dungeon. I am glad that the feeders are finally going to get some help, but I'm also afraid Clark will come after me for causing trouble.

I am about to say something to that degree when the double doors swing open again, and a flourish of laughter hits my ear. I turn to see a strikingly beautiful raven haired woman float through the door on the arms of two handsome men. One has blond curls that frame his thin face. He is almost lovely in his elegant beauty. The other has dark hair and looks a lot like the woman, though he has a sharper nose and square jaw. He is more muscular than the blond, though nothing like Rainer.

"Who is that?" I ask, feeling my stomach twist into a knot. Something tells me I already know who she is and who the blond is, though I don't know why she's here… at the castle.

"That's Prince Jacob of the Clan Maxwell, from Scarlett Thunder," he explains, and I know he means the dark-haired man. "The other fellow is Prince Luther Alexander, otherwise known as Lex." I nod, seeing only a faint resemblance to King Kane but having heard a description of the prince before.

"And who is she?" I ask as the woman stops laughing, her sapphire eyes turning to look right at me. I gulp back my apprehension.

"Princess Opaline Maxwell," Rainer says. "The king's… fiancée."

My eyes widen as I shift my gaze to look from her to Rainer. "His… fiancée?" I ask.

Just then, Opal asks in a loud, high-pitched voice, "Who the fuck invited a mangy dog to our dinner party?"

All of the blood leaves my face as I feel myself begin to react. I'm not sure if I should hide behind Rainer or throw a plate at her, but something tells me Princess Opal and I are not going to get along.

DINNER AND A SHOW

Emory

"WHO THE FUCK invited a mangy dog to our dinner party?"

Princess Opal's words hang in the air as the rest of the room goes silent. It's as if the rest of the guests are all waiting for me to respond to the loud, offensive statement, including Rainer, though I believe he's just as taken aback by the assault as I am.

Either that or he's just choosing to let me wage my own war.

But as I settle on a witty remark to politely say back to her, my voice is drowned out by the confident reply that comes from my right.

I can't see him through Rainer's large frame, but I don't have to in order to know who is speaking. He must've come through his own entrance and taken us all by surprise, including Opal whose face shifts slightly at the sound of his voice.

"As far as I know," King Kane begins, "no one invited a dog to dinner, but I did invite a wolf."

My eyes lock with his about the time he stops next to his fiancée who is standing across the table from me, both of her escorts having dropped her arms as her betrothed approached.

I have to avert my eyes. I can't hold his gaze while he's standing next to her. It's too shocking, too unsettling as I get a glimpse of how beautiful the two of them are together. It seems absolutely ridiculous beyond measure that I even let my subconscious entertain the possibility that the Vampire King might see me as anything more than a prisoner.

I manage to glance up, but no higher than their chins, as the princess rests her hand on his chest and flutters her eyelashes at him, I'm guessing, probably smiling innocently. He bends down and kisses her cheek. It's nothing more than a peck, but I feel a twist to my gut that seems both ridiculous under the circumstances, yet very real.

King Kane pulls Opal's chair out for her before adding, "Let's all be kind to my guest. Princess Emory has had a trying day."

It's then that I feel the weight of his eyes on my face again and know I am compelled to look back at him.

When I do, our eyes lock for only the briefest of moments, but it is enough for me to register a few emotions running through his mind, the primary one being sympathy. He honestly does feel badly for me, that I've been betrayed by my family, that I am even here. But there's something else, too, something I can't quite understand. Is it the hint of an apology? Or could it be… a trace of… longing?

Whatever it was, he shores up his emotions quickly enough as he moves to the head of the table, and though he has been kind enough to pull out his fiancee's chair for her, a waiter jumps to pull his back for him, and he takes his place, and then the rest of us may sit. Opal slides around her chair and is pushed in by her brother before he is seated.

Rainer helps me with the awkward chair, both pulling out the large, heavy piece for me, and pushing me in, which I could've managed since I am exceptionally strong, but I appreciate his help anyway.

As my abdomen hits the edge of the table, I think I hear a low rumble but it's just a whisper, and I'm not sure what to make of it, so I ignore it. The sound reminds me slightly of the noise Darius made at school whenever he saw me speaking to my friend Freddie.

Rainer also chooses to ignore it, though when I glance over at him for a split second once he's settled, it seems he has a surprised, amused hint of a smile on his face. Whatever is happening is a mystery to me, and there is a flourish of dinner etiquette happening around me that is more important than trying to figure out if King Kane truly just growled at his friend for helping me with my chair.

I have attended dozens of formal dinners over the years at various palaces, and they are all slightly different when it comes to decorum. I do my best to follow along with everyone else when it comes to when to place the napkin in my lap, how to choose a utensil, all of those things, but when the waitress present us with our plates, mine is much different than everyone else's.

They all have three large goblets in front of them while I only have two. All of us have water and red wine, but they have one for blood, and as the thick, crimson substance is freshly poured by the servants designated to each vampire, the scent hits me and makes my stomach twist slightly.

I've never been squeamish, but having seen the state of the feeders' dungeon first hand, and thinking about how much blood had to have been harvested to feed this many people an entire goblet full... it makes me have to look away slightly.

The servant behind me stands with his hand on top of the silver cloche until the signal is given, and then they are all lifted at once.

My plate is much different than the others as well. While they all have small portions of red meat swimming in its juices, as well as small portions of sides, my plate is huge. I have a massive steak, a huge potato, a salad on a separate plate, and a vegetable I'm not sure I can identify. Asparagus wrapped in bacon, possibly?

I don't know what to think of the situation, but I don't have much time to process it anyway before Princess Opal lets everyone know that an oddity has occurred amidst the dinner guests.

"Holy hell," she practically shouts as a giggle escapes her lips. "It's no wonder you're such a big girl. That's a lot of food."

My eyes widen in slight horror as I process what she's said to me. I take a breath, trying to decide what to do. Rainer already has food in his mouth, not that I think it's his place, or anyone else's, to stand up for me to the bitch.

I decide it is best to be polite. I don't want to give anyone here the reason to think that I am the problem. "Yes, well, one never knows when they may need to defend themselves, so it's best to keep one's strength up." I hope that my answer is both polite and to the point—she ought not to mess with me; I'll snap her hand off.

But she only giggles and her brother asks, "Perhaps Clark is here after all, and we simply can't see him. Are you sitting on him?"

Both of the guests from Scarlett Thunder laugh at this, as do several other guests, including Prince Lex, who appears to be attempting not to.

I've never had my physical appearance made fun of before, and I'm not sure how to process it. My combat training has required me to keep my body muscular and in shape. I've had to eat quite a bit of protein each day in order for that to stay the case. But it's not fat. It's not excess. And considering how short my pack is on food sources right now, recently, it's been a challenge to even find enough protein —for all of us. So no, I'm not large. At least, I don't think I am.

"Enough, Opal," King Kane says, not looking at either one of us. "You're being ridiculous."

"Oh, I'm just poking a little fun," she says with a shrug. I refuse to look away from her, to drop my gaze and submit. "Mother always taught me it's polite to play with my food."

That gets another laugh out of everyone within earshot, except for Rainer.

And the king.

"Princess Emory is not your food, Opal." He takes a drink from his goblet of blood and somehow manages to do so without a trace of the substance adhering to his lips or teeth. "Princess Emory is off limits to everyone in the castle. Didn't you receive my decree?"

She pulls her eyes off of me to look at him; I feel the shift in the weight on the side of my face as I am having a hard time looking away from him myself. The king is looking at his fiancée, though, and when she says, "Yes, yes. I heard something about it, though I didn't pay it much mind. The three of us were out in the garden still, looking at where to place the blood bar for the reception."

"I suggest that whenever I make a decree, you do pay attention." His tone is direct but not otherwise harsh, and when Opal shifts the topic of discussion from me to her wedding plans, I feel inclined to begin my meal.

I'm not hungry. As much as my body is longing to replace the calories I burned beating the hell out of those guards, I can't seem to make room in my stomach for much of anything. The knot there is so intense, and the thoughts that plague me about all that's happened throughout the day restrict my ability to get more than a few bites down.

It's just as well. As soon as Opal is done explaining how the ice sculptures will be mechanized so that they will display the king and herself turning toward one another and kissing over and over again, her brother has a question for me, "So, you're the daughter of Bernard Moonraker? Is that right? Sworn enemy of Crimson Peak clan?"

I am taking a sip of water when the question is asked, so I have to swallow before I can say, "Yes, Prince Jacob. That is correct." Although, at the moment, I'm not sure I want to claim Bernard as my father.

"And how, exactly, did you come to be here?" he continues. "Not at the dining table. I know that King Kane is far too generous to let someone of your status end up in the dungeon for what her father has done to his people, but are you here to help facilitate peace?"

I stare at him for a long moment, confused as to why he's asking the question. I think everyone here knows why I am at the castle, including him. It's like he just wants to hear me say it.

His blue eyes are locked on my face, unblinking, as I choose my words.

But there's simply no reason to be anything other than honest. "No," I say. "My father offered me in exchange for his debt. To become a feeder for the king."

Jacob has a satisfied look on his face, as if he'd been hoping that is exactly what I would say, but Opal begins to laugh loudly. "How awful!" she blurts. "To have your own father do something so… harsh. You must feel terrible."

"Opal," King Kane say, looking at her sharply. "Be polite."

"Oh, I'm sorry. Sometimes I forget that wolves have feelings." She clears her throat. "But seriously, that is too bad."

"She's not telling you everything," Rainer says beside me. It's the first time he's addressed them when they've spoken against me, and by the way his words leave his mouth, I can tell he's been holding back, though I'm not sure why. "Her father wasn't trying to trade her. He was trying to trade another family member, and she stepped in on the other girl's behalf."

I can't look at anyone now. My eyes drop to my lap, and I take a few deep breaths so as not to remember what has transpired. I feel Rainer's hand on my leg, a squeeze, and a release. He hasn't meant to upset me, I know that. He's trying to get them to leave me alone, for them to see that I've been through more than they realize, and to understand that I am brave or something.

It doesn't work.

"Unbelievable," Opal says. "Your father is a bigger asshole than I even imagined."

"Opal—" the king says, but she doesn't deter.

"Well, he is your enemy, isn't he?" she asks King Kane. He says nothing, and I'm not about to raise my head to see his reaction. I have managed to blink back my tears, though, so when Opal continues, I am looking at her. "I've always thought that werewolves cared very little about anyone other than themselves. I suppose this just confirms it."

"The fact that Emory stepped in to spare her younger sister confirms that for you?" It's the king himself who is questioning her logic now. I feel my chest both tighten in sadness as I think about Lola and swell with pride that he is standing up for me and my people, something he shouldn't feel compelled to do. We are his enemies, it's true, and we have been at fault this entire time, it seems.

"Oh, my," Opal says, and I can tell she truly is shocked this time. "I certainly hope someone is there to protect the girl. Otherwise, I can't imagine what your father might do in his rage."

Her words are meant to get a reaction out of me, and they do. I feel hot tears springing to my eyes as I contemplate the same thing. I want to get up from the table and run away, to hide, to cry in my despair, but I can't move.

I no longer have the freedom to do any of that without permission, and when I turn to the king to see if I should ask for his consent to leave, I see that he is seething.

1 2

OPAL IS OUT OF LINE

Kane

IF I OPEN my mouth to reprimand Opal right now, a rivulet of curses will be released into the world the likes of which no one has heard before. I have already tried politely, asking her to stop verbally assaulting Emory. When that didn't work, I ordered her with a mind message, one she clearly chose to ignore in the same way she failed to mind the decree I sent out earlier. No, Opal is out of control, and she's doing her best to push me beyond my limits.

I should've known better than to bring Emory here. I knew that Opal wouldn't like it. Despite our agreement that neither of us is romantically limited in our relationship, Opal sees any other female I take any interest in whatsoever as a threat against her position as the future queen of Crescent Peak. So even if Emory really was over-weight as Opal tried to imply, if she had a snaggletooth and beady eyes, body odor and excessive mucus issues, Opal would see her as a potential rival.

And Opal loves the energy a rivalry brings her. She thinks it puts her in her element, that it makes her seem more powerful as she uses what she would refer to as wit to poke and jab at her enemy. It's nothing but bullying, and for Opal, it tends to work because there are few with the same station that she holds. Those beneath her feel subservient already, and her chiding just makes it worse.

It's better for me to keep my mouth shut and make it through this dinner than to try to defend Emory because it will do nothing but cause an argument, and though there are no other visiting dignitaries at the table, I know better than to cause a scene in front of my mother. She may be queen only in name now, but I still respect her. Already, she is giving me sharp looks from the other end of the table.

"Opal," I try again, breathing deeply, "why don't you tell us more about the wedding?" It's the only topic that is safe at the moment.

As Opal begins to describe various aspects of the wedding, I finish my blood and sit back in my chair. I won't be attempting to eat any food tonight, not after the day I've had. Food is fine for vampires, generally speaking, but it doesn't do us much good nutritionally, and it is often tricky for our bodies to digest when we eat in excess. The way I'm feeling right now, I may as well ensure I don't cause myself any unnecessary suffering later.

Listening to Opal causes enough suffering for even a vampire's lifetime.

My eyes fall on Emory as Opal discusses the problem with the moon we settled earlier. Emory appears to be paying attention to the princess, but I don't think she truly is. She isn't really eating. It's more of a march of food around her plate, with the occasional small bite slid between her lips. I can imagine a day like this would leave one without much of an appetite.

I don't like the way Rainer is protecting her. He's sitting too close to her. He's made one too many overly protective comments to Opal or Jacob. It's not that I don't appreciate him sticking up for Emory, but he seems to be taking a liking to her beyond his normal accepting self. Rainer knows a good person from a bad one from the moment he meets them, and he will embrace a good person as if they have always been friends while making life miserable for anyone who doesn't meet his moral criteria. It is why he hates my brother so fiercely but would do anything in the world for me.

He knows that Emory is a good person, so he will do whatever it takes to make her feel welcome here, and to me, that looks a bit too much like… something else. Like genuine interest.

I don't like it.

Opal pauses to take a drink of her blood, and Jacob takes the opportunity to steer the conversation in a new direction. "You have a sister?" he asks Emory, and I immediately sense her body tensing up, even from two seats away.

Quietly, she says, "I do."

"But you have different mothers?" It's more of a statement than a question when Jacob asks. I wonder why he suddenly knows so much about Moonraker pack. He never took any interest in them when we were actively waging war against them. I was on the battlefield nearly every day for two years. Where the fuck was he? We are allies, after all.

"That's right," Emory says, and Rainer's right hand disappears beneath the table again. Is he… touching her?

"Was her mother a breeder?" Opal blurts out. "I've heard about those creatures before, women who make a living out of bedding rich, powerful werewolves. Was something the matter with your mother?"

"Opal?" I say but I don't get any other words out before Emory answers.

"No, my sister's mother wasn't a breeder. It's not for me to say what transpired between my parents." I can hear the sorrow in her voice, and I am regretting bringing her. I should've known better.

"Is that why you wanted to become a feeder?" Opal asks, poking again. "For the same reason your kind becomes breeders? Were you hoping to gain power and position?"

"Opal!" This time it isn't a question. "You know this wasn't her choice. Why would you ask a question like that?"

"Just because it didn't appear that it was her choice, that doesn't mean it wasn't," she says, as if I've been duped. "Who knows what a werewolf will do."

"She's not a werewolf," I correct my fiancée. "She's a wolf shifter.

There is a difference, you know? Werewolves don't even exist. And I strongly suggest both you and your brother stop asking Princess Emory questions as you are irritating me by upsetting my guest."

"Well, I'm sorry." And there it is, the tone I was looking to avoid. "I guess I didn't realize she was so very important to you. Princess! She's not a princess. She's an Alpha's daughter. I'm the only princess here."

"All right, Opal." My tone alone is enough to make her curl in on herself slightly. "Let it go."

"Your Majesty?"

Emory's sweet voice has me ripping my eyes away from Opal's glare. I take a deep breath, already knowing what she's going to ask me. "Yes, Princess Emory?" I emphasize the title I have bestowed upon her. Whether she was a princess or not when she arrived, she's one now because I said so. I could proclaim my untouched fork a princess and that would speak it into existence.

"May I please be excused?" Her voice quivers slightly, and I can tell she's trying to escape the table before she begins to cry.

Without answering her directly, I signal for the servant who has been assigned to her to escort her to her room.

Before the man can step forward, Rainer says, "I'll take her."

I meet his gaze for a moment, contemplating whether or not I should allow it. My best friend taking a troubled guest back to her room makes perfect sense. So why do I find myself saying, "That won't be necessary."

Rainer takes a deep breath, holds it, considers arguing with me, but by the time he picks his poison, the servant has already helped Emory out of her chair, and she is making her way out of the dining room at such a pace, it is unnecessary for Rainer to follow. He shakes his eyes at me, a sign between us that he disagrees with my decision, but I have no reply.

I am about to end this entire fiasco anyway.

The woman who had been sitting next to Emory all night, an older woman who has been a member of the court for decades says, "Thank god she's gone. Now I can breathe again," and several of the people sitting near her laugh.

I am taking names now. Those people just ate their last dinner at this table.

As for Opal, she has a very satisfied look on her face as she daintily wipes her mouth with her napkin, and I want to reach across my brother and slap her.

Lex, who has been unusually quiet for him, also has an completely placid look on his face I can't quite understand, but I won't create more problems by asking him why he's so happy. Instead,

I excuse myself from the table, ready to end this catastrophe of a dinner.

<hr>

EMORY

I DON'T MAKE it too far out of the dining room before the tears begin to streak my face. I swipe them away and continue to march down the hallways, trying to remember which direction I'd come from. I hadn't been paying that much attention when Rainer led me in since we'd been chatting, and I'd foolishly assumed he'd escort me back to my room—or someone would anyway.

The servant who has been assigned to take me back to my room does not seem so excited to be doing so, and he's a good ten feet behind me when I reach a hallway I'm unsure of. Did we come from the left, down by that suit of armor, or the right, by that painting of a peacock with blood dripping from its mouth?

"It's a right, my lady," the servant says, and I turn to nod in thanks as I turn to the right and go past the peacock. At the end of this hall, there's only one way to go, and when I reach the end of the next hall, I remember the painting of a blood red ocean.

After that, I recognize where I am so I am able to make it to my room without the servant's help. I find the door with the butterflies and flowers and knock. I'm not sure why. No one answers, so I let myself in and find that Helga and Nellie are not here.

It's just as well. I'm not in the mood to explain to anyone what has happened anyway. I was making it through dinner all right until the questions about Lola kept coming up. After that, I couldn't keep my emotions in check anymore.

Opal is a raging bitch.

I can't imagine why in the world someone as intelligent and understanding as King Kane would want to marry her.

Pulling my earrings off, I manage to kick out of my heels and lower myself to the ground. The necklace I'm wearing seems to weigh at least ten pounds, so when I remove it, I literally feel like a weight has been taken off of my shoulders.

For me to think that King Kane is anything but evil is a complete change from my feelings toward him only a short time ago. It just goes to show that there truly are two sides to every story.

Taking deep breaths, I decide to focus on getting to bed. I am exhausted in every way, and I hope that, when my head hits the pillow, I can sleep for at least ten or twelve hours.

I do my best to reach around and unzip my gown, but I can only get it down about an inch or two, then, I can no longer reach. I am flexible, but it's a stretch even for me, and then, the zipper sticks. "Oh, come on!" I growl, thinking I am going to rip the dress.

It's certainly not the most comfortable thing I've ever had on, and I can't imagine sleeping in it. I try again, but I can't quite get my hands in position to work the zipper down.

Cursing, I think I will have to figure out where Nellie or Helga are.

A soft knock on my door makes me think that perhaps they've felt my distress or otherwise been ordered to come to my room.

I throw the door open, but it's not my maids standing on the other side, and when I lock eyes with him, all I can think to ask is, "What in the world are you doing here?"

13

TOUCH ME, KING KANE

Emory

THE QUESTION LINGERS in the air between us as I stare into King Kane's eyes, trying to figure out why he's followed me to my bedroom. It doesn't make any sense. Isn't he expected to still be at dinner with the rest of his guests?

If anyone from dinner were to follow me, I would've assumed it would have been Rainer. But it's not his blue eyes I'm staring into as the king leans against my door jamb.

He clears his throat, a moment of hesitation that is out of character for him. "I wanted to make sure you were okay," he says.

"Oh." I take a deep breath and step back once, almost tripping over my discarded shoes. I catch myself, seeing an eyebrow arch in concern. "I'm fine."

"Are you sure?" He doesn't come into my room, and I'm assuming that's probably because I haven't invited him in. But he is leaning further in than he was before. "Opal can be such a… bitch."

I want to agree with him, and I also want to demand to know why he never mentioned to me that he had a fiancée. I found out that another princess was present in the castle just before dinner, and I even got the feeling there was something going on between the two of them, something I probably didn't want to know about. But no one had told me they were getting married, and that hadn't made its rounds to my pack lands through the usual gossip circuit.

"I'm fine," I tell him again. "I'm just really tired." I try to smile, but it's hard, so I give up.

He nods sympathetically. "I'm sure you are. It's been a long day. Tomorrow will be better." He is quite a bit taller than me, and now that I am barefoot. I feel that even more as I look up at him. How did I get back over here, so close to him? He is still using the doorway as support, one arm cradled against it as he casually hovers there. So... I must have moved toward him, which isn't too surprising.

I seem to be drawn to him in a way I can't explain and probably don't want to admit.

He says tomorrow will be better, but from my perspective, I'm not sure how that will be true. It's just one more day away from everything I've ever known. The first day that I won't see Lola at all. Likely, the first day I will fulfill my new role—as a feeder.

Is that why he's here? Didn't he get enough blood at dinner? My bottom lip quivers thinking about it.

I haven't spent too much time thinking about what it will be like to feed the king, though I was trying my best not to imagine feeding anyone else, like those assholes in the dungeon. But feeding him... that would be different than feeding anyone else. He's the king, after all.

My eyes drop from his piercing gaze to his lips. Soft, pink, warm... I can only imagine what it would be like to have them on my body. I assume, he'd drink from my wrist, but what if his mouth found its way to my neck? Would it hurt when his teeth pierced my flesh, or would other sensations override the pain?

He stands up straight, and I realize he's about to leave. I don't want him to. Despite my exhaustion, I feel like the moment he walks away, the world will come crashing down on me again. At least, while he is here, I have enough of a shelter to protect me from the splintering explosion that is my life.

"Do you need anything before I go?" he asks, his voice just above a whisper.

My first instinct is to shake my head no. I don't want to be a bother. But then, I remember there is one thing I need. I can't ask him, though. He's the king.

He sees that I'm not being completely honest with him before my head even stops moving. "What is it?"

"Oh, uh… my dress," I admit. "The zipper is stuck. But… I'll find one of my maids."

He glances around the room. "They're not here?"

"No. They probably didn't expect me back yet." I shrug. "It's not that big of a deal. I'm used to taking care of myself. I just happen to have a persnickety zipper."

"Nellie and Helga's room is right through there." He gestures at a door I didn't notice before. "But I'll get it."

My mouth drops open at his last sentence. "You, uh, you… don't have to."

Without me inviting him, he steps into the room, closing the door behind him. I suppose he doesn't need my permission to come into any room in his own castle; and he does own me, too, after all.

"I know I don't have to," he says, taking me gently by the shoulders and turning me around. "But if the dress is ripped, this way, it'll be my fault, and who would dare get mad at me for such a thing?" he asks with a chuckle.

His touch is a bit colder than what I am used to as his fingertips graze my shoulders through the fabric of the gown. The way he has turned me, I am looking into a mirror. I don't think he's noticed.

I remember reading a book when I was younger that said vampires won't show up in reflective surfaces because they don't have souls. Well, that's clearly not true.

Much of what I know about vampires isn't true….

Especially this one.

I can see him; I can most definitely see the tall, dark haired man with the features of a god as he stands behind me, his lose hair moving slightly around his shoulders as his fingers graze my skin above the zipper. He gives it a slight tug, moving it down just a bit before he carefully lowers it to the small of my back where I will be able to reach it myself. Again, his hands touch me only in passing as the zipper is moved, but I feel his essence lingering on my skin, even after he has released me.

My eyes lock onto his in the mirror, and I can't help but bite my bottom lip. He feels this, too, doesn't he? This… chemical reaction, this longing I can't quite quantify, this… whatever it is that has my knees wanting to fold in on one another and a tightness in my core radiating down into a dampness I've never experienced before.

His hand is back on my shoulder, but this time, the material has slid down enough that nothing separates his skin from mine. His eyes move away from my reflection as he leans toward me, and my eyes fall closed. I turn my head slightly, not to put space between us but to give him access, my body betraying my desire.

His breath is warmer than expected as it fans across my skin. His thumb slips to the back of my neck, his fingers cradling around my throat. I want to feel his mouth on me. I want to give him whatever he wants, whatever he needs. Whether it's the hot liquid spilling through my veins or the slickness I feel between my legs, I want him to command me.

It isn't his mouth I feel on me, though. When he finally brings his head down, he is resting his forehead on my shoulder, and his hand slides down my arm to my waist as he holds me close to him. I lean back into a solid wall of muscle that is surprisingly more flesh-like than I would've thought as he seems to be contemplating a world of perplexing choices beyond my comprehension.

Is it Opal?

Is that why he hasn't put his mouth on me? Is he afraid that he will do more than feed from me if his lips touch my skin?

I have no way of knowing, and I cannot ask, but the strength of his arm around me, of being pressed against him, allows me to feel safe for the first time since before I left home early this morning.

My hands can't help but reach for him. I want to feel him, too. I want to caress his skin and hold him, but I can't be too forward, too presumptuous. I lift a hand to place on top of the one he has cradled around my waist, and just as before, when he took my hand in the dungeon, the sensation of a thousand electric pin pricks dance up my arm. It nearly takes my breath away.

His other hand slides around my hips, and he pulls me even tighter into his grasp. A sigh escapes my lips as I feel his need pressed to my back. So I'm not imagining any of this—the connection is there. I lean my head against his shoulder, breathing in the scent of bergamot and a few spices I cannot name that I have already come to associate with him.

Of its own accord, my other hand lifts to touch him. Silky black strands run through my fingers as I discover his hair is as smooth as it looks. His cheek is like porcelain, though a bit cold, and when I turn my head and our faces meet for the first time, all I can think about is how good it would feel for him to brush his lips against mine.

He stays unmoving though, and I realize he's barely breathing. I don't think he needs oxygen to stay alive, so that's not too surprising, but I can't figure out why he is so very still. His hand at my waist is so very close to my breastbone, the longing for him to slide it up only a few inches, to touch me in places no one ever has before, has a gasp leaving my lips. I have to bite down again to keep from moaning, and he hasn't even kissed me.

After a moment, his countenance changes. He stands up, moving his hands around my body in a more controlling, yet careful, way. He turns me to face him, his hands on my shoulders now. I grasp the top of my dress to keep it from sliding down as my straps are useless now, hanging loosely around my elbows.

"Emory." The way he says my name has me longing to reach for him, but it's clear to me now that whatever spell he was under a moment ago has dissipated, and I am the one left with her head spinning in the clouds. "Forgive me. I've gotten carried away. It won't happen again."

He swallows hard, his eyes still on my face, and then, he is gone, out the door, erased from my room as if he was never even here.

I am left standing in a draping gown, feeling much colder without his touch than with it, wondering what happens now.

Why would I need to forgive him for touching me when I wanted it to?

And... what if I want it to happen again?

14

LUSTFUL THOUGHTS

Kane

Vampires don't have fated mates.

In fact, most people don't think that vampires even have souls. I'm not sure what I think of that since I was born a vampire. It's not as if I were once a person who was killed by a vampire and my soul was released to hell or where-have-you, and now I am something else. No, I have always been a vampire, so if I am a soulless, earthbound creature, then so be it.

Right now, I think there is something deep inside of me that is driving me toward Emory Moonraker, though, and I have no idea what it is—but it is persistent.

Back in my room, after I nearly took her on her first night in the castle, I am lying in my bed, staring at the ceiling, trying to determine what to do about it.

It's not true that vampires don't sleep. We do. I do, anyway. Perhaps there are some that don't need to, but on average, I need at least five hours of sleep each night to function. Otherwise, I am a monster the next day—literally.

The other rumors about vampires, that they have high sex drives and are into all sorts of kinky things in the bedroom are true to different levels. I believe I fall somewhere above average but am nothing like my brother—or Opal.

The thought makes me wonder if my brother is fucking my fiancée.

He pretends to hate her whenever she's not around but still seeks her out. He escorts her to dinner every night, along with her brother, who is into anything and everything in the bedroom…. I wouldn't be surprised if Lex isn't fucking Opal.

Tossing an arm across my forehead, I wonder why I care and decide it is only because I don't like the idea that they are doing something so intimate behind my back. People that will screw each other behind your back are more likely to throw daggers when you're not looking as well, and while my brother can say it doesn't matter to him that he'll never rule, I know that he actually does care. He does have designs to be king. If he could get Opal pregnant before me, he would at least solidify his own child's place on the throne, assuming I never find anyone else to bare me children.

It's all too much to think about, so I don't.

Nor do I want to think about that bastard Clark….

Putting him on house arrest doesn't seem like enough. I should've ripped his fucking head off. Especially after his response to, "Why did you take her to the feeders' dungeon?" was, "Well, she's just another fucking bitch feeder. Who the hell cares what happens to her?" I had smacked him across the face hard enough to draw blood. Vampires must be struck very hard to draw blood. Now, I had his mess downstairs to clean up and his problematic ass to deal with.

Really, it had been a shitty day.

Except for Emory herself.

I shift on the bed again, my hand trailing down my bare chest as I think about her, settling my palm just north of the V beneath my boxers. The scent of roses fills my mind; not the ones from the flower garden where Opal was throwing her fit, but rosewater… and lavender.

Emory smelled divine, and the way she looked in that dress.... It was no wonder Rainer couldn't keep his hands off her.

She was gorgeous, and she had absolutely no idea what she did to every male who looked in her direction. The way she'd handled herself in that prison was impressive, too. I never want to make her mad enough to grab my balls—not like that anyway.

But I had wanted her to touch me, and I knew she wanted me to touch her, too....

I can't explain what this magnetism is. Why do I ache for her now? The moment is gone. Normally, if I decided not to take a woman in such a moment, it would fade from my memory and become background noise until it dissipated altogether. But now, I find myself replaying those moments with Emory over and over again. The thump of her heart, the feel of her skin, the way her hand felt on mine, her cheek pressed to my face, her fingers streaming through my hair.

It's all I can do to keep my hand still as I harden beneath the sheets.

I know I've done the right thing in walking away from her. She is emotional and exhausted. Her entire world has been torn apart, and it will take some time for it to be put back together. I may own her, but only as a feeder. She is not my whore. I can't make her feel obligated to service me in that way, and I know, if I try to feed off of her, I will not be able to control myself. The rush of placing my lips on her body will drive me toward an unbridled lust I will not be able to control.

I can't fight my body anymore. With an image of her beautiful face in my mind, my hand dips below my waistband, and I thrust into my palm, thinking of how exquisite it would feel if it were her hand or her mouth on my body.

When I hit my release, it comes hard, but I can only imagine that if I were actually with her, instead of all alone, it would be earth-shattering.

Satisfied and exhausted, I clean up and then roll over, determined to sleep. My hope is that the morning will bring new clarity to all of us, and she can figure out where she belongs in this new life. She is the daughter of my enemy, likely has her own fated mate back home, and I am engaged to a she-demon.

Wherever her place is, it's likely best if it isn't in my arms. But one thing about vampires that usually is true is that we are selfish creatures who have trouble with impulsivity.

And right now, all of my impulses are telling me I need that woman in my mouth and in my bed.

EMORY

I SLEPT WELL, despite my new surroundings and all of the confusion that washes over me every time I close my eyes. My body was just exhausted the night before, so when I lay down in my bed, after King Kane left, I immediately went to sleep, and now, as I open my eyes and blink a few times, I realize I've slept longer than usual. The clock says it's past 9:00 in the morning. I am usually up by 6:00.

Trying not to think about everything that happened the day before, I take a shower and get dressed. I decide to pin my hair up off my neck, which is probably not the wisest decision in a castle full of vampires, but it seems like a warm day outside for this part of the world, and the sun is actually shining. My understanding is that it is almost always cloudy here, as it was yesterday when I'd arrived. If there'd been any sun the day before, I hadn't noticed, though I had spent some time beneath the ground.

My eyes wander over the makeup the ladies brought the other day, and I decide to put on just a little. I have no idea what I'm doing, but when I'm finished, I decide I look presentable.

I'm also starving.

I am about to go knock on the door to the maids' room when mine opens. Nellie is there with a tray. "Oh, good. You're awake now," she says, bringing it in and setting it on the table. "We came by earlier, but you were still sleeping." Helga follows her in, gives me a curt nod, and heads to the bathroom, to clean I suppose.

"I'm sorry," I say. "I was very tired."

"That's understandable. We brought you some food." She gives me a reassuring smile.

I can smell the bacon and eggs and move to the table. Since I hadn't eaten much the day before, I am famished.

As I eat, the two of them clean the room, and by the time I'm done, it's pristine again. They are quite fast and accurate.

"What would you like to do today?" Nellie asks me.

I arch an eyebrow. I have just assumed my job is to stay in this room, since I am a prisoner, and just wait for the king to want to feed on me—or whomever he allows to do so. "Do?" I ask.

She nods. "It's a beautiful day outside. We could go for a walk in the garden."

"Am I allowed to do that?" I ask her.

She giggles. "Of course. And you're dressed for it."

I glance down at my red sundress and strappy sandals. "All right," I say. "As long as you're sure the king won't mind."

"No, he won't. He gave a decree yesterday that no one can harm you, so you shouldn't worry about that either."

She seems very confident that everyone listens to the king. I hope that is the case. In my pack, as far as listening to the Alpha is concerned, it's more of a question of will one get caught.

Nellie and I go out to the garden, through the door that Rainer showed me the day before. I am beginning to get the layout of the castle a little better now. The sunshine feels good on my skin, and the roses do smell divine. There are other flowers present, too, and Nellie seems to know all of them. As we walk, she tells me their names. I've never heard of most of them, but it's a nice conversation starter, and I can ask her questions about them.

Eventually, I ask her, "How do you know so much about flowers?"

"I use to work in the garden," she explains. "When I was a human, back when King Michael was our ruler, before he died."

It takes me a moment to process that. She looks like she is my age.

She even acts young—but she's over a hundred and fifty years old. It's such a strange concept to me. Wolf shifters live to be about eighty or ninety at the oldest. Lately, thirty has become our median age in my pack because of the war.

"How did you become a vampire?" I ask her.

"The gardener, Mr. Castaneda, took a liking to me." She speaks of it now like it's nothing. "He bit me... even though it was against the rules. He was killed for it, but Queen Agatha allowed me to live. She had always liked me."

"I didn't realize a person could be in trouble for being turned into a vampire," I stated as we made our way down the cobblestone path that twined between the flowers.

She nods. "Oh, yes. King Michael was very strict about population control. Back then, it was difficult to get blood to feed the vampires in the villages. Now, it's no problem because we are wealthy enough to buy it, but much of the wealth of the pack has come under King Kane's reign, not his father."

I am about to respond when I hear a snapping sound and look down to see my shoe strap has broken. "Oh, no," I mutter.

"What is it?" Nellie asks, dropping down to look. "These are new!" she declares.

Sighing, I hobble to a bench. "I guess I'll just take them off and go back inside."

"No, no, it's fine," Nellie says, standing next to me. "I'll run in and get you some new shoes."

"You don't have to do that—"

"You are enjoying the garden and the sunshine." She lovingly pats my arm. "I'll be right back."

I smile my thanks, and she takes off like lightning.

Sighing, I look around me. It is quite lovely and secluded here. This would be a wonderful spot to get lost in a book.

Just as I begin to daydream about sitting here, reading a nice romance novel, I hear voices and realize I'm not alone. I recognize them a moment too late for me to get up and dart away, even with my broken shoe.

Opal appears from around the corner, flanked by a bunch of other vampire women, with her brother and Prince Lex as well.

"What do we have here?" she says, a snide smile on her face. "If it isn't the fucking feeder bitch."

I am in trouble.

15

SHIFT FOR US, FEEDER!

Emory

"THIS IS HER?" a blonde woman with a pointy nose asks, her raised finger barely sharper than her beak. "This is the fucking breeder?"

I take a deep breath, not wanting any trouble. I am obviously outnumbered, and while I have no problem kicking Opal's ass and her friends' asses, I have a feeling I can't take Prince Lex and Prince Jacob. Not at the same time anyway. I imagine they've both got some sort of warrior training.

"Good morning, Princess Opal," I say, tipping my head down. "Prince Lex, Prince Jacob… ladies."

"Don't you know you're supposed to stand and curtsy when you're in the presence of your superiors?" Opal says, kicking me in the leg with her shoe. It's not hard enough to hurt, but it doesn't feel good.

"Oh, but don't you recall, sister dear," Jacob says, pulling her back by her arm. "She's a princess, too, remember?"

That gets a laugh out of most of them, though when I look at Lex, he's not laughing. In fact, he looks a bit concerned, like this is going to go south soon, and he'll be blamed for it.

93

"That's right!" Opal says. "She's not just a princess. She's a queen! She's Queen of the Bitches!" Another laugh surrounds me, and I begin to wonder how fast I need to run to get away from them.

If I were able to shift, I could leap over the rose bushes better than they could. Or if I could mind-link to Rainer or Nellie, perhaps I could get help. The maid herself wouldn't be able to save me, but she could bring guards or something.

At the moment, I am trapped here, though, and I honestly hope that Nellie doesn't hurry back. She could get caught up in this. I imagine that King Kane has rules against harassing the staff, but I don't know if this mob of brats would care about his rules.

"All right, let's go, " Prince Lex says. "You guys were going to show me where you were thinking of putting the ice sculpture." He tugs lightly on Opal's hand, and she lets her finger linger there in a way that seems a bit too familiar for a soon-to-be sister-in-law.

But she doesn't budge. "Lex!" she says. "Don't drag me away from the fun just yet! Oh, I know what we should do! We should get her to shift!"

"What a wonderful idea!" a dark-haired girl whose eyes are too close together for her to be considered classically beautiful declares.

"Why in the world would you want that?" Jacob asks as I try to slide my foot out of my broken shoe, still thinking of escape. "Filthy, mangy dogs. They're disgusting. Drooling everywhere. They smell like shit."

"She already smells like shit!" Opal declares, and the women actually bounce up and down with laughter.

I get my broken shoe off, but now I will have an uneven surface with each step, so I need to figure out how to get the other one off.

"Have you seen a werewolf in real life, then?" This girl has red hair but it's more orange than red like mine. "Prince Jacob? Were you frightened?"

"Of course, I've seen them, hundreds of them," he says, scoffing at her. "I served in the war, you know?" I don't know which war he's talking about. Perhaps he fought against my own pack. I have no idea. He is allegedly King Kane's ally, after all. "I've killed hundreds of them, for that matter. Sliced them open, ripped out their entrails." He looks at me, his gaze narrow, and I know he's trying to intimidate me, but I'm barely listening as I try to get my foot free. The shoe slips slightly. Perhaps I can get it off.

"Shift, stupid bitch!" Opal says, kicking me again, this time in the shin, harder.

Her foot is like a piece of stone, and I wince as I feel myself instantly bruising. I may have to run with one shoe on and hope that it falls off. Maybe I can use this shifting bit to my advantage.

"It's against the king's law for a wolf shifter to change into their wolf form in the castle or on its grounds," Lex reminds them. "You know that."

Opal waves one hand at him. "Please! I am the king's fiancée, the queen-to-be. If I give her permission to shift, she can do so. It's fine!"

I don't want them to know that I'm unable to shift, in case that secret becomes valuable someday. But if I could shift, I would've done so by now, king's law or not. I would have shifted and leaped right over their heads, racing back to the castle over the tops of the highest bushes.

But I can't shift, and telling them that might just sign my death warrant.

"Shift!" Opal shouts again, kicking me in the same place as before. My leg burns, pain radiating up and down my shin.

"Fine!" I shout back at her. "Let me take off my shoes." I reach down to unbuckle the one I still have on as she whines about why I need to do that. "They're new," I explain to her. So is the dress, but if I were to shift, it would be shredded.

"Well, they're hideous," beak-nose says. "You may as well ruin them!" They all laugh, except for Lex. He looks worried.

I get up, my leg screaming at me, and step around them so that I am closer to the castle than them, my shoes still in my hand.

"Wait!" Opal says. "How does it work? You can control it, right?"

"No, not really," I tell her. "I mean… not at first. You probably ought to step back."

Lex tips his head to the side and studies me as Jacob says, "What do you mean you can't control it? Of course, you can!"

"Not me," I tell him. "I'm new at this and… messed up. It's, uh, inbreeding." I nod, and he seems to buy it.

"That makes sense," the brunette with the strange eyes says. "It's no wonder she's so ugly."

They back up about ten feet, Jacob folding his arms in protest that he's budged at all, and Lex watching me carefully. He steps a bit in front of Jacob, and I have to think there's a reason for that.

"All right," I say. "I will have to leap into the air, and that's when I shift. Stay back. I don't want to hurt you!"

"Just get on with it!" Opal demands, but she seems scared. She steps behind her brother and grabs his arm.

With a deep breath, I bound up into the air, thrusting myself backward, not forward. At the same time, I let my shoes fly, aiming for Opal's face and hoping one of them misses Lex and hits Jacob. I throw them as hard as I can as I simultaneously spin around and take off running down the path toward the castle.

I can't look back to see what's happening, but Opal screams, "Ouch! You fucking bitch!" and then I hear what sounds like a platter hitting the ground in an empty dining hall. I turn to see that nearly every single one of them has landed on the ground, their stone-like bodies ricocheting off the cobblestone to make that sound. The only one still on his feet is Lex, and if I'm not mistaken, his leg is protruding in front of the rest of them, Jacob and Opal anyway. He is shaking his head at me, but it won't take long before the others are up, so I turn back around and run as fast as I can.

"Get back here, fucking bitch breeder!" Opal is shouting, and I can feel the reverberation of their footsteps off of the sidewalk as they fly toward me.

I am fast. I am not that fast.

I see the castle in front of me and know it will take me a moment to get up the steps and through that door. Even then… I'm not sure what I will do.

A second later, I see the door open. Nellie is standing there, but she isn't holding my new shoes, and she looks mad, not confused.

Still, she has to know this isn't safe. "Run!" I shout at her. "Run!" She isn't, though. She's just holding the door open.

I turn my head to look behind me. The vampires are coming fast. They are just blurs, except for Lex, who is running after them but at a much slower pace. I am about to die, and Nellie is going down with me.

I turn back around, hoping to have reached the steps so I can navigate them, as quickly as possible, but I slam into what feels like a brick wall, and it is only the fact that the wall has hands that dart out and surround me that keeps me from bouncing back several feet.

"Get inside," Rainer tells me, shuffling me off to Nellie who is beside him now, and I hear the other vampires come to a halt in front of the king's best friend. "What the actual fuck are you doing?" he shouts.

Nellie is pulling me up the steps and into the castle as a mass of guards come flying down the hallway. I don't have time to think about the pain in my head or whether or not Rainer can hold them all off while the guards arrive. I just have to keep moving.

We reach my room, and Helga is there, waiting for us with the door open. Nellie moves me to the bed and lays me down. "Get some ice, Helga," she says, and it's then that I realize despite Helga's harshness, Nellie is her senior. She's probably even much older than Helga in reality.

"Where are you hurt?" Nellie asks me, and I'm not even sure. My leg hurts the worse, that and my head. I ran right into Rainer, head first, after all.

She assesses the damage. "Your left shin, your forehead, and your shoulder," she says. "I'll get you some medicine." She moves to the bathroom, and I struggle to catch my breath. I almost died. Those bitches would've torn me apart....

Helga is back with ice and Nellie is telling me to swallow some pills, but the room is spinning, and as the adrenaline leaves my bloodstream, I can't hold back the tears. I need to thank Rainer. I need to thank Lex. I hope he doesn't get in trouble for this. I don't know why he helped me….

"How did you know?" I whisper to Nellie.

"I was on my way back with your shoes, and I heard them. I knew Rainer would know what to do, and he came himself." She smiles and pats my cheek lovingly. I see a new pair of sandals in her apron now. "You're safe now."

I nod, but I'm still crying, and I don't feel safe.

"You should rest." Even Helga looks concerned.

I know they are right, but how can I sleep when I can't stop the shuddering that wracks my body?

I turn onto my side, balancing the ice on my head and my leg, and close my eyes, but a few moments after I start to calm down, I hear a familiar voice say, "Leave us," and my breath catches again.

What is he doing here?

16

JUST A TASTE

Emory

MY HEAD IS ACHING, and my shin is throbbing, but when I look up to see King Kane standing near the side of my bed, it's like all of the aches dissipate, and the only thing that matters now is him.

I start to sit up, but he stops me with a motion of his hand. Helga and Nellie are gone, and it's just him and me now. I don't move, but he comes to sit next to me on the bed so that his hip is right next to mine.

"Are you all right?" he asks, his voice full of concern as he gently brushes my hair away from my face.

I am lying in an awkward position to be able to talk to him, and I do feel it is necessary that I let him know what happened, at least to a degree, so I roll my hips toward him and scoot up a bit on the pillow, while holding the ice bag in place over the lump on my forehead.

He takes it from me, and once again, his fingers touch my skin, just briefly, but it is enough for a fire to begin to grow in my flesh, rippling through my body to create a knot in my core.

"I'm all right," I assure him. "Thanks to Nellie and Rainer."

At first, his expression only darkens, but then, he nods slowly, and I think I see a bit of relief on his face. "Opal did this?" he asks me.

All I can do is shrug at this point. I don't want to stir up more trouble with her than what's already gone on. I'm sure Rainer will tell him, though. "They scared me. I'm not sure they were going to do anything. But—"

"What happened?" His voice commands me to answer.

I sit up further, tucking my dress beneath my legs and working the ice pack so that it's nestled against the bruise on my shin. He pulls back the bag on my head until I'm situated. Then, he replaces it on my bruise, holding it for me. "I was in the garden, waiting for Nellie to bring me some new shoes. My strap broke." He doesn't move, like he has no idea what I'm talking about, so I continue. "Opal, Jacob, your brother, and some other women came along and started asking me questions."

"What sort of questions?" He slides closer to me and his thigh is against my folded knees now. I can't breathe for a second, and it has nothing to do with my injures.

"Uhm, just silly… teasing questions. Lex actually tried to get them to go on and leave me alone, but then Jacob and Opal wanted me to shift."

"To shift?" he raises his eyebrows. "They know that's against the law on castle grounds."

"Yes, and Lex pointed that out. Opal said—" I stop myself. If I quote her exactly, she will hate me. "She said it would be okay."

He only shakes his head. His hair is down right now and I watch how the light plays off of it as he moves, momentarily mesmerized, like I am watching a shooting star. He notices and moves so that our eyes are connected. "Then what?"

"Well, I didn't think it was in my best interest for them to know that I can't shift yet. I'm not twenty-one yet, so… I don't have my wolf." He nods, clearly aware of that already. "Right. So… I got up like I was going to shift, but since I was afraid they might try to hurt me either way, whether I told them I couldn't shift or I just didn't shift, I threw my shoes at them and ran."

His face is unmoving for a beat as I realize how absolutely juvenile I sound. "You… threw your shoes at them?" he repeats. "And ran?"

I nod, biting my bottom lip. He must think I am ridiculous.

A chuckle escapes the back of his throat before he says, "That's brilliant. I do hope you hit them with your shoes."

Stunned at his comment, I'm not sure what to say at first, but then I manage, "Well, I didn't get a good look because I was trying to get away. Nellie had come back and heard what was happening and went for help." He is nodding again, so I guess he knows this. "I was checking how close they were to me when I ran into Rainer."

"That's how you got the bruise on your head?" he asks.

"Yes, and my shoulder." That one doesn't hurt as much.

His fingertips slide beneath the strap of my sundress, moving it slightly out of the way, and I can't help the little gasp that escapes my lips. After he's inspected the bruise, he puts the strap back.

"Well, I'm certainly glad that Nellie and Rainer kept you safe," he says, but I see that same look in his eyes that was there last night at dinner when he was mad. "Those assholes from Scarlett Thunder, though…. And my brother of all people!"

"Oh, actually," I interject, lifting a hand to his bicep. As soon as I touch him, I know it is the wrong move. My hand is now magnetized, and I am unable to pull it away from him. I stare at it, and he shifts his eyes to look at it as well before looking back at me, waiting with an eyebrow arched.

I want to pull my hand away, but I can't. I'm not sure why. Perhaps it's because he's not as cold as I always imagined a vampire would be or as rock hard. It's odd. It's like he has flesh over marble, like it's only their bones that are unyielding. But then, I never gave much thought to touching vampires except for to kill them.

"Emory?" The sound of my name on his lips does nothing to dislodge the distraction I am caught in. He lifts his other hand so that one finger is beneath my chin, and he pulls my eyes back to meet his face. When his hand leaves my skin, I can breathe again, and my hand slips away from his arm. "Actually… what?"

"Right. Actually… your brother was trying to help me, I think."

"My brother?" He sounds like he doesn't believe me. "Lex?" I nod, smiling at him as he's clearly taking this a bit too far. "Blond guy, little shorter than me, thin, with a pretty face."

"I know what your brother looks like," I assure him, still giggling. "Though I will admit the two of you look nothing alike."

"Oh? I'm not pretty?" he asks. "Or am I not thin enough?" He fakes sucking in a tummy he doesn't have, and I am beyond the ability to speak because I am laughing too hard. He's having trouble keeping the ice on my head because I'm shaking so much. I reach up and take it down, thinking it probably won't do much good now anyway.

"I'm sorry, Your Majesty," I say. "You're not thin—you're quite muscular. And… I wouldn't say you're pretty either."

He feigns being hurt, pretending that tears are welling up in his eyes. "I'm not pretty?"

"Sorry," I tell him, and then I'm touching him again, my knuckles brushing the smooth surface of his cheek. I stop laughing now. "You're not pretty, but you are very… handsome." A thousand other words rush to mind, some of which are very inappropriate to say to your king—sexy, godlike, fuckable? I could never….

A grin replaces his fake tears. "You think I'm handsome?" He moves toward me, and for a moment I think he might kiss me again, the way that I thought he might the night before.

I nod, looking up into his eyes, and his smile widens, but he stops a few inches short of me and brushes a curl behind my ear. "Don't let Lex fool you."

"Why do you say that?" I ask, trying to concentrate on the words and not the lips they are escaping.

"Because… he only does what serves his purpose. If he seems like he is helping you, it's to move forward with his own agenda."

I hear what he's saying, and perhaps that's true even in this instance, but it helped me, so I don't think that Lex should get in trouble for it. "He tripped them," I tell Kane. "At least, I think that's what happened. When they started running, after I threw my shoes, they all fell down except for him, and he had his leg out, like he was the one who knocked Jacob and Opal over and into the others. I think... I think he meant for me to get away."

Kane holds my gaze for a second and then shrugs. "Maybe so. But don't let that make you think he's your friend. There's a good chance he was just trying to keep his own ass from getting in trouble."

I open my mouth to say something else, but I don't know what else to say. He certainly knows his own brother better than I do.

"You need to sleep," he says. "You've been through a lot in the last few days. I can't even imagine how you're dealing with it."

Just the statement makes me want to burst into tears again. "I'm not," I assure him. I don't want him to leave. I'll say just about anything in the world if it will make him stay. "What about you?" I ask him.

He cocks his head to the side and stares at me for a second before he asks, "What do you mean?"

"I mean... whether you wanted me or not, I belong to you now. I'm yours to... do whatever you want with."

"That's not true." He readjusts so that there's more space between us, and I instantly regret my words. "I agreed to the trade with your father because I didn't think it was in your best interest to go back home with a man who would do something like that, who would sell you. And as for what I can do with you, well, I bought you as a feeder, Emory. Nothing more."

I hear his words, and they send a crack splintering through my heart. Nothing more.

Tears come to my eyes, but I look away. Maybe he'll think they are because of how it hurts to know my father sold me. Or because I am thinking of my sister with no one to protect her.

"Em?"

I look up at him, but I can't stare into his eyes. It hurts too much. I have already completely lost myself in him, and I have no idea why. Is it because he's shown me kindness when he didn't have to? Or is it something else? I don't know, but the pain of being so close to him when he's just said he doesn't want me for anything but to be his feeder aches worse than any external bruises.

And then... his lips are on mine, and the confusion is lost to the spell of his kiss.

17

I DON'T LOVE HER

Emory

KANE'S MOUTH is smooth and warm as his lips move against mine. Once again, I'm surprised that they're not cold, but the longer he holds himself against me, the more those thoughts fade from my mind, and all I can think about is how badly I want this man who is touching me in a more intimate way than anyone ever has before.

No fear resonates within me as his tongue taps against my bottom lip, prompting me to part mine. His tongue touches mine lightly, and my body is ablaze as tingles radiate down my spine and out through my limbs, causing a tightening in my core. He takes his time, his hand on my cheek as he steadies us, and I keep my eyes closed to savor the feeling of him, the taste of strawberries and cinnamon, not at all what I was expecting, the way his intoxicating scent wraps around me.

When he pulls away from me, I find myself leaning forward, unwilling to release him, but the moment has passed, and as I open my eyes, I see a very serious expression on his face.

"I need to go," he says, but he's not moving.

I nod. My lips are still prickling with energy from his touch.

105

"I need to go speak to Opal."

The way he says her name sends a bolt of clarity through me, and I am suddenly aware of the fact that he has a fiancée.

He's marrying her—not me. Opal. The horrid woman who does nothing but scream at me and make fun of me.

"Why?" I ask him, and I realize as soon as the word slips out of my mouth that it's not only none of my business, it's rude of me to ask. He's the king. He can speak to whoever he wants to.

He tips his head slightly as he says, "I need to talk to her about what happened. With you. Outside in the garden."

"Right." I drop my eyes to my lap where I am absently rubbing the hem of my dress between my fingers. I don't want him to leave at all, but I most definitely don't want him to leave to go to her. "Why… are you marrying her? I mean, not that you owe me an explanation. It's just… it doesn't seem like the two of you have that much in common."

"Unfortunately, we have a lot in common," he tells me. "We are both born vampires, which is a rarity. We are both the oldest sibling, which means she will rule her father's kingdom as soon as he is ready to step down. We've both been in aristocracy our whole lives. We both know the importance of alliances and staying strong against our enemies. There's a lot more to this than meets the eye."

I consider all that he's saying, and it seems like all of his words are political, occupational, and none of them are personal. "But… do you love her?" I ask him.

He scoffs at me and pulls his eyes away from my face. "Do I love her? Do I love Opal? Fuck no, I don't love her. I can't stand her."

The clarity his words give me makes me breathe a sigh of relief, as he has spoken with conviction, and it leaves no doubt in my mind that he most definitely does not have romantic feelings for Opaline.

"But you're marrying her anyway? Don't you worry about the unhappiness that will bring you? Do you even want to have children with her?" I can't help but wrinkle up my nose. The idea of that woman raising children makes me sick.

The idea of the two of them having sex in order to make those children makes me even sicker. I wonder if they already have had sex.

He shakes his head. "It's not that I necessarily want her to be my wife or the mother of my children, but my choices are limited, Emory. A born vampire can only mate with another born vampire, as far as we know. Granted, there aren't a lot of us around to find out, and most vampires don't particularly like children, in my experience. No, I would not want Opal raising my child."

"How would you keep her from it?" I ask, remembering that he said he needed to go, but I am not ready for him to leave yet.

"I am hopeful that after the wedding, she will return to her kingdom, and we will only see each other once a month until… we have a child. Then, once she gives birth, the child will come here and live with me while she stays in Scarlett Thunder."

"But…." I shake my head, trying to process. "Who will raise the child?"

"Someone who loves children," he tells me. "Someone… who is not Opal."

I want to ask him how he can even bear to have sex with that woman, but I suppose he is a vampire, and my understanding is that sex is such a high for them, they'll screw just about anyone, or anything.

Maybe that's why he kissed me.

But then… he did stop before more could happen between us.

And he didn't have to.

"What about that man from the meeting yesterday?" he asks, changing the subject on me so abruptly, I'm not sure who he's speaking of. I stare at him, unblinking. "The tall one who was standing behind you."

"Oh. Darius," I say with a nod. "He's my Beta. Will be my Beta. Was supposed to be my Beta." I take a deep breath, reminding myself that everything is different now, that the life I believed to be mine yesterday is gone now.

"Beta?" Kane repeats. "You mean… you were going to rule the pack?"

I nod. "That's what I've been told my whole life. I am the oldest, after all, and Colt is… a loose cannon. But now, I suppose Darius will be Colt's Beta, and who knows what will become of the pack. I wouldn't care at all except for...." I have to stop talking as emotion overcomes me.

He squeezes my hand, knowing what I'm talking about. "Was he your mate?" The question is gentle, meant to steer me away from thoughts of Lola, I imagine.

"I don't know," I admit. "I thought I might find out on my twenty-first birthday. Darius has already turned twenty-one, so sometimes we can tell if one mate isn't old enough yet, but he says he wasn't certain."

"Did you want him to be?"

I want to ask him why he wants to know, but the words spill out of my mouth without time for a question. "At one time, I did. But now... obviously, I'd hate to be away from my mate for the rest of my life."

Kane mulls that over for a minute before a slight grin forms on his face, and he says, "If you see him again and determine that he is your mate, maybe I can capture him for you. Make him a feeder, too." He chuckles, and I feel it in my soul.

I shake my head, a smile on my face. "That's all right. I think... I'll start my new life without any remnants of Moonraker pack. It seems like my entire existence there was a lie. I hated you immensely until yesterday morning, but as soon as I realized everything my father had ever said to me about both himself and you was a lie... you were able to show me that you're not a complete and utter asshole who wants to kill all wolf shifters and rule the world." I'd come to that conclusion in the dungeon, before the guards showed up, and it was a bit remark-able how quickly it had happened.

"So... I'm only a partial conceded asshole then?" he asks, winking at me.

"Something like that," I tell him, my face heating up again.

"I was honestly surprised at how quickly we won you over," he admits. "I thought you'd be angry and bitter, refusing to speak to any of us for weeks, maybe months."

I can't explain it either. It seems ridiculous when I stop to think about it, but I was wounded by my father and the rest of my pack, and Kane and Rainer were instantly nice and welcoming to me.

And then there was this heat, this pull, this magnetic connection I felt for the vampire king the moment I arrived here, as if we were meant to be together. It makes no sense. He's a vampire; I'm a wolf shifter. It's not as if he could be my mate, and even if he was, I wouldn't know it until I turn twenty-one.

I think he must simply have that effect on everyone. Except for maybe Helga. She doesn't seem very vampire-like when it comes to sex drive. Not that it's for me to judge.

"Earlier, when you said you wanted to leave your old life behind completely, you didn't mean your sister, though, did you?" the king asks me.

I swallow the lump that quickly rises in my throat and shake my head. "No, I didn't mean her."

He nods. "I'm sorry I had to send her back with your father. If I'd been thinking clearly, I would've gotten her, too. As much as he owed me, I would've been able to. I was just in shock that he was trading his children for drakes." He pauses for a moment and then corrects, "Not that you're not worth the sum and more by yourself."

I hadn't even thought of his statement that way. I can't help but smile at him.

"Well, I will let you rest. If you need anything, send for it. Your head looks better already. You wolf shifters really are quick healers." He pats my leg in a fashion that is incompressible to me. "And don't worry about dinner. Tonight. I'll have it sent to you." And then he is gone.

I lay back down, trying to close my eyes, but I can still smell his scent in the air. I can still taste him in my mouth, and I can still feel his touch on my skin.

Maybe I'll fall asleep and dream of him....

18

WHAT WERE YOU THINKING?

Kane

Kissing Emory was likely a mistake, but as I rush down the hall to the room where my brother, Prince Jacob, all of Opaline's consorts, and the princess herself are awaiting my arrival, I can't say that I regret my actions. The warmth of her lips lingers on mine, and I can still taste her on my tongue.

She may regret letting me kiss her, though. It seems she is confused about the relationship I have with the princess from Scarlett Thunder, and I honestly can't blame Emory for not fully understanding something I can't comprehend myself. It doesn't make sense that I would marry someone I hate simply to have a child unless I thought I was going to die and leave my throne to no one, but I plan on living a great deal longer, and my brother can always rule in my stead if I decide this isn't the life for me.

I will have a child because it is expected of me....

I push those thoughts aside and try to do my best not to think of Emory either as I enter the room off of the library where I asked Rainer and the guards to assemble them.

When I walk in, the three women that go practically everywhere with Opal are sitting on a couch, and at least one of them is crying. Opal is sitting in a chair, looking out the window with an expression on her face that says she's bored. Her brother has his arms folded as he sits with his feet up on the coffee table, and my brother is pacing back and forth behind the desk near the window. Rainer and five guards are lined up against the wall next to the door, and when I walk in, I don't believe I've ever seen anyone so relieved to see me as my best friend.

"Thank god," he mutters. "What, did you get trapped in a pit of quicksand?" he whispers to me so as to prevent the others from hearing his consternation.

"Yes, that is exactly what happened," I say, shaking my head. "I had to check on the victim."

I see his eyebrow twitch and know what he is thinking, but he will get no answers from me as it is not his business. I see the way he looks at Emory. Rainer is always friendly and kind, but I do believe he has his eye on her.

Who am I to tell him hands off when I'm engaged to the demon in the chair by the window?

"Stay, won't you?" I say to him, and he glares at me.

"Fine." That's all I get from him as he resumes his stance by the wall.

"Guards, wait in the hall." The five of them move at my command, leaving me alone with the troublemakers and Rainer.

"Who would like to tell me what the fuck was going on in the garden today?" I ask as I stand in the middle of the room, my hands folded behind my back.

"I'll be happy to tell you, darling," Opal says, "just as soon as you calm the fuck down. Why the hell are we being held in here like prisoners when it was that goddamn feeder who caused the problem to begin with? I mean, really, look at my face! I'm scared for life! I've been brutalized!"

I have excellent eyesight, but I don't even see a mark on her face from across the room. I step closer to her and look again. "What are you talking about, Opal?"

"See, I told you you couldn't see anything," Jacob chimes in. The woman who has been crying is just sniffling now, but it is still annoying, and I wish she would just fucking stop it already!

"Look!" Opal says, dragging her hand across the center of her face. "Can't you see it? That beast of a woman struck me with her shoe! She threw it at me, hitting me right in the face. Another one hit poor Jasmine, and she just can't stop crying."

I look at Jasmine, the blonde, and while her eyes are puffy and red from all of the crying, it isn't clear to me that she has any sort of mark on her face either.

"Why did Emory feel the need to throw her shoes at you to begin with?" I have to ask, though I already know the answer.

"Because she's a horrid bitch!" Opal proclaims, turning in her chair to completely face me now. "She's a monster! We were just walking by, minding our own business, and she leaped up and started taunting us, telling us she was a werewolf, and she was going to rip our throats out."

I know every word that is coming out of her mouth is a lie, but I am too intrigued to stop her.

"So then, Lex reminds her that it's against your rules for her to shift, but that doesn't seem to matter to her. She says, 'I don't give a fuck what that asshole King Kane says. I'm a wolf, and I'll show you my claws!' So she leaps up off of the bench, but for some stupid reason, she just throws her shoes at us and takes off running in her human form."

I survey the room and see that her three friends are nodding. Jacob looks confused, and Lex still looks uninterested.

"Well, naturally, I wasn't going to let her get away with tossing her shoes at me, so I grabbed them up and went after her to give her a piece of my mind, but all of us took off at the same time and tumbled into a big pile on the sidewalk, so by the time we caught her, Rainer just happened to be coming out the door, and he assumed we were the bad guys." She glares at my friend. "But that is obviously not the case."

When she is done, Opal drags her fingernails along the sleeve of her dress and resumes her window staring, obviously just assuming that I will accept her story as the truth.

Looking to the others, I ask, "Is that what happened?"

Immediately, the three girls say, "Yes, that's exactly what happened," or some variation thereof.

I look at Jacob. He says, "I don't have a very good memory, but I trust my sister to fill in the details. I do remember her sitting on the bench, yelling at us, throwing her shoes, and running."

"And she did this without being provoked by any of you?" I clarify.

Jacob's face splits into a wide grin, and he snickers at me. "Not that I recall."

I have nothing more to say to the lying asshole. I turn to look at my brother, and I know that expression on his face. He's not intending to tell me anything right now, not in front of the others. He may have fooled Emory into thinking that he was on her side, but Lex never does anything without an ulterior motive.

All I can say is, "I don't believe you."

"Seriously?" Opal whines, slamming her fists down onto the chair next to her legs. "Of course, you will take her side! What is she to you? Some sort of a pet now? Is she a stray you've taken in? A little poodle?"

With every question her tone becomes more and more annoying until I finally have to tell her, "Opal, that's enough!" She is seething as her narrow eyes pierce through my skin. "I saw the way half of you acted at dinner last night, the three of you that were invited." I know my comment is a slam to the three women on the couch, but I don't care. "And I know how unbelievably cruel you can be. Why would I believe that you would just pass by her without making a single remark when the possibility of ganging up on her and attacking her presented itself?"

Opal opens her mouth and closes it before she begins to fake cry. No tears are running down her cheeks as she says, "You never believe me! I bet you have already taken her into your bed, and you insist that we wait until we are married!"

"I don't believe who I sleep with is any of your concern, Opal, as we've discussed in our premarital agreement. Otherwise, I would need to be taking stock of everyone you've spread your legs for recently." I fight the urge to look at my brother, but I have a feeling he would give himself away if I did. I don't want to know. "The bottom line is that I have given an order that the girl, Emory Moonraker, is not to be harmed in anyway. That means no assaulting, teasing, bullying, etc. Do not touch her, do not pretend to touch her, do not think about touching her, and if you see her, do not speak to her. Do you all understand me? My motivation is none of your fucking business!"

"Fine!" Opal stands up in protest, flipping her skirts around wildly. "Is there anything else?"

"No, you may go." I am calm again, and as she files out, muttering under her breath that it's not fair that she got in trouble for something that "awful bitch" started, I am rethinking most aspects of my life.

My brother waits until the others are gone, and I stop him.

Lex looks at me with mirth in his eyes as he asks, "Yes, my King?"

I clear my throat and give the others a chance to get away from the open door so that perhaps he'll be more inclined to tell me the truth. "Emory is under the impression that you may have done something to help her out during this… attack."

"Oh?" he asks. "That's… interesting." I see a twinkle in his eyes and know that Emory is not mistaken after all.

"Listen, brother," I say, choosing my words carefully. "I know that the only person whose interests are important to you is you. So… whatever motivation you have for assisting Emory, know that I am watching you."

Lex rests a hand against his chest. "Brother! How could you? Am I completely heartless?"

I choose not to answer that. Instead, I say, "You and I both know they won't stop. If anything, this will just add more fuel to the flames. So… if you protect her, I will repay you."

"Why can't you just protect her yourself?" he asks me.

I shake my head. "I will do my best to keep her safe, but Opal and Jacob trust you. For some reason, they think you like them. Why, just yesterday, you were calling her every name in the book. Now, here you are, all buddy buddy again."

He shrugs. "I need to have something to do around here."

"Yes, well, if something else happens, please step in. I will make it worth your while."

"Oh?" he asks. "How so? Half your kingdom for a wolf?"

I snicker. "No. But… I haven't forgotten that you have your eye on Chateau de Rouge, that castle of father's near the ocean."

"I do love it so, but it's in disarray."

With a small shrug, I say, "I'll fix it for you."

"Completely?" He can't believe his ears as he stares at me, his mouth left hanging agape.

"That's right. But if anything happens to her on your watch… I'll ship you off to Hell's Eaves in five seconds flat."

He shakes his head at me. "All right, dear brother. We have a deal. I'll keep your new pet wolf safe, and you fix up that house I love." He offers his hand, and I shake it before he walks out with a grin on his face.

"What are you doing?" Rainer asks. "You know he's likely to start a problem for Emory now just so he can pretend to solve it."

Shaking my head, I say, "I don't think so. He's too smart for that. And not brave enough." Rainer heads toward the door, unconvinced, and I tell him, "Besides, you'll be watching her, too."

"That I will be," he agrees. "That I will be."

I try not to acknowledge the pangs of jealousy coursing through my middle.

19

WHAT'S WRONG WITH ME?

Emory

AS I EAT MY DINNER, I contemplate whether or not I am letting myself get carried away with the feelings I am developing for Kane. I have heard about women becoming obsessed with their captors before, but it doesn't seem like he is my captor. On the contrary, in many ways, it seems like he is my savior.

I sit at the table in the little dining area, eating a nicely prepared game hen, as well as several sides, and wonder whether this is what they are eating in the dining room tonight as well or if this is especially prepared for me. Last night, I hardly ate anything since I was so nervous, but tonight, I am practically swallowing my meal whole. I am glad to see I also have a slice of chocolate cake. Perhaps it is easier for me to eat without goblets of blood sitting everywhere.

Helga and Nellie are in the room, but I think their cleaning is really more just to keep me company. They meander around, dusting things, moving items from one spot to another, not really doing anything. I should probably tell them they can go, but I don't find the words just yet as I am considering asking Nellie a question I think she might know the answer to since she has known Kane for so long.

Yet, at the same time, I am nervous to ask because I don't want her to know how I am feeling….

"Your head looks better, Princess," Nellie says with a smile. "I'm glad you healed so nicely."

"Thank you," I tell her. "That nap helped tremendously. I still don't know what I might've done if you hadn't gotten help when you did."

She shrugs and her face turns a bit pink. "It's nothing, dear. I'm just glad I was able to help."

I smile at her. She seems like the sort of person I can confide in. I'm not sure about Helga, but she's on the other side of the room and might not even be paying attention. She seems very interested in the books on a shelf there, and I think she might be sorting them by color or something.

With a deep breath, I say, "Nellie, can I ask you something?"

"Well, of course you can, dear," she says with a friendly grin. "I might not know the answer, but I'll do my best."

I use my foot to push back the chair across from me and invite her to sit down. My shin is still a little sore, but I'll live.

Nellie looks hesitant to sit down on the job, but she does so. "What is it, Princess?"

"Well… this may seem like an odd question, and I won't try to explain my reasons for asking, so I hope you won't try to guess them."

She shakes her head slowly with a shrug, an inclination that she won't. "Go ahead, please."

"Well…." I say again and try to regain my composure so I won't sound silly. "I was just wondering… King Kane?" I pause, as if she might not know who I am talking about and wait for her to nod. "Is it… uhm… typical for all of the women who are in his presence, I mean, that see him. Or work with him—for him—that stay here…." I sigh and take a deep breath before I begin again, "Do most women like him?"

I hear a snicker from across the room and turn my head toward

Helga, but she looks innocent as she is moving books about on the shelf.

When I return my attention to Nellie, she is also smiling at me. "Do you mean is it common for women to be attracted to His Majesty?"

"Yes, I suppose that's what I'm asking, but I don't just mean women who've worked here for a while, or visiting dignitaries who think they might have an opportunity to marry him, or something like that. I guess what I'm asking is, does it tend to happen quickly and without explanation?"

"I don't know if I'm qualified to say how quickly it happens for most, dear, but I do think most women who spend much time at all in the presence of the king tend to catch some sort of feelings for him. I don't suppose it's without reason, either. Not only is he a strikingly handsome man, he is a good man as well. He cares about his people, does his best to keep them safe and provide for them, all of that sort of thing. He's intelligent and brave. Honestly, what is there not to like? Even Helga's been known to swoon a little when she catches His Majesty without a shirt."

"I've never!" Helga says, but I see a twinkle of truth in her eyes.

Nellie and I giggle at the statement before she continues. "I'm not saying that you are developing feelings for the king, dear, but if you are, I wouldn't think it too shocking. You have been through a traumatic time these past couple of days, and he has been there to help you. No, I wouldn't find it odd at all."

I take a deep breath, glad to hear her assessment of the situation. That does make me feel a bit more like I'm sane, that I'm not losing my mind.

"What does surprise me," she continues, gaining my full attention at once, "is how quickly he seems to have become smitten with you."

My eyes nearly bulge from their sockets and my mouth drops open. "Wh-what?" I ask her, and Nellie giggles again, a mischievous look in her eyes.

"Careful now!" Helga warns from across the room. "Don't go saying things you can't take back, Nellie."

"Oh, hush!" Nellie says, swatting a hand at her coworker. "I'm not saying I think he's ready to call the wedding off or anything, but I have noticed the way he looks at you. The way he checks on your well-being, the way he… dawdles."

"Dawdles?" I repeat, not sure what she means.

"Yes, he's a busy man with an entire kingdom to care for, yet he has more time for you than anyone else I've ever known him to spend time with." She shrugs. "That has to mean something."

I'm not sure what to say to that. It seems like I've hardly spent any time with him at all. Surely, he spends more time with Rainer than me. But then, that's got to be for work.

"He put Clark on room arrest, where he still sits, after hundreds of years of service to the family. Granted, this isn't the first time Clark has made a major mistake, so it might just be the last straw, but… I think if it had been someone else, perhaps the king would not have acted so swiftly," Nellie says.

"You don't know that, Nellie! Quit speculating." Helga comes over to join us but doesn't sit down. Instead, she stands with her arms folded behind Nellie.

Since I don't know what to say or do, I decide to start eating my cake.

Nellie isn't done yet, though. "He also got rid of those three guards who assaulted you yesterday. I am shocked about that as well. Not that they didn't deserve it, but generally speaking, the king can't be bothered with that sort of business. He has far too many other tasks to tend to."

I am confused by what she means. 'Got rid of?" I repeat. "What are you talking about?"

"He had them executed," Helga says in a matter-of-fact tone that almost has me choking on my cake.

"Executed?" I repeat as soon as I can speak. I take a drink of my water, a better choice than my wine at the moment. "Really?"

Helga and Nellie both nod. "Yes, this morning. He has the new jailor interviewing the other feeders to see if they can identify anyone else who may have taken advantage of them over the years. He wants the place cleaned up now, thanks to you."

I am glad to hear it, but I am sad that it is because of me. I also don't know what to think of those three men being killed. They do deserve it; my rational mind knows that. But... it's too much for me to process at the moment. I'm just thankful they'll never be able to hurt anyone else. I can only imagine what they must've been doing to the feeders who were too weak to fight back.

That night, when I go to bed, dressed in a pair of boy shorts and a camisole in a light blue, I can't help but think about how I was sitting right here when Kane kissed me. I wish he were here now, that his arms were around me. Even with Nellie's assessment of the situation, that I'm not being silly for having feelings for him, and that he may be interested in me as well, I can't help but think it's too soon.

My whole life, I've grown up believing in the mate bond, that the Moon Goddess has one person destined for each of us. If it's true that I could fall in love with Kane so quickly, then how can that be the case? He can't possibly be my mate—he's not a wolf.

I close my eyes, hoping I will dream of him. If I can't be with him in real life, then a dream is the next best thing.

Kane

DINNER IS ABYSMAL. I can't wait for it to end. Opal spends the whole evening talking about wedding plans. My eyes keep flickering to Emory's empty seat. The Duchess of Heartstone had wanted to sit there, but I wouldn't allow it. The woman who joked about her last night and all of those who laughed are gone, so there are plenty of empty chairs. But that one belongs to Emory now and will remain empty until she reclaims it—whenever she is comfortable enough to do so.

After the meal, I take a stroll around the gardens, noting that Opal is right about one thing. The rose garden does look lovely bathed in direct moonlight. The moon isn't full, but it's still bright, and it makes me wish I weren't standing here alone.

I should go to bed. I should lock myself in my room and stay as far away from the feeder as possible. If I move on instinct and go to her now, nothing good can come of it. She's only been here two days—not even—and she will grow to hate me for taking advantage of her.

But I know she wants me, too. I felt it in her kiss, can see it in her gaze.

As my feet begin to move of their own accord, I know I can no longer fight the craving I have for her, and this feeling has nothing at all to do with her blood. It's not the crimson liquid that flows through Emory's body I want.

It's her—completely and irrevocably.

20

HE CAME TO CLAIM HER

Emory

I AM TRYING my best to fall asleep, but my mind continues to spin with thoughts of Kane and the kiss we shared earlier in the night. The feeling has faded from my flesh, but it continues to burn in my mind, and I can't help but wonder if there's any possibility he is still thinking of me.

Dinner has to have ended long ago, so I wonder what he is doing now. I imagine him sitting behind his desk in his office or lying in his bed sleeping. Vampires do sleep a bit, don't they? My father used to say they did, so it would be the perfect time to attack, except he never figured out how to take advantage of that.

I sigh and roll over, thinking I will force myself to sleep when an odd feeling settles around my middle. I feel a tightening in my core, and my breathing becomes shallow.

Immediately, I sit up, my eyes focused on my bedroom door. I sense that he is there before the door even opens. He steps into a beam of moonlight filtering in through the window, standing there with his iridescent skin shining in the light, streaks of silver seeming to dance in his hair as it falls behind his shoulders. He doesn't need to speak in order for me to know precisely why he's here. My body sings for him, and as he closes the distance between us, I push the blankets down and come up to my knees, my essence longing for his.

His eyes are locked on mine as he unbuttons his shirt. I think he's already barefoot, but my eyes don't leave his face except for to sneak glances at his perfectly chiseled chest. He tosses his white shirt aside, leaving him only in his black pants, and as he reaches for me, I catapult myself into his arms, our mouths crashing together in a hungry kiss.

Kane's lips roll over mine as our tongues collide in a wet, messy, beautiful dance. I run my hands along the marble ripples of his chest and abdomen, feeling every divot, every crevice of his perfect muscles.

Breathing deeply, I inhale his scent and immediately feel my eyes rolling to the back of my skull. My eyes are closed so I can fully take in every brush of his fingers over my blazing skin, and I feel myself beginning to float away before he's even inside of me.

His touch is sensual, every caress full of purpose as he further ignites my flesh on fire. His mouth slides to my neck, and I let him kiss and suck on my most sensitive areas without reservation, knowing the vein right beneath the surface must be thrumming for him.

His hands slip beneath the hem of my top, his fingertips running along my sides and up slightly until he takes hold of the bottom of my shirt and smoothly pulls it upward, moving his mouth away only long enough to free me. Then, when his mouth is on me again, I am silently begging for him to make his way to my breasts. My nipples are already hard, begging to be sucked. He is taking his time, though, and I know I will have to find a way to be patient.

Running my fingers through his silky strands, I can't help the moan that escapes my lips as his hands finally find my breasts. He lifts them carefully at first before kneading them slowly and then concentrating all of his attention on my nipples, his thumbs rolling over them, plucking them gently at first and then a bit harder.

I can no longer support myself and swoon backward onto the pillow. I think I hear a chuckle escape his lips as he looks down at me. He still says nothing as I grin up at him. Then, he kisses me deeply once more, and I hold the back of his head, pulling him closer, wanting everything there is to have of him and more.

When he pulls away, he kisses a trail down my neck, between my breasts and around them, each peck a spark that leaves cinders behind. His tongue lashes out to find a nipple, and I cry out for more, the ache between my legs growing ever stronger.

His tongue is a magic wand that elicits a need within me that cannot be satiated. Again, Kane is taking his time, sucking, licking, and lapping my sensitive peaks, one and then the other, before he moves on, working is way down my abdomen to my waistband.

The weight of his gaze has my eyes slitting open, as I realize he is asking my permission. A moan is enough since I am not capable of forming words at the moment. He hooks his thumbs into my shorts and yanks them off, baring me to him.

I hear his gasp of delight as he takes in my body, and when he runs his hands along my thighs, spreading them, I comply. The wetness there is heavy, but he seems to like it as he licks along my thighs up to my center.

Again, he is in no hurry as his tongue meets my outer folds. I've never felt anything like this before. Tiny whimpers of pleasure punctuate each passing of his mouth against me, and when he makes it past my first barrier, I am ready for him to take me in every way possible.

He licks between my inner folds and then probes inside of me with his magnificent tongue before he takes my clit between his lips and sucks, rolling it between his lips. "Goddess! Kaaaane!" I cry, thinking we are past formalities at this point.

Alternating between sucking on my clit and probing me with his tongue, he continues to lap up my juices, bringing me closer than I've ever been to an orgasm. I feel my muscles tighten, my pussy begin to spasm around his face, and I want to come so badly, but I'm not sure if it's okay when he hasn't even taken his pants off.

Kane sits up, kissing my stomach before he slips two fingers inside of me. "You're so wet," he says, not probing very far. I can't respond. I can hardly breathe. He uses his thumb to massage my clit as I rock back and forth on his hand, and it's all it takes to send me falling over the edge. I am a panting, moaning, writhing, untethered beast, only from his tongue and his hand. I can only imagine what he can do with his cock.

Once again, he pauses to kiss me, and this time, I taste myself all over his mouth. I pull him closer and deepen the kiss, attempting to find his taste in there somewhere, the taste I am craving, and after a moment, that hint of cinnamon and strawberries is there. I don't want to let him go, but I hear him unhooking his belt, and then, when I hear his zipper, I am ready.

I know this will hurt a bit at first. It becomes more evident when he takes off his pants and boxers, revealing that he is long, thick, and his member is every bit as solid like marble as the rest of him. But I am ready for the pain to get to the pleasure, and though I feel a bit selfish for not taking him into my mouth, I know that having him buried to the hilt inside of me is the only way I'm ever going to extinguish this fire that has my core alight again.

He settles on top of me, his cock poised at my entrance, and I run my hands down his back, still too shy to touch what I'm sure is the finest ass the world has ever seen, which is ironic since his tongue has been inside of me, and he is about to bury himself deep within me, but I wrap my arms around his back, and he locks his lips onto mine before he begins to thrust inside of me.

The pain begins with the first movement as his head enters me, but when he finally works his way past my barrier and stretches me full, I can't help the little gasp of pain that escapes my lips, but then, suddenly he freezes on top of me, and I open my eyes to see his are wide.

"King Kane?" I ask, wondering what's the matter. What have I done wrong?

He says nothing, but instantaneously, he withdraws himself, not only from my body, but from my bed. Without a word, he grabs his pants from the floor and hastily puts them on.

"Wh-what's the matter?" I ask him.

"I… have to go," he says, picking his shirt up off the floor as soon as his pants are fastened.

"Did I do something wrong?" I whisper, grabbing the blanket and pulling it over my body.

He doesn't turn to look at me as he heads for the door. The only thing I hear him say is, "This was a mistake."

And then… he's gone.

I sit there, staring at the closed door for several seconds, trying to wrap my mind around what has just happened. I can't figure it out. I didn't do anything, did I? Nothing different than what I was doing. Did I move wrong? Did I touch him in the wrong place?

I can't figure it out. I thought… we were having a good time. More importantly, I thought that we had a connection, a deep one.

One that was worthy of me giving him my virginity.

Whether it lasted five seconds or a minute, I couldn't say for sure, but my virginity was gone. I had given it to him, and there was no getting it back.

With tears streaming down my cheeks, I go to the bathroom to use it and clean up. I still can't understand what's happened. When I wipe, there are streaks of red, and I know that's because I was a virgin, not because he hurt me.

I go back to my bed and see that there's a crimson stain on the bedsheets. It's not much, but even in the dim light of the moon, I can see it.

Perhaps he was afraid I was too inexperienced for him. Or perhaps he wasn't sober until that very second, though he seemed completely sober to me.

I get dressed and scoot over on the bed to a spot where we were not lying, my mind still going over everything. I begin to wonder if this wasn't all a dream. Maybe he wasn't here at all, and when I wake up in the morning, I'll realize it was all just a pleasant dream turned into a nightmare.

But I know that's not the case. I can still smell him in the air around me, and I can still feel his touch on my skin.

No, King Kane came to my room, intending to claim me as his own, and when he did, he became so completely and utterly disgusted with me, he ran away, telling me this was a mistake.

Maybe now, he will think that me being here at all is a mistake....

Then, what will become of me?

2 1

SHE WOULD BE DEAD

Kane

I WALK BACK to my room, collecting the shoes I'd left in the hallway, my shirt in my hands, thinking about what a horrible fucking person I am. There's simply no way to ever explain or justify what has just happened, not to anyone who isn't a vampire anyway, and I completely deserve it if Emory never, ever wants to speak to me again.

Thankfully, the hallways are mostly empty, except for the occasional servant passing through them. None of them dares to speak to me when encountering me in such a state, and I can imagine servants working this shift have a multitude of information to keep to themselves about the comings and goings in the castle.

All I want to do now is climb into my bed and hide under my blankets for a long while, until I figure out a way to go back in time and change what's just happened—after I have a large glass of blood, anyway. I can still taste her; I can still feel her on my skin.

I can't let myself think about how she tastes sweet like morning dew or how I've never felt like that before, not once, in all of the encounters I've had. She felt like her body belonged wrapped around mine in every way imaginable.

"A fucking virgin," I mumble as I reach the double doors that lead to my room in a secluded part of the castle. I shake my head, still trying to process everything that has happened. It is a lot to take in.

Before I even open them, I know that someone is in my chambers. I can sense another life force. I have a feeling I know exactly who it is, too, though why the guards let her in, I don't know. Oddly enough, they are both absent from the outside of my room right now, and all I can do is swear under my breath again.

Now is really not the fucking time.

I see her shadow draped over my settee and choose to ignore her, walking to my kitchenette and opening the fridge instead. I pour myself a glass of blood from the stock I always keep on hand and warm it for a few seconds before I turn to face her.

By now, she's up and has slunk her way over to the island. It appears that she's wearing the same long yellow gown from dinner, the one with the full skirt that makes her look like she's as old as she truly is, and when she hops up onto the island, it falls around her thick legs like a lampshade.

"Why are you here?" I ask gulping the contents of my glass quickly to try and satiate my need for blood. I'd been so close to losing control before, to taking it the wrong way. When the liquid hits my fangs and I take it in, the burning within my veins begins to lessen immediately. It's definitely not the same as taking it from another person, but it'll do. For now.

"I thought you could use a companion," she purrs. "You seemed… troubled… at dinner."

"I'm surprised you even noticed anyone else was at dinner, what with all of your wedding preparation stories." I take another drink, relieved that the burning is beginning to fade.

Opal snickers. "I'm always aware of you, my King. Always."

"Well, then, you should be aware that I don't want you here, Opal." I try to keep my tone even. I see no reason to launch an argument with her at the moment. All that will do is bring me grief. But I'm still pissed at her for what she did earlier in the day, and she has to know that.

A light giggle escapes her lips, and it reminds me of the sound a fairy might make, if there were such things. "You don't mean that. Especially not in the state you're in now. What's the matter? Did the little whore reject you? I smell her all over you—but I can also sense you're frustrated. I don't smell your release at all."

She makes a keen observation that is absolutely none of her business. "I don't ask you what goes on in your bedroom, and you don't need to know what goes on in mine—or any I happen to frequent." I finish off the blood and move to the sink to rinse the glass. "Seriously, Opal. It's late. Go to your room."

"It's clear to everyone that you're obsessed with her," she continues to purr as if I haven't just told her to drop it and get out of my room. "I can't pretend to understand why."

"It's not your business." I sigh and lean back against the counter, wondering if I'm going to have to physically remove her. "What did you do with my guards anyway?"

Another ripple of laughter leaves her. "Let's just say they were easily bribed."

The fact that she can do that makes me think I need to do a thorough investigation of all of my soldiers and not just the ones who work in the feeders' dungeon.

"You should go," I say again, but she's still not moving.

"Oh, come on, Kane," she says in that sultry voice that works so well on other men but leaves me nauseated. "Don't be like that. We're getting married soon. We should go ahead and consummate this relationship, make it real. It's clear you're horny as hell, and I am always up for a good time." She runs one hand down her exposed cleavage and leans back, arching like a cat, as her other hand begins to gather up her skirts.

"Not anymore, I'm not," I tell her. "We've already talked about this, Opal. I'm not interested in fucking you. We'll do it when we have to, when it's time to conceive children, but your attitude completely turns me off, in every way imaginable, and unless and until you become a more attractive person to me, I'm not sleeping with you."

"Kane!" She says my name like it's a curse. "You're being ridiculous. You have to know I'm a good fuck. Look at me!" She continues to gather up her skirts until they are mid-thigh. "Your stupid feeder is just a nasty dog. Why do you fucking want her so badly? She's not even pretty."

"I'm not having this conversation with you again." This isn't the first time she's tried to seduce me, though it is the first time she's brought up Emory or any other woman, and it's also the first time she's gone so far as to break into my room.

As I move toward her to try to remove her from my island and send her on her merry way, she finishes gathering her dress up so that it's at her waist now, and she isn't wearing any panties. Spreading her legs, she reaches down and fingers herself. "Just fuck me already," she says, her voice full of lust.

I don't want to go anywhere near her now for fear she'll manage to latch onto me, and I'll have to fight her to get her off of me. "Opal...." While I'm not sexually attracted to her at all, I have just pulled out of a woman I very much want with my dick hard as a rock, and it's clear Opal is doing her best to take advantage of this situation.

But Opal is not Emory—not even close—and sex with Opal would be some kinky circus act that would probably leave me with even more regret than I'm feeling now, and that's saying something.

"Come on," I say, walking away from her and heading toward the exit. "It's late. You should go."

"But—" she whines, dropping her gown down enough to cover herself now that I'm no longer able to see anyway.

"Just go. Don't bribe my guards again, and stay the hell away from Emory." I open the door and motion for her to go through it.

Reluctantly, she drops down off of the counter, sighing heavily. "You're making a huge mistake. You're going to regret this. Once we finally do consummate our relationship, you'll wish you'd fucked me a long time ago."

I want to tell her I feel like she's been fucking me all along, just not in the way that she means, but I say nothing only continue to motion for her to leave.

She walks out the door but pauses in the hallway, turning back to look at me. "That woman is going to be your undoing if you're not careful."

I slam the door in her face, knowing she's probably right, but it's not her concern. Turning the lock that prevents anyone from coming in, I head to my room and drop down onto my mattress, still smelling Emory, still tasting traces of her even after I've drank enough to rinse her away. She will not go quickly in the night….

It's fitting to me, as I put on a pair of clean boxers and climb into bed, that the woman who has managed to wind her way through my thoughts nearly every moment since she arrived here has now wrapped her way around my body in a way that makes her impossible to release.

As I lay in bed, praying to whoever listens to such thoughts to send sleep to claim me, I can't help but pray that Emory is already asleep. But I have a feeling I have left her confused, hurt, and feeling more alone than she has since she arrived here.

For that, I am terribly sorry. I owe her an explanation, and I will give her one as soon as I think she's ready to hear it, but for now, I just have to focus on the fact that I did what I had to do.

As angry as I am with myself for treating her so poorly, I am thankful that I was able to have enough self-control to fight every last ounce of my instincts and leave when I did.

Most wolf shifters think of us as monsters, and for the most part, they are wrong. We are more human than beast. But in moments like this, it's easy for me to see how we've earned such a reputation.

I can't remember the last time I felt more like a monster than I do right now.

If I hadn't left that room the second that I had… there'd be no way I could explain anything to Emory because, while I still haven't tasted her blood, the scent of it was enough to let me know if I had lingered even one moment longer…. she would be dead.

ALL ALONE

Emory

I WAKE up sore in places I've never felt before, and it takes me a moment to remember why. I try not to even roll over because of the muscle pain I feel in my core. Blinking against the sun streaming in from between the splits in the curtains, I feel a pain that radiates from my forehead, where I'd crashed into Rainer the day before, through my skull, and out the other side. But that pain is nothing compared to the one I feel in my heart.

A groan escapes my lips as I note I can still smell him on the bedding. I can still smell him on me. I push my head beneath the pillows, wondering what time it is but simultaneously not caring. I want to go back to sleep and wake up three days ago when I still had some control over my life. I want to remember all of this so I can avoid making the same mistakes twice. I want to take Lola and run away from home, but when my father tells me we are coming to visit the Vampire King to discuss his spoils of war, not his debt that he is rightfully owed, mind you, I want to tell my father no, that I'll never come to Castle Graystone, that I never want to meet King Kane

Alexander, and I never want to feel the highs and lows of longing, lust, and love I've experienced ever since my world got turned upside down.

With my face buried in the sheets, I realize that none of that is true, yet all of it is true, at the same time. The way that Kane makes me feel, how he can look at me in such a manner that my body springs to life in ways I've never known existed, how he can touch me and set me aflame, do I really want to go back to a time when I didn't know those things were even possible? Would it be better to have never experienced such things at all than to be where I am now with my heart torn in two and my body aching from both his touch and the loss of it simultaneously?

After a half an hour or so of contemplation, I pull myself from the bed and head to the bathroom, still seeing faint hints of blood when I wipe. I take a shower, hoping to rinse him off, but even if the smell completely dissipates, I will not be able to restore my body to the way it was before he touched me.

Getting out of the shower, I wrap a towel around myself and look at my face in the mirror. I have a faint bruise on my forehead, but otherwise, I look about the same as I always do. Except for my eyes. I can see the sadness within them, their lack of life and vibrancy. I have bags beginning to form as well from lack of sleep, and my eyeballs are red from all of the crying I did the night before.

Deciding that sleeping all day will likely help with at least two of these problems, I head back to my room to find something to wear. That's when I realize Nellie and Helga have arrived. A glance at the clock tells me they've likely been in earlier and let me sleep, like the day before, but I can tell by Nellie's expression as she puts fresh sheets on the bed that she's concerned.

"Are you all right, Princess?" she calls to me.

"I'm fine, thanks," I tell her. "Just... tired."

She arches an eyebrow and nods, but I know I haven't fooled her. Why does she think something is wrong? She may smell Kane on the bedding, but he was in here earlier in the day yesterday, and she knows that. Perhaps she smells my arousal. That doesn't mean anything. I could've been having a dirty dream.

I'm in the closet, pulling a comfortable looking outfit of an oversized T-shirt and joggers together, glad that not everything in my closet is fashionable, when I realize what the problem is.

Going back out, I see that the bed is made up with fresh linens. Even the duvet has been switched. "I, uh… started my… period," I explain to her. "Sorry for the mess."

"Oh," she says with a nod, and when I glance at Helga's face, I see that she doesn't believe me. I suppose neither one of them does. "Well, as long as you're not in any pain, dear. If you are, there's plenty of medicine in the cabinet in the bathroom."

"Thank you," I tell her, but I know there's nothing on the shelves that will fix the pain I'm feeling.

"Your breakfast is ready when you are, dear," she says, gesturing at the tray on the table. I'm not hungry at all, but I thank her again and go to get dressed.

When I am ready, I come back out to the table to see a plate of fruit and pastries. At least the food isn't something that needed to stay warm. I nibble on a strawberry danish and eat a few grapes, but I'm not hungry, and forcing myself to eat will only make me feel worse.

Both of them keep giving me sympathetic looks. I know I must look pathetic for Helga to care enough to look at me that way. But I don't feel like trying to explain myself, not at the moment anyway.

"Do you have any plans for the day?" Nellie asks me with a kind smile.

"No," I tell her. "I think I'll just stay in here and sleep. Maybe read a book or two." I remember the shelf Helga was straightening the day before and consider asking her for recommendations, but I stop short of doing so. It's not as if I'm actually planning on reading anything.

"We will leave you be, then," Nellie says. "If you need anything, just knock on the door between our rooms, and one of us will be here in a moment."

"Thank you," I say, remembering that they are nearby and

wondering if they heard anything the night before. I doubt it. I haven't been able to hear anything from their room or even the hallway with the door closed, but it does seem like they know my story is a lie. I just don't know if they are aware of the exact truth or not.

Eventually, I fall back to sleep for a bit, awoken when Helga brings in my lunch tray. She asks me if I need anything else, and I say no, so she goes, but she's continuing to look at me like the witness at an accident scene. She seems to want to help but doesn't know where to begin, and I feel that in my soul.

I don't know either.

After lunch, I am back in bed, my mind running away with me as I try to figure out what to do with my life now that all of my dreams have been dashed, and I've been rejected, when I hear a knock on the door.

At first, my heart leaps into my chest with the idea that maybe it's Kane. But I quickly push that hope aside, knowing it can't be. I would have sensed him if it were him, like I did the night before.

On unsteady feet, I walk to the door and pull it open, relieved to see Rainer standing there. "Hey!" he says with a big grin on his face. "How are you?"

I let him in, and he immediately wraps his arms around me. Suddenly, I find myself melting into him, the tears I've been fighting all day springing to the surface. It's like I've found solace in the arms of a friend or a caring sibling instead of a man I just met a couple of days ago, and I already know as soon as he asks me what's wrong, I'm going to spill everything.

"Are you… still not feeling well?" he asks me, clearly confused by my tears. He doesn't try to get away from me, though, only holds me and lets me cry until I am done, and then I realize that even though I am regretting ever coming here, I am thankful for a friend like him.

When I can finally breathe again, Rainer quietly asks, "What happened?" He's clearly figured out by now that it's not my health that has me crying.

With a loud sigh, I free myself from his grip and go to the sitting area, and he follows me. I fold myself into one of the chairs, and he lowers his massive body down into the other. "I guess he hasn't said anything to you?"

His bushy eyebrows raise for a second as he tries to decipher my cryptic statement, but once he has it, he shakes his head. "No." That's all he says.

"He, uh, came in here last night… after dinner." Rainer nods, and I swipe at my tears. He gets up and grabs a tissue from the box near my bed and hands it to me before going back for the whole box. I thank him and take a minute to clean up my face before I go on. "We did… stuff. But just when he, uh…." I am making some sort of gesture with my hands, but I don't know if he's getting it, and I can't bring myself to say it.

"Hit a hole in one?" he asks, and I am now the one who is confused. "Insert his tab into your slot? Plugged his cord into your outlet?"

I feel my face turning bright red as I hold up a hand for him to stop. I'm not sure what else he's got on the list of descriptive ways to say penetration, but I don't think I want to hear them.

"Yeah—that," I tell him. "When he did that… he was only in there for, like, two seconds before he immediately got off me and rushed out the door, telling me this was a mistake and just leaving me lying there, naked and alone." The words bring tears to my eyes again, and it's all I can do to keep from having yet another break down.

"Oh, shit," Rainer mutters, shaking his head. "That really sucks."

"Yep, thanks." I don't know what else to say. My nose is starting to run, so I wipe it on a tissue, and I hope that Rainer has some insight, but honestly, I'm just glad to get it off of my chest.

"Well," he begins, leaning forward in his chair so his elbows are on his knees and his hands clasped together. "He didn't say anything to me about it, but then, he probably wouldn't. We don't talk about sex much, believe it or not. And he didn't say anything else? Nothing that would give you an indication that he got a message from someone about an emergency?"

I shake my head. "Wouldn't you know if there had been an emergency last night?"

He concedes that he would know. "Yeah, probably so." He sits up in his chair. "That's so bizarre. I mean, he has been denying that he has feelings for you, but that's not unusual. And we can all see right through it anyway."

I'm not sure if that should make me angry or cause me to blush. My face goes with the latter. "Maybe I just wasn't what he was expecting. He's probably used to girls with a lot of experience. I was probably just a huge disappointment to him." I need a fresh tissue. Mine is disintegrating. I pluck another one from the box.

"I'm sure that's not it," Rainer assures me. "Besides, how would he be able to tell you were inexperienced from just one thrust. Unless—oh!" His eyes grow to the size of saucers, and he stares at me for a moment.

I suddenly begin to think I must be the worst person in the world when it comes to having sex that people can just tell I'm awful from two seconds of being with me.

Then Rainer asks me, "Were you a virgin?"

Were you a virgin. That word seems so strange. I'm so used to being a virgin, it seems like I still should be, especially since that two seconds of sex shouldn't count. But I nod my head.

He is nodding, too. "Yeah, that explains it."

"It does?" I ask him, still confused.

"He didn't know before, did he?"

"I didn't tell him, but I didn't *not* tell him...." I had just gotten the impression he knew. We had talked about how I hadn't found my mate. "Why?" What am I missing?

"The blood, Emory," he says, and while I am still confused, when he finishes his statement, I'm up to date. "In that aroused state, assuming he didn't feed on you first, as soon as he smelled that blood, he knew if he didn't leave—he would've ripped you apart."

23

WHY HE RAN AWAY

Emory

I AM LISTENING to Rainer's words and trying to digest them, but I'm not completely sure I understand what he is saying to me.

"It was the blood?" I ask him, and he nods at me. "But… there was so little of it. Less than whenever I am menstruating by far."

When he shakes his head, his dark curls dance around his face, and I can see why some women would find that alluring. He really is a handsome man.

"It's not just that it's blood per se. Menstruation blood is… unappealing to us. I won't go into detail, but it's not something that most of us would want to drink. Kind of like bad coffee for humans, I guess. Even regular blood doesn't get us in quite a tizzy the way that particular kind of blood does."

I stare at him for a moment, trying to understand, but I'm not sure I do. "That kind of blood?"

"Some people call it cherry blood." He seems slightly embarrassed to be talking about this with me. His cheeks are a bit pink. "The blood

141

released when a woman loses her virginity is filled with aphrodisiac scents for us but also drives our hunger. I'm not sure why. Perhaps it's because back in the day, before we could easily syphon blood from humans, we had to bite them in order to drink, and the easiest way to do that was during sex. So whoever the hell created vampires made it so that when we smell that scent, we want to drink the person we're with. And… we want to drain them dry. In fact, a lot of times, it becomes a savage situation where the virgin literally has her throat ripped out. It's not pretty."

Unable to respond, I just continue to look at him for quite some time before I finally ask, "And Kane didn't feel it was necessary to ask me if I was a virgin before he went through with this?"

He smirks at me. "Yeah, one would think." He runs a hand through his hair making his wild curls even more unruly. "But in fairness, I don't think he intended to come here last night. I think it was more of a whim. Maybe he was just coming to check on you, and other things happened?"

It is a question, as it should be because it's way off from what actually happened. It's clear to me that Kane came here the night before with only one thing in mind.

But I see absolutely no reason whatsoever to tell Rainer that. So I only shrug. "Who knows? I just wish he would've said something to me. I wasn't trying to keep my state a secret to him, but when he left like that, I thought I must've been the worst lover in the history of sex."

That causes him to start laughing, but once he reins it back in, he says, "I highly doubt that's the case. Just… give him some time. He'll figure out how to go about apologizing and making it up to you."

I think about those words. Do I need an apology? It would make me feel better, but at the same time, as long as I have an explanation, that's really good enough for me. I don't necessarily need him to say that he's sorry. But if he could confirm that what Rainer is saying is the truth, I would feel better.

And there's really only one way to make it up to me. I think about how I felt before he tore out of the room, what it was like to have the king's face buried between my legs, and I feel myself growing heated. I know my face is turning red, and I can feel that familiar ache beginning to grow between my legs.

"I guess… you thought of a way he could make it up to you, huh?" Rainer asks.

I feel like a ridiculous woman-child, and I can't look at him. He's chuckling again, and I just have to let him. What am I going to say? If the king wants to bury his tongue in my pussy to show me he's sorry, he can do that anytime!?! I think better of making that statement.

"Well, uh, thanks for stopping by to check on me," I say, thinking Rainer probably needs to go before I let my mind fall any deeper into the gutter.

"Of course," he says. "I hope this is the last of any trouble you have with those assholes from Scarlett Thunder. Lex has agreed to help keep them from bothering you, so keep that in mind. Not that Opal and her brother know that." He shrugs, and I'm not sure what he's talking about. I had thought all along that Lex was trying to help me. Maybe Rainer is just confirming that.

"All right," I say, and he stands. I feel a little less weak in the knees now and manage to walk with him to the door.

"Sorry my chest is so hard," he says, his way of apologizing for the bruise on my head, I'm guessing.

"It's okay," I assure him.

At the door, he stoops to kiss the top of my head, and a rush of warmness shoots through me. It's not like when Kane kisses me by any means, but it's nice.

"See you," he says.

"Bye." I give him a wave as he heads through the door before I close it behind him. The temptation to look out into the hallway to see if I can spy Kane anywhere is difficult to ignore, but I manage.

I go back to my bed and toss myself down, thinking it may take a while for the Vampire King to realize he's made a mistake. In my experience, most men with power don't like to say they are sorry, and while it's clear to me that Kane isn't anything like my father or any other man I've met that's at his level of authority, he's still the king. And he's still a man….

It could be a day. It could be a week. It could be never.

All I can do now is wait.

———

Kane

I should apologize….

I should go over there to check on her at the very least.

But I don't. Instead, I spend the morning doing the usual tasks that keep me busy. I spend the afternoon digging up new tasks to keep me busy, and by the evening, I am too busy getting ready for dinner, or so I tell myself, to stop by and see if she's all right.

On my way back to my room to get ready for the nightly event, I see Rainer for the first time all day. He has a look on his face that makes me think he knows something.

"Well, you fucked up," he says with that chuckle he rarely gets to use on me. Most of the time, he is the one who has messed up, and I'm the one telling him he needs to fix it if either of us is in a position of making a mistake.

I stop in the hallway and squeeze the bridge of my nose, trying to figure out how to respond to that. Eventually, I just blurt out, "What are you talking about?"

"Yeah, go ahead and pretend like you don't know." He folds his arms and leans back against the door. We are standing right next to the library, one of the most magnificent rooms in the castle, and as we are speaking, a few servants come out with their selection of books, they bow their heads and scurry off, and the interruption gives me a moment to think about what he's saying.

"Did you speak to her, then?" I ask, hoping it's that and not rumors. Who knows what Opal has been telling people?

"I did. I think I calmed her down some, but dude, she was really upset. Like... thinking she'd done something wrong."

"Shit," I mumble under my breath, letting the fact that he has just called me "dude" slide.

"Seriously, an apology is in order. Or at the very least an explanation. But I think you need to do something to make this up to her. Why didn't you ask?"

I shake my head. "I don't know. I didn't intend to go there. I just got caught up in everything." There's simply no other way for me to explain it.

"Well... I wouldn't wait too long to let her know that you care about her, assuming that you do. And if you don't, that's cool, I guess, but you should probably let her know that, too."

He knows that I care about her, and as he pats me on the shoulder and walks away, I have to think there's a pretty good chance he cares about her, too, so I'd better get my shit together before he's the one who swoops in and steals her away from me.

But how? I've never been one for apologizing. Not that I never make mistakes. It does happen from time to time. But when it does, people usually just pretend like it never happened because I am the king.

No, this time I'm going to actually have to think of something to fix this if I want Emory to be able to trust me again.

I head off to my room, thinking about how amazing she tasted, how tight she was when I slid inside of her, how responsive her body was to mine.

In my room, I turn on the shower and check the time. I have an hour before dinner is ready. That's plenty of time to think about how to fix this—and plenty of time to think about Emory in the shower. I can't help but wrap my hand around my hardness as the warm water flows over me. This time, I don't have to wonder what it would feel like if it were her tight cunt around me instead of my hand. I already know.

And it feels amazing.

It feels so good, I know I will be on the brink of losing control if and when I'm with her again. But this time, I hope there won't be any surprises.

I wonder if I can figure out a way to make this up to her quickly because my hand is no substitute for her perfect pussy, and I need her again.

I need her now.

24

A LETTER FROM THE KING?

Emory

IT'S ALMOST DINNER TIME. But I'm not going back to the dining room today. I haven't been told by King Kane that it's okay for me to skip again. Maybe I need his permission. Maybe I don't.

I figure, if he wants me to know I should be there, he can come and tell me. And if he realizes he wants me there after dinner has started, well, he can send someone for me. I'll just tell them I'm not feeling well.

Either that, or I will show up at dinner wearing my baggy T-shirt and joggers.

For most of the day, I've sat in the reading area with a book on my lap not looking at the words. Nellie asked me if I wanted to go to the library. She says it's spectacular, with hundreds of thousands of books, and plenty of comfy areas to sit and read a book. There's even a loft with a lovely view out the window of the lake on the east side of the castle.

It did sound nice, but I'm not going anywhere. If my job now is to hang around the castle until the king or one of his noble people is ready to feed on me, then that's exactly what I'll do. I'll stay in my room and wait. I'm not doing anything wrong this way. And if I was still in the feeders' dungeon, I'd be doing the same thing. At least then I'd have other feeders to speak to.

My mind goes over everything Rainer said to me earlier in the day, and I hope he's right. I wish I could confide in Nellie, but I would feel so stupid telling her what happened after the conversation we had yesterday. It's better if I just keep this to myself.

I wonder if Kane will ever apologize. I doubt it. He will probably just find another feeder, another woman that he wants to have sex with. It would probably be better than coming to me to say that he's sorry.

With nothing to do, I am wondering how Lola is and wishing that I could see her, hear her voice. I am second guessing all of my choices in this world. I am wondering if Opal has a shoe print on her face and how she will get back at me for the way I embarrassed her yesterday.

My thoughts are interrupted when I notice a bright red piece of paper lying on the floor near the door.

It catches me off guard. How long has it been lying there? I don't remember seeing it when I walked over here an hour or so ago, but then, I wasn't really looking at the floor. Nellie and Helga cleaned up after lunch and then left a few hours ago, saying they'd bring me dinner later, so if it had been lying there when they were in here, they would've picked it up, right?

I wonder if one of them dropped it when they left, but I don't even know if they went out this door or the one that leads to their room.

Curiosity gets the better of me, and I go over to pick it up.

It's a note.

Handwritten with thick black ink, it's short and to the point. I take it back over to where I was sitting and drop down next to my book to read it over.

"Dearest Emory,

Please meet me in the library in the loft at 3:00 AM. I want to make last night up to you."

K."

Puzzled, I turn the paper over and over again. That's it. That's all it says. It makes no sense to me. Why would he leave me a note instead of just telling me what he wants me to do? It's not like Kane is the sort of person to beat around the bush.

It is possible he's chosen to do it this way as part of his grand gesture to show me that he's sorry? I don't know, but the situation seems a little strange to me. And why 3:00 in the morning?

I have no idea what to think of any of it, but I'm so absorbed in trying to figure it out, I don't hear Helga and Nellie come in until Nellie's voice says, "What you got there, dear?"

I nearly jump out of my skin. Turning around, I see her approaching from behind me, peering over the couch.

Hastily, I shove the paper into my book. "Oh, uh, just a bookmark," I tell her. I don't think it's any of her business what it is. I don't even know if I'm going to go. What would the king do then, if I didn't show up to his invitation?

I stand up and walk over to where Helga is setting my dinner up. "That smells good," I tell them.

"Pork chops, potatoes, and mixed vegetables," Helga announces.

"With apple pie for dessert!" Nellie smiles at me. "With whipped cream!"

I can't help but smile back at her. She's trying to make me feel better, and I do appreciate it. "I'll just go wash my hands," I say and head to the restroom.

When I come back a few moments later, Nellie has my book in her hands. I narrow my gaze at her, but I don't ask. Was she reading the note?

She sets the book on the coffee table and picks up a throw pillow to fluff it. "Just tidying up, dear," she says with a smile that looks a bit guilty to me.

I nod and head to the table to enjoy my dinner. As awful as I've felt for most of the day today, I am hungry. I decide to enjoy my food and not worry about Kane for now.

The maids clean while I eat, and when I'm done, they take the tray away. "Will there be anything else?" Nellie asks me.

I shake my head. "No. I'll probably just read a little and then go to bed early."

She nods, but I see doubt in her eyes. It's like she can see right through me. "All right, dear. Let us know if you need anything. Otherwise… goodnight. And… stay safe." She gives me a pointed look, and I have to wonder if she thinks there's something going on.

But then, I managed to get myself into trouble without even leaving my room the day before, so maybe she doesn't need to know about the note to warn me to stay safe. I'm pretty sure they've figured out by now that I'm not actually on my period. I haven't used any other pads today. I'm not about to cut myself in a castle full of vampires just to fake my period.

Once they are gone, I do try to read for a bit longer, but I can't stop thinking about the note. Am I going to go? Why does he want me to go? What's going to happen when I get there? If he apologizes, will I forgive him?

I'm pretty sure I know the answer to that last question, but that doesn't mean I should be so fast to forgive and forget. He put me through a lot of pain for absolutely no reason. All he needed to do was ask a simple question and/or give a simple explanation.

A couple of hours after the maids leave, I decide to go to bed, leaving it to fate. If I fall asleep and manage to wake up in the middle of the night in time to get ready and go to the library, then I will take it that the Moon Goddess has this in store for my life.

If I sleep right through, then I will know that I am not meant to go.

And if I cannot sleep at all and just lie there for hours staring at the ceiling, feeling like a tortured soul, then I will get up in time to get dressed and head to the library.

With the moonlight reflecting off of the white ceiling of my room, I do finally fall asleep, but not for long, and when I wake up and glance at the clock, I see that it's 2:12.

That gives me plenty of time to get up, get dressed, and go to the library to see what it is that King Kane wants.

Sighing, I push the blankets off of my legs and head to the bathroom to start getting ready. I shower quickly, put my hair up in a twist with a gold clip I find in one of the drawers, and put on some makeup. I'm still not that good at it, but I'm getting better.

I put on some nice lacy blue lingerie and then go to the closet to pick out a dress. I find a black one and decide that it will look nice on me, and I can manage the zipper by myself, not that I would mind having Kane unzip me again. I decide on some black heels that have no straps that are easy to get in and out of.

When I am finally all ready to go, I head to the library with about five minutes to spare. I'm not exactly sure which way it is at first, but then I see a landmark that Rainer pointed out to me, and I turn that way. My heels are loud on the marble tile as I walk through the dark, deserted hallways.

I reach the library door and pull it open, peeking my head inside.

The room is huge, and I can't help but gasp at how beautiful it is. Even with the lights off, I can see most everything as the moonlight pours in through a giant, circular skylight in the top of the room, with crystal cut glass that creates dancing prisms that bounce off the walls and bookshelves. A huge crystal chandelier hangs in the middle of the room as well, catching the light and casting rainbows off the other surfaces.

The bookshelves reach all the way to the ceiling, which has to be at least three stories high. The fine wooden carvings remind me of my door. The place smells like paper and book glue, which invites me in.

Walking across the room, I see all sorts of cozy places to curl up with a book—Nellie was right. The seating options are endless, some by fireplaces, others near windows with lovely outside views, and I can't picture a more amazing place could ever exist.

I see the ladder that leads up to the loft. I can only imagine how amazing that place must be based on how the rest of the room charms me. I don't sense that Kane is here just yet, but I have to think he must be coming soon.

With my heels on, I have to be careful as I ascend the ladder. I take it slowly, keeping my dress gathered out of the way as well.

At the top, I step onto a solid wooden floor with a railing that almost reaches my waist. The view of the library is nice, but when I turn to look out the window, I can see the lake sparkling in the moonlight, and it truly is one of the most beautiful scenes I've ever taken in.

The loft has a few seating choices, including a couch and a chaise lounge. The books up here look to be well loved as the covers are worn and the binding doesn't appear to be solid. I can only imagine how many people have called this their special place over the centuries.

The sound of someone climbing the ladder has my heart skipping a beat and my throat restricting in anticipation. But even before I see a head pop above the surface of the floor, I know something is wrong.

I don't have to see the man's face to know that it isn't Kane. Instinctively, I back away from the ladder. But it's the only way up or down except for a long jump to the library floor below. I pray it's a friend, someone I can trust, someone who's just come to tell me the king is running late.

And then, he steps onto the loft floor, and my worst fears are staring me in the face.

"Hello, feeder," he growls.

I have to be strong and brave, so I look him right in the eye and say, "Hello, Your Majesty."

25

THE PAIN OF DYING PREMATURELY

Emory

JACOB'S pale skin catches the moonlight as he comes toward me, his pace surprisingly human now, a bit cautious. I can't anticipate what he's waiting for, but I wish I knew. Maybe then, if I had some kind of an inkling as to what he's up to, I would be able to do something to get away from him.

My eyes immediately go to the library floor below me, but it's so far. Even if I had my wolf, which I don't, I am pretty sure I wouldn't be able to make that leap and walk away unscathed. I wouldn't mind breaking all four of my limbs if it meant getting away from Jacob, but there's no point in contemplating something I can't do anyway. I can't shift, and if I did, I would just be easier for him to catch with four broken legs.

Vampires can easily leap down from heights of this distance with no problem whatsoever.

Me, in my human form? Nope.

Still, he feels the urge to say, "I wouldn't even think about it, bitch.

You jump down there, you're just going to die a more painful, slower death."

I know he's right, but I also don't want to let him kill me. I think I can fight him. I fought those three guards in the feeders' dungeon, but he is probably more skilled than they were. After all, he's likely participated in battles, or at least trained for it, and those guards had not. Didn't Jacob say something the other day at dinner about killing wolves?

"Stay back," I warn him, stepping out of my heels. "I will hurt you."

"Oh?" he asks, his eyes dropping to my feet. "Are you going to throw more of your death-shoes at me?" He snickers, and when he opens his mouth wide, I see that his fangs are already beginning to elongate. They must be two or three inches long already. I don't remember ever seeing vampire fangs this long, and they're continuing to grow.

"No, I'm not going to throw my shoes at you. I don't need to." I'm still trying to sound tough. "I took on three trained guards in the dungeon the other day. I can handle you."

That chuckle resounds throughout the library again, but this time, he's not the only one laughing, and behind his shoulder, I see Opal appear. She's wearing an evening gown, likely the same one she wore to dinner early, and she looks more like she's on her way to a ball than to murder me.

I know that I'm screwed now. She may look like an untrained, domesticated housewife type, but I'm sure that's not the case. Besides, she has the natural fighting instincts of a high-born vampire.

I'm not going to give up, though. Maybe if I stall long enough, someone will hear the commotion and come to help me. I'm not above actually screaming for help. I don't want them to see that I'm afraid yet, though. So instead of yelling, I knock over a bookshelf. It thunders to the ground and shakes the entire loft. I do the same with one of the chairs, throwing it between us.

Both of them are amused. "That's a nice try," Opal says, "but it's not going to work."

I have my back to the window now, as Opal stands between me

and the chairs, and Jacob is between me and the railing. He must think there's still a chance I might jump.

An idea sparks in my mind, and without hesitation, I try it. Picking up a lamp off of the table in the reading nook, I throw it at Opal a hard as I can.

She's not fooled this time. Her hand darts out, and she catches it before it can hit her. She nonchalantly tosses it over the railing, and it shatters all over the floor. She seems confident that the noise won't alert anyone.

"The guards that patrol this part of the castle have all been paid off," she explains. Taking a step forward, she says, "No one is coming."

My eyes widen as I realize she's telling me the truth. What am I going to do?

"It's one narc, bitch werewolf against three vampires," Jacob says. "I think the odds are in our favor."

"Three?" I repeat. That's when I realize there's another vampire on the floor near the first bookshelf, the one closest to the balcony. I can barely see him from back here by the window, but I don't have to see him to know who it is.

Lex.

Kane and Rainer had said he would be willing to help me, that I could count on him. Maybe he's just falling prey to peer pressure at the moment.

I'll try anything.

"Lex!" I shout. "You know that your brother is going to be furious when he finds out about this! You can't let this happen. It's your duty as next in line for the throne to obey the law of the land!"

Opal giggles. "No one is going to find out that Lex or either of us had anything to do with this, silly little bitch. We've already got our cover up plan in place. When they find out what happened to you, the guards who are responsible will be easy enough to track down, Jacob will be fucking his maid, maybe his butler as well, and Lex and I will be in bed together, our naked bodies wrapped in the sheets."

My mouth drops open as I realize what she's saying. She's sleeping with Kane's brother—Lex is sleeping with her.

He won't help me. Why would he? He must have feelings for this insane woman to be sleeping with her.

"King Kane is smart. He'll figure it out," I tell them.

"Is he as smart as you are?" Jacob asks, pulling a red piece of paper out of his pocket. It's the same kind of paper that they used to lure me here, and I have to wonder if they haven't done something to try and trick Kane, too. Maybe he's far away in another part of the castle, thinking I am waiting for him or on my way to meet him.

No, he wouldn't fall for that, and they are not stupid enough to try that. Jacob is just trying to make me feel stupid for falling for this.

Well, I'm too busy being scared to feel too stupid.

If I'm going to make a move, I have to do it now. I dart toward Jacob, getting Opal to move that way. Then, I loop around and head for the ladder. I think Lex will let me go if I can get down, but Opal is there, her hand rushing out to reach for me. She grabs my arm and yanks me back. I throw an elbow and hit her right in the chest. Wincing, she loosens her grip, but by then, Jacob has me by the other arm.

They're not holding me the same way those idiot guards had me. I can't swing my legs over the top of them. So, instead, I kick. I bring my leg back into Jacob, aiming for his groin. He side steps and twists my arm behind my back hard enough that I hear the bones snapping.

Pain consumes me as my arm shifts out of its socket. I can't think about anything else as the blinding fury lashes up my arm. But then, I remember that if I don't fight, I'm going to die. I try to kick him again, but he has my leg pinned between his now, and it's like trying to draw my thigh out of a vice.

It's not budging.

I turn my attention to Opal, but she's got my other leg. It's like they've done this before.

Her fangs are a good four inches long now, and I know this is it for me. They will drain me dry, killing me within a few minutes.

"Help me!" I scream. "Lex, please! Kane! Nellie!"

I am still screaming for all of the people I can think of when I feel the piercing sting of Opal's teeth sinking into my skin. She's tearing into the flesh between my neck and shoulder. A moment later, I feel the same horrid sensation near my jugular.

I try to scream, but I can't. No sound will come out of my mouth as Jacob rips deeper into my throat. The only noises I am able to make now are a wheezing sound when I inhale and a gurgling sound in the back of my throat.

It all seems to be happening so fast and yet in slow motion as well. As the blood rushes out of my body, my limbs begin to grow cold and tingly first. Then, I feel as if I am no longer connected to my body.

My brain takes a bit longer to fade as a flood of memories fires off in my mind's eye. I see my grandmother before she passed away, baking cookies in her kitchen, and everything smells like warm, chocolatey goodness.

I see my mom in the back garden of our house, a bouquet of purple lilacs in her hand as she talks about how the garden is coming in nicely this year.

My brother and I are tearing through the woods, racing, trying to see who can get to the swimming hole fastest, both of us dreaming of the day when we'll be able to do this as wolves.

Our nanny is holding Lola, all wrapped up in a pink blanket, a huge smile on Corinne's face as she shows me my baby sister's scrunched up, red face. I kiss her on the cheek and promise her, "I will always protect you, Lola."

Friends from school flash by in waves, some standing out more than others.

Darius, his hands in the pockets of his jeans as he asks me if I think it would be a good idea for the two of us to go to the school dance together—since we are going to be ruling the pack together one day. I accept—for that reason only.

I'm standing in a throne room, nervous, waiting to hear what my father is about to say, when the most enchanting man I've ever seen steps before me, and my eyes lock on his. I never want to look away.

Kane is on top of me, looking down, passion flickering in his eyes as he assures me with just one look that everything is going to be all right, that he's about to make love to me because he cares about me; this isn't just sex for him.

A scream breaks loose from my throat as everything fades to black around the corners—the bookshelves, the sitting area, the window, the moonlight....

"Stop! Stop right now! I command you!"

I hear a voice from below me. I think it's Lex. But no one seems to care what the king orders, so why would they care about the prince?

And then, everything is dark, and cold, with just a haze in my line of sight, as if I'm floating through a dark sky in a bank of clouds.

I am falling. The sensation of the floor rushing up to meet me penetrates the darkness. I can do nothing to stop myself from falling, just as I can do nothing to stop myself from dying.

I want to say his name one last time, but I have nothing left.

There's nothing left.

26

SAVE HER

Kane

I AM WALKING through a meadow in the darkness. The tall grass waves in the breeze as the moonlight glints off of the trees in the distance. A slow fog rolls in from the edges of my vision. I am all alone, yet I know that Emory is somewhere nearby.

I'm not sure if I'm looking for her or if I'm just cognizant of the fact that she is here, but as I near the tree line, she steps out, barefoot. Her hair is blowing in the same wind that stirs the trees, and the light makes her jade eyes glow.

She looks lovely as always, but also a little wild as she stands there in a long green dress, her hands folded in front of her.

"You should have told me," she says.

"I know. I'm sorry." She has to be talking about the cherry blood, how I nearly tore her apart because I didn't know she was a virgin and had to leave the room before it was too late. "I have been wanting to speak to you all day. I just didn't know how to say it."

"Like you just did," she says, her tone very direct. "I accept your apology."

A smile slips over my lips. "I'm so glad to hear that. Maybe that means we can try again?" I take a few steps toward her, but she retreats.

"No, it's too late," she says, her hands up between us. "It's too late for us to try again now, King Kane."

I pause, questioning why she says that. "What do you mean?" I ask. "If you want to wait until we know one another better, we can. I just… want to be with you. We've got all of the time in the world."

She shakes her head. "No, we don't. You do. But I don't. My time is over. And you're too late, Kane."

"Too late?" I repeat. "Wh-what do you mean?"

"You're. Too. Late. Kane!"

With that, Emory goes flying up through the trees, as if he's been wrenched back by some unseen force, her arms and legs whipping forward as her eyes widen and her face morphs into a silent scream.

"Emory!" I shout after her, running through the trees, trying to keep up with her, but she's moving so fast, it's impossible, even for someone with my speed.

I keep running though, even when she fades from my line of sight. And then a familiar odor hits my nose.

It's the smell of blood.

Her blood.

I tear through the trees, looking for her, crying out her name.

Then… I see her.

She's impaled on a tree, high above my head, a branch piercing her right through the navel. Blood drips down from the wound, but it's also pouring from her mouth, her nose, her eyes, even her ears.

"Emory!" I scream, beginning to climb the tree. I need to get to her before all of her blood is gone, before she completely fades away.

My fingers and toes bite into the bark as I scale the tree as quickly as I can, but when I finally get to her, it's clear, she's already gone. Her eyes stare straight ahead, her head lolling to the side.

"Emory?" I whisper her name as tears begin to stream down my cheeks. "Emory?"

In my head, all I hear is, "You're too late—Kane."

"Kane! Kane!"

I sit up on my couch, my lungs whooshing as they fill with unnecessary air. I look around. Where is that voice coming from.

"Come on! I need you! In the library! Are you asleep? For fuck's sake!"

Lex. It's my brother shouting at me. Whatever the fuck is wrong it, must be really bad. My stomach tightens as I immediately think it must be Emory, though I don't know why she would be in the library.

The cup of blood I'd been drinking when I fell asleep sits cold on the coffee table. I scurry to shove my feet back into my shoes and take off for the door. Throwing it open, I nearly collide with Nellie and Helga.

"Thank god, Your Highness. It's Emory!"

"In the library?" I ask them, and they confirm that as I rush right past them.

I am in the library in a matter of seconds, throwing the doors open and rushing over to my brother who is sitting on the floor, cradling her.

"I called for Dr. Martin," he says. "I didn't know what to do."

"Wh-what—" I can't finish the sentence as I see that she has two deep bite marks on either side of her neck, and her arm is clearly broken, torn from its socket. I drop to my knees. "Who did this?" I ask him, but I already know.

"Opal and Jacob. I sent the guard after them. I... I..."

He can't get any more words out. I know how quickly a vampire can drain a wolf shifter of all of their blood, so I don't doubt that my brother did everything he could within his power to call help, but I don't understand why he doesn't appear to have a scratch on him.

I have no time to stay here and ask him questions. I scoop Emory into my arms and take off for the infirmary. She needs a blood transfusion, and she needs it now. Every second that her organs attempt to pump blood that isn't there is a second closer she comes to complete organ shut down, something she will never recover from.

Wolf shifters heal differently than humans, and for Emory, it's more like an engine with no gasoline that will need to be primed before it can start again as long as she has some blood in her body. That blood will pool in her brain, heart, and lungs, trying to keep them functioning for as long as possible while the other systems go into full failure.

She's still alive for now. I can hear her heart but only faintly. I'm shocked. I can't believe Opal would stop unless she was completely dead, but they might've been frightened off by the appearance of all of the guards. Either that or Lex managed to get Emory's heart working again. I can't ask right now. I have to get her to help. Then, I will worry about what happened and how to track down the two miserable bastards who did this.

Rainer is coming at us down the hallway in a rush. "Do we know where they went?" he asks.

"No. Ask Lex."

I see him look at Emory as we breeze past him, and his eyes narrow for a moment before a look of anguish takes over. I don't have time to analyze my best friend's feelings for her at the moment either. He's already told me about the discussion he had with her earlier, after all, and I get that he's trying to be my friend and hers—maybe more for her. If she lives, and she wants to be with Rainer, so be it. For now, I have to get to step one first.

A nurse holds open the door to the clinic for me as I burst through the doorway. "Room five, Your Majesty," she tells me, and I carry Emory straight there, lying her down on the table as Dr. Joe Martin comes through the door, rolling up his sleeves to his elbows. He's followed by several nurses carrying blood bags.

Immediately, the nurses strip her torn gown from her, throw on a hospital gown, and start the IVs, one in each arm, while the doctor checks her vitals. I stand back trying to keep out of the way while I still need to see absolutely everything that goes on.

The doctor and his team work quickly to get the blood flowing back into Emory. At the same time, they patch up the marks in her neck where she was bitten, and the doctor sets her broken arm and puts it in a cast. He says, "Her shoulder was dislocated, but now that it's back in place, I believe her body will heal itself fairly quickly because of her shifter DNA, so long as we get enough blood in her to do so."

"Is this shifter blood?" I ask him, and he nods.

"Yes, I always keep some on hand. It's from the shifters in the feeders' dungeon, and it's all type O, so she shouldn't have any problem with her body rejecting it."

I trust Dr. Martin completely, but I know he's not used to working on shifters. He does get the occasional injured human, but most of his work is with vampires, and there's not too much that can be done when a vampire gets hurt. Setting bones perhaps, but our bodies heal so quickly, if we are able to heal from whatever wounds are inflicted, there's not much for a doctor to do.

Still, there's a reason I keep him and his staff around, and it's for times like this.

"Thank you," is all I can say to him, and he nods, knowing he will be well paid for his services, as will his entire team.

"I believe she will make a full recovery, Sir," he says about a half an hour after we've entered the infirmary. "It may take a while for her to wake up since she lost so much blood to her brain and other vital organs, and when she does awaken, she may have some trouble remembering everything that happened, but I will be surprised if she doesn't pull through. Clearly, she is a strong woman."

I think about everything Emory has been through in the last few days, since her father sold her to me. The doctor has no idea just how strong she truly is.

The staff clears out of the room, and I sit on Emory's good side, the one where her arm isn't broken, holding her hand, hoping that she is okay.

I think about the dream that I had right before Lex and Nellie woke me up, and I wonder if it was really a nightmare or if somehow Emory managed to reach me in my dream from the other side. Could she have been dead for a while?

I have no idea, and I won't dwell on it, but I know that all of this is my fault. I failed to protect her in her own home. I failed to fish out all of the corrupt guards, and I failed to make sure that my word was enough to keep everyone within my jurisdiction from being harmed.

With her hand in mine, I make a silent vow that I will ensure that nothing like this ever happens again, not to her or anyone. When she wakes up, if she can forgive me, I will do whatever it takes to make sure she is safe and that she knows how very much I care about her.

In my mind, I hear another message, this one from Rainer.

"Guess who I just found?" my best friend says. "What are your orders?"

Initially, my thought is to tell him to kill them both where they stand, but I still have to consider they are both the children of a powerful Vampire King. Do I want to start a war over this?

I do—but I won't, not unless I have to.

"Bring them in if you can," I tell him, "but if you can't… go ahead and end them."

"You got it, Your Highness," he says, and I can hear the bloodlust in his voice.

27

TRACKING THEM DOWN

Rainer

THOSE TWO FUCKING assholes had a head start on me, but that doesn't stop me from tracking them down. It's not too hard. I just follow the trail of dead bodies they leave in their wake. Lex was able to get the guard on their trail as they left the library, so as I rush after them, I encounter one dead guard after another, leading through the field outside of the castle into the woods nearest the side of the castle that faces their home kingdom.

I have a feeling I know exactly what these fuckers are trying to do. They could run all the way back to Scarlett Thunder, but I have no doubt they've got some sort of help waiting for them at some point on the other side of the wall that runs along our lands. They will do their best to get over that wall and into a waiting vehicle, I'm guessing, and since I can't drive through the woods, they're hoping I won't be able to catch them before they get to their escape vehicle, likely driven by someone from their own pack.

Crescent Peak has warriors throughout our lands, and I've sent a message to those that are stationed along the border, but there are so many back roads and winding paths through here that there's a good chance the Maxwells will be able to sneak through if I let them get to that car before I stop them.

Lex was with me, but I outran him about four miles ago, so I know I'm on my own when I finally do catch up to them. I'm not afraid at all. They've got to be beaten down from the number of guards they've encountered, and I have no doubt Opal is no match for me anyway. Jacob likes to talk a big game about how many shifters he's killed, but I think he's full of shit.

I've run past all of the other guards as well, which means it's up to me to track their footprints now, and I see them clearly in the forest floor, as well as a path of snapped branches.

The wall is less than a mile away when I emerge from the woods and see the two of them running in the distance. I am gaining on them, and with every stride I take, I get closer to taking them out. Opal is ahead of Jacob, and he is limping slightly. He's likely done the majority of the fighting. I have to wonder why he even let her talk him into this to begin with. Sure, he probably loves this sort of game, finding someone weaker than him and picking on them, but he has to have known that Opal was signing his death certificate with this scheme.

As I run, I check in with Kane, knowing he wishes he was the one out here hunting them down, but he has to stay with Emory. He has to make sure she's okay. I can hear it in his voice when he responds to me that she's alive. Otherwise, the fury within him would be raging even hotter than it is when he tells me to try to bring them back alive.

I will do my best, but if I have to kill one or both of them I will.

Jacob pulls up as Opal continues to run behind him, and I can't help but curse under my breath. This is the worst case scenario. He is sacrificing himself for his sister. She will be able to get away if I can't bring him down immediately, and even though he's wounded, it won't be an instantaneous death for him.

The wall is high, almost thirty feet, and it's nearly smooth. But it's not meant to keep vampires in or out. It's partially meant as a deterrent to vampires attacking us, to slow them down, but it's mostly to protect our villages from the wolf shifters in the area. Wolf shifters are powerful creatures and can jump high, but they couldn't possibly leap over that wall, and they wouldn't be able to scale it either. And wolves don't climb ladders....

Opal will find a way to get up it if she has more than a couple of minutes....

"Well, it looks like the king sent his best chum to do his dirty work," Jacob smirks at me, standing in a fighting position with his hands out in front of him.

Is this really the same asshole I was sitting across from at dinner just a few hours ago? How did we get to this?

"You really wanna die for her?" I ask him, as I continue to run at him full speed.

"You only think you know what happened, but you're wrong. It wasn't Opal who planned this. It was Lex!" he yells back at me.

"The hell it was!" Lex shouts about a quarter mile behind me. Our hearing is superior....

Jacob keeps his hands up as I fly at him, slamming into him. He tries to kick me away at the last second, but I am ready for it. I grab hold of his leg and whip both of them out from under him, bending the one leg up as I slide past him. I hear a sickening crunch as his leg snaps. He falls backward, onto the ground, his head landing near my hip as he groans in pain from the break.

Releasing his broken limb, I move around quickly so that I am on top of him just as Lex whizzes past us. "Get her! There's gotta be a car!" I tell him.

"I'm going!" he shouts back. I don't hazard a glance in Opal's direction when I have her brother in my grasp like this, but I know she has to be close to the wall.

I flip Jacob over so that he's prostrate on his stomach and grab his arm. "How the fuck do you like it?" I shout at him and pull on it, twisting it behind him the same way Emory's arm had been twisted when I'd seen Kane carry her past me in the hallway.

I intend to dislocate Jacob's arm, but in my fury, I accidentally rip it off. Dark blood and ash come streaming out as I look at the limb and decide there's nothing more to do with it, so I toss it away.

His screams of agony fill the night sky, and in the distance, a flock of birds takes flight, terrified by the sound.

I want to kill him now so that I can help Lex with Opal. I glance over my shoulder and see that she is at the wall, leaping up, trying to find some sort of crevice or crack to wedge her fingers into. It won't take much. If a bird or a hailstone has hit it hard enough to chip away at the flat surface of the rock, she will find a place to work her fingers in. Then, she can use that divot to rocket herself higher up and over the wall.

I see a group of guards coming through the forest, and I hope these are more competent than their counterparts who are littering the ground every three feet between here and the castle. We seriously have to look at our guard program, that's for damn sure. How can we have the world's best army but such piss poor guards?

A few of them are running faster than the others, and I am tempted to hoist Jacob up and carry him back to them, but I don't. Instead, I wait for them to get there and take him into custody. They chain his one remaining arm to his body and lift him since he can't walk on his broken leg. It's beginning to heal already, but it's still twisted.

When I am assured they will get him back to Kane alive, without him managing to escape again, I turn to check out the situation behind me.

Opal is at the top of the wall, thrusting one leg over the top. She turns and flips Lex, who is about halfway up, the bird and says, "It was nice fucking you, fucker," and then she disappears over the other side.

"No!" I shout, outraged that she's getting away. We need to get her. She has to pay for what she's done.

I'll address her comment to Lex later.

By the time I reach the wall, he is almost at the top. I make short work of following the exact path that Opal used to the top, seeing the places where her fingers and toes bit into the surface since she's chipped away slightly more at the rock.

When I reach the top, I toss a leg over and survey the situation.

I do not see her anywhere.

"Fuck," I mutter as Lex joins me, dragging himself over. He almost slips and falls all the way back down, but I grab the prince's hand and help him up.

"Come on!" he shouts, ready to run after again, but two things are stopping me. One, I see a puddle of fresh oil on the ground on the asphalt near where we are sitting, and two, I can hear the roar of an engine in the distance. We don't have much need for vehicles when we can run almost as fast as one, so I'm certain that car is the one she's in.

"We're too late," I tell him. "Unless our guards can stop them at the border before they pass back into Scarlett Thunder, she's gotten away."

"Fuck, no!" he yells, slamming his hand into the top of the wall. It rumbles a bit but doesn't break. It's made out of strong enough materials to keep us from just pounding right through it.

"I'm afraid so," I tell him. "And you and I both know that getting her back is going to take a declaration of war."

"He'll do it," Lex tells me, saying what I already know. "The way he feels about this girl, Kane will tell Opal's father that if he doesn't send her back, he'll fight him to the death."

I feel a slight pain in my heart as I know that Lex is speaking the truth. Emory is special to me, too, for reasons I can't quite explain, but I know how she feels about Kane, and I know how he feels about her. I've already determined I have to resign myself to the fact that the two of us will have to remain friends.

Still, I understand why Kane will not hesitate to start an international incident in order to get justice for her. She deserves it. What did the girl ever do to anyone?

Lex, on the other hand…. "You were fucking your brother's bitch fiancée? All that talk about how you couldn't stand her, and this whole time, you were screwing her?"

The prince looks ashamed for one of the first times in his life, for as long as I can remember. "I know. It's just… she's a good lay. And

Kane isn't interested in her like that, so I figured he probably never would bed her."

"Not even after they were married? She was supposed to have his baby, remember? That was the whole point in this."

"Oh, I'm aware," he snaps back, and I am reminded that Lex never did like the idea of Kane having a child. That would prevent the younger brother from ever taking the throne. "I just didn't know if he'd ever do that even, and besides, there are other methods now days to get women pregnant."

The image of a turkey baster comes to mind, and if I wasn't so fucking pissed, I might actually laugh. I look off in the distance one more time in the direction that Opal disappeared in before I say, "Let's head back to the castle. We've got to make sure Jacob doesn't get away." I pause for a moment wanting to ask Lex if he was screwing him, too, but I decide I don't want to know, not because I care that Lex is bi but because, at the moment, I hate Jacob so much, I don't want to think about it anymore.

I leap down off of the wall and land with a thunderous boom that shakes the trees in the distance. I wonder how Opal managed not to do that. But then, she's not nearly as big as I am. Lex's landing isn't quite as loud as mine either.

As we walk back toward the castle, I do say, "You've gotta take this as a sign that it's time to grow up, Lex. You're well over a hundred years old. Stop acting like a teenager, and get your head out of your ass."

"Don't worry," he promises me. "I get it. I can't trust anyone anymore. I thought those two just liked to have fun and act stupid like me, but they took it way too far."

We enter the forest, and I say, "You did do the right thing in calling for help." He nods, but he doesn't look like that's much of a consolation. "Your brother will be happy about that."

He shrugs. "Unless the girl dies. Then it won't matter what I did. Nothing will be good enough. As usual."

2 8

———

AM I DEAD?

Emory

I HEAR A BEEPING SOUND, faintly, in the background, and I know that it's some kind of machine. I remember hearing them in the hospital when Lola was born. For a moment, I am back there, and I am wanting to hold the baby but also want to see her mother, and I'm told that she died in childbirth. Sadness washes over me as I wonder who will take care of this little girl. Then, I vow it will be me.

"Lola," I mumble, but the voice I hear in response isn't hers. It's another familiar one, a voice that stirs all kinds of feelings within me as I begin to process the events of the last few days.

"Emory." He sounds relieved, like he wasn't sure I'd ever speak again. "You're okay, Em. You're safe. I'm right here."

Kane. He's with me. Wherever I am, with all of this beeping, he's by my side. In fact, I'm pretty sure I can feel his hand in mine.

I can't feel much else, though. I wonder if that's because those two bastards drank all of my blood. I remember now. I remember the note that led me to the library, the moment Jacob showed up, followed by his sister, and then Lex, on the floor, not willing to help me.

171

Or had he?

Why am I not dead?

I remember them both attacking me, Jacob snapping my arm, and then their razor sharp teeth pierced my skin on both sides. I tried to scream but I couldn't, and then, everything slowly faded to black.

I'd seen my family, including sweet baby Lola.

And I'd also seen Kane.

Another vague memory comes to mind, but it can't be real. I am in a forest, barefoot, and he's standing in front of me. I want him to know that it's too late. I want to tell him that we could have been together forever, but I can feel all of the blood draining from me, and then that world had darkened too. I was whooshed away from him, then, there was only pain and darkness.

My eyelashes flicker open. Bright lights have me unable to open my eyes completely. Kane shouts something to someone, and the lights are off now. I can focus enough to see his face.

His forehead is crinkled, his eyes a bit puffy and red, and he looks like he is ready to rip someone's head off, but he has my hand in his, and when he sees my eyes, his face cracks into a smile.

"Emory," he whispers. "Thank… the Moon Goddess."

I almost laugh because I know he doesn't believe in the Moon Goddess, but obviously I do. Laughing seems like too much work at the moment. I can't believe I'm still alive.

"Why doesn't it hurt?" I ask him, meaning my body in general. "Is it because I don't have any blood left to feel with?" My voice is hoarse and crackles with each word.

"No, you have blood now, baby," he says, smoothing back my hair, his fingertips cold on my face, which feels refreshing. "We gave you lots of it. You're almost full again." He smiles at me, like I am a container they are dumping blood bags into. "You can't feel the pain from your injuries because of the medicine Dr. Martin gave you."

"Oh," I say. That makes sense. Our pack healer relies mostly on herbs and other plants to heal people, but I can see vampires being different. They've always been more advanced than we are. "What's wrong with me?"

"Do you remember what happened?" he asks before answering my question.

I nod the best I can without being able to feel too much of my body. "Jacob and Opal ambushed me in the library."

"That's right," he says. "They broke your arm, dislocated your shoulder, and then drained you. They must've thought you were dead when they tossed you over the side of the banister."

I cringe even thinking about that fall. "How did I not break more bones?" I ask.

"Lex caught you," he explains. "He called for the guards. He sent Nellie and Helga to get me. I'm so sorry I wasn't there, baby. I was asleep." He shakes his head, like sleeping is a crime. "I should've known you weren't safe. I thought—"

"It doesn't matter," I tell him, wishing I could lift my hand to stroke his cheek. "It's over with now. What matters is I'm not dead, right?"

That makes him crack a smile, as if I think he has to contemplate whether or not that is the most important thing. "Yeah, absolutely," he says. "That is definitely the most important thing." He bends down and presses his lips to my forehead, and again the difference in his skin temperature is refreshing to me.

"Did you catch them?" I ask him.

His eyes drop my gaze as he stares at the floor in front of his feet for a few moments before shaking his head. "No, only Jacob. Opal got away."

"Really?" I say, surprised. "I would've thought that it would have been the other way around." Opal never struck me as particularly strong or fast, but Jacob…. Just thinking about how easily he ripped my arm backward makes me shirk, and at the moment, it feels like I don't have arms at all.

"He sacrificed himself for her," Kane explains. "They had a car waiting on the other side of the wall, closest to their clan lands. Jacob slowed Rainer up so that Opal could get away. She's gone now, and I'm pretty sure she managed to slip through our border patrol, too. I'm going to go call her father as soon as I am sure you're all right."

I want to tell him I'm sure I'm fine, but I'm not completely convinced that's true. As much as I want to believe that all of the threats are gone with Opal and Jacob out of Crescent Peak, for all I know, there could be others with designs on angering the king who would even break into the hospital to kill me.

"What about her entourage?" I ask, thinking of those other girls that were always with her.

"We have them all under arrest," he says with a confident nod, "even her maids. The ladies-in-waiting insist that they didn't know anything about this scheme, but I don't have any way of knowing that for sure. They will all be punished for the way they've treated you."

"Not the maids, though, right?" I ask. "They didn't have anything to do with any of it, did they?"

"Well, no, not them," he clarifies. "But her friends, those bitches are going to wish they never stepped foot in Crescent Peak."

The way he speaks when he's angry is very sexy, and even though my body seems to be somewhere else at the moment, I still feel a stirring within my core. "I'm sorry," I tell him, and I watch as his expression tumbles back into confusion. "I'm sorry I didn't tell you that I was a virgin."

"No," he says, interrupting me as I state the last word. "Baby, you've got nothing to apologize for. That was all my fault. I should've asked you. I should've warned you. I just... when I came to you that night, I wanted you so badly, I wasn't thinking clearly. I should've come later to tell you the reason I acted the way I did, but... I was... embarrassed."

My eyebrows arch as I contemplate the truth of that statement. The Vampire King was too embarrassed to tell me something? That didn't quite seem right, but I believe him. "I hope that you'll never hesitate to tell me anything important ever again," I say to him. "Regardless of what we are, King Kane, I want to be someone you can trust. I've never felt this way about anyone before, ever, and even if you don't feel the same way about me, even if you're too busy being the king of the world to have much time for me, or if I become a nuisance to you as someone you have to spend valuable resources keeping safe when you never wanted me to begin with, I hope you'll know I'll always be there for you, no matter what. No matter how big the problem is, I'll always be your soft place to fall."

He stares at me, unblinking for several seconds, and I feel a rush of heat to my cheeks as I contemplate whether or not I am the one who should be embarrassed now, but when he speaks, he says, "That was the most thoughtful thing anyone has ever said to me, Emory Moonraker. Thank you."

I can't help but grin at him. I try to shrug again and fail. The attempt makes him chuckle, which makes me laugh as well. "It's true," I tell him.

"I never meant to buy you, that's true," he says. "But I'm glad that I did. This is going to sound awful, but I'm glad that your father is a fucking asshole."

I know what he means, and we both laugh again. I want to kiss him so badly, but I can't reach him, and I know he's afraid he's going to hurt me.

"How long was I unconscious?" I ask him, wondering what day of the week it might be.

"Just a couple of hours," he says. "You wolf shifters heal quickly. Not as quickly as we vampires do, but still pretty fast."

I'm relieved to hear that. I yawn and can't raise my hand to cover my mouth, so I feel silly, but when I look back at him, he has a thoughtful expression on his face.

"A lot of people are waiting to see you, but I think you should rest first."

I agree with him, but there's one person I do want to see before I go back to sleep. "All right," I say. "But can I talk to Lex for a minute? Alone?"

His eyes widen, but then he nods. "Sure."

Kane leans over and presses his mouth to mine softly before he stands. It's difficult for me to let go of his hand because it's just a mass of warm tingles, but before I release him, I ask, "Does this mean the wedding is off?"

He looks at me for a long moment, and his expression is unreadable. My gut tightens. "I need to talk to King Peter." He lets go of my hand and exits the room, leaving me, once again, wondering what the hell that means.

Can he still have a baby with the woman that tried to kill me?

29

THANK YOUS

Emory

LEX LOOKS different when he comes in. It's not just that he's got smudges of dirt all over him and his clothing is torn, something I can't imagine from the polished Lex I saw at dinner the other night and in the library earlier, but his countenance has changed.

"Hello," he says as he walks to the foot of my bed. He doesn't sit in the chair his brother vacated about ten minutes ago, nor does he find another one. He just stands there, with his hands folded in front of him. "How are you?"

I'm starting to get my ability to feel my body back now. I am still a bit tingly in the extremities, and my shoulder is starting to hurt a little, but I don't want more medicine because I don't want to lose my ability to feel, so I haven't told the doctors.

In response to Lex's question, I say, "I'm better, thank you."

"I'm glad to hear it," he says politely. "Dr. Martin is very good."

I nod. I haven't had a chance to meet the man yet, not that I remember anyway, but I am looking forward to thanking him and his staff for saving my life. But right now, I'm more concerned with the man in front of me. "You helped me." It's not a question, but he reacts like it is.

"I tried to reach Kane, but he was asleep. Nellie and Helga were nearby, in the hallway. They said they knew something was wrong, so they'd followed you to the library. I honestly didn't know what the plan was when Jacob and Opal told me they had invited you there. I knew they weren't up to any good, but I went with them, hoping I could make them stop. They just told me about it a few minutes before they left the room where we were all hanging out."

It sounds to me like he's trying to apologize for the role he played in all of this, but that's not why I asked him here. He could've done a lot of things differently, and I would be dead right now, so I don't feel like he owes me an explanation.

"I just wanted to thank you," I say, my voice just above a whisper. "I wanted to thank you for helping me."

He shrugs before he shakes his head. "You shouldn't be thanking me, girl." I'm not sure if he doesn't know my name or if he just doesn't want to use it. "I helped you because my brother expects it. That's all."

He suddenly seems cold, as if he's aware that I almost caught him having feelings, and that's too human for him.

"I guess I don't really care why you helped me," I say, though that's not quite true. I just don't want him to feel uncomfortable. "I'm just glad that you did. So… for whatever reason. Thanks. And if there's ever anything I can do for you…."

He scoffs, a bleat of a laugh exiting his mouth. He really is nothing like his brother, I note. "You help me?" he asks. Again, he's shaking his head at me. "I highly doubt we will ever be in a situation where you can help me."

"You're probably right." I give that to him. He may well be right, and I might never be in a situation where I can repay him for what he's done. But a person never knows. "Well, I won't keep you. I just wanted to thank you."

"Yeah, sure," he says, and then, he heads for the door, but a few steps away from the exit, he turns and looks at me again, and for a moment I think he's going to say more, but he doesn't, and then he's gone.

I take a deep breath and blow it out slowly, thinking I should ask for some medicine to help me sleep now. I've been so tired the last few days, it should be easy enough even without the medicine, but my shoulder is aching a little, and I feel drained, but my mind is blasting off at a million miles a minute.

So when Rainer sticks his head in, I am both thrilled to see him and also a bit disappointed that it's not the doctor. I was hoping to ask for sleeping medicine.

"Hey, there she is!" he says, still just leaning in. "Got a minute?"

"Well, I am very busy right now," I say, making a joke. He chuckles as he approaches the bed and sits in the same chair that Kane had occupied not long ago. "I have a full schedule of meetings and other important events."

"I bet someday you do," he says, "but I think I'll have your secretary go ahead and clear out the rest of your day so you can get some rest—just this once."

I love that we can joke around like we've known each other for years, rather than just a couple of days.

"You know, you look pretty good for someone who was basically dead a little while ago," he tells me, patting me gently on the leg through the pile of blankets.

"Thanks," I tell him, meaning it. "I feel okay for someone who was basically dead a little while ago."

"How's your shoulder?" he asks. "Last time I saw it, it looked like it was on backward."

That makes me cringe a little. "It didn't feel very good last I recall either," I admit to him. "But it's fine now, thanks to the doctor and his staff."

"Good, good," he says. I notice his hair is damp and figure he's gotten himself cleaned up after the run. "If they'd have left it to me, I would've probably managed to get it stuck behind your back or something."

I laugh because I know he's just being silly. "Thank goodness you're not the doctor then," I chide.

"No shit!" he claps his hands down on his muscular thighs. "Other than that, you're okay, kiddo?"

It's an odd nickname for him to use for me, but then, he is a lot older than me I suppose, even though he doesn't look it. That's one thing it's easy for me to forget about here. Especially with Kane.

"I'm fine," I tell him. "I hear you got Jacob. Thanks for that."

He makes a face, his nose and upper lip scrunched together, as he shakes his head. "That fucking asshole," he mutters. "I wish I would've killed him when I had the chance. I did rip his arm off, though. That was payback for what he did to you." He points at me for emphasis.

"That's amazing," I tell him, wishing I could clap for it. "I'm sure he'll be wishing he were dead soon enough." I recall the murderous look Kane had on his face when he left here.

But Rainer doesn't seem that sure. He shrugs. "Yeah, we'll see." I recall what Kane said about Opal, and I want to ask Rainer if he thinks he may actually marry her even after all of this, but I say nothing about it because I don't want to know the answer, not right now when I feel like shit.

"I just wish I could've got to Opal. I'm sorry I didn't get her, kid." He shakes his head slowly, and I can tell he really means it. I bet he would've destroyed her, given the chance. Her brother might've been the brawn behind what happened to me, but she was definitely the brains.

"It's okay," I say. "I think… she'll get what's coming to her. One way or another."

"I like your optimism," he says. "But… unfortunately, in my experience, bitches like Opal tend to get away with this kind of shit."

"Maybe you're right," I tell him. "Only time will tell."

"Well, listen," he says, clapping my leg again, though not hard. "I know you're tired. I'm gonna get out of your hair. I know Nellie and Helga want to say hi, but they are back in their room for now. They said they wanna make sure you get plenty of rest before you spend any time speaking to them."

I can't help but feel warmth spread throughout my chest at the thought of my two maids, my friends. "That's so kind of them. They really are lovely." There are so many people here that are kind, it turns out, and I'm slowly beginning to realize that having my father sell me isn't the worst thing in the world that could've happened to me.

I do wonder what would've happened if Kane would've taken Lola instead of me, though. I'm sure he would've been kind to her, but he would still be in a situation where he was tied to Opal and had no choice but to go through with the wedding.

Now, I have to imagine he has some pretty strong reasons to tell King Peter that he's not going to go through with it after all.

But with the way he left here, there's really no way for me to say.

"Is there anything I can do for you while you're napping, Emers?" he asks me. This nickname makes me chuckle a bit.

"Uh, not that I can think of," I say at first, but then something does come to mind, and he can see it on my face.

"What is it? Anything you want, you name it!" He winks at me, and I tend to believe there's not too much he wouldn't be able to do for me.

"Well," I begin, "I don't want to upset the delicate balance between pack and clan politics, but would it be possible for you to call the Beta's house in my pack and ask his wife, Margaret, if Lola is okay?" I hear the pleading in my voice, and I see him soften.

"Of course," Rainer says. "I'm sure she's fine. Probably misses you, no doubt about that, but she's probably doing all right. I'll check and let you know."

"Thank you." I smile warmly at him, so glad he's in my life. He's a great guy. I hope one day he meets the right girl, and they fall madly in love and live forever happily together.

"See you later, Princess," he says, and I wave goodbye, smiling at the thought of him.

It's not long after he leaves that I begin to doze off again, but after a few moments, a nurse comes in to check on me. "Do you need anything?" she asks.

I am not rude enough to say I wish to be left alone so I can sleep. Instead, I say, "Thank you, all of you, for taking such good care of me. Is there anything that might help me sleep better?"

"You're quite welcome, dear," she says. "Yes, I have something. I can put it in your IV."

"Thank you," I say, noting I have a tube coming out of my left arm still. My right arm is the one in a cast.

She returns and puts the medicine in the bag along with the clear fluid I suppose is meant to keep me hydrated so my organs can keep functioning, and within a few moments, I feel the medicine begin to take effect, and I am drifting away again.

I hope this time I have happy dreams, dreams of me and Lola, dreams of me and Rainer, and most importantly, dreams of me and Kane.

3 0

GETTING HIS HEAD ON STRAIGHT

Kane

I’s difficult for me to decide what to do first, call Vampire King Peter to see if he has Opal and demand justice for what his bitch daughter has done here or to go interrogate Jacob. In the end, I decide to head to the dungeon first. I want to see the face of the asshole who tried to kill my Emory. Even though I can’t kill him like I wish to because it would essentially be an act of war, that doesn’t mean I can’t hurt him.

I wish that Rainer would’ve killed him in battle, to some degree. After all, if that was the way it had played out, Jacob would be dead, and I could use the fact that he broke my laws and ran from my guards as an excuse for his death. His father would still be mad and come at me with his military, no doubt, but Jacob wouldn’t be alive to know about it.

I’d originally told Rainer to bring them both back alive if possible because I wanted to hurt them myself. Now, I am fairly certain I will kill him if I’m not careful, and I don’t want his father to be able to use this incident as a way to unite other clans against me. As it is right now, he will be standing in a very bad light when the other vampires hear what has transpired here, even though I'm sure he'll try to spin it one way or another. But if I kill him while he's imprisoned, and it gets back to Peter and then the other clans, it will not look good for me, no matter how heinous Jacob and Opal's crime is.

I find him in a back room in the prison, writhing on the stone floor in pain. He's naked from the waist up, barefoot, and missing an arm. His leg is twisted at an odd angle, and I imagine it's trying to reengineer itself into the correct angles needed for him to function, but since it wasn't set properly, his cells are having troubles with it, and chances are, it will take weeks, if not months, for it to straighten itself out unless we rebreak it and fix it.

But I'm still not convinced that Jacob has weeks or months to live, so I suppose it doesn't really matter.

When he senses me entering the room, he stops grunting and groaning and looks up at me. The man looks nothing like the fellow I'd had dinner with only about seven hours ago. He looks like a common criminal or worse. He looks like a prisoner of war. He's covered with sweat, his eyes glazed over, and dried blood streaks his chin.

That's not his blood, though, and when I see it, I can't help but walk over to him and ram my boot into his face, kicking him right where Emory's blood still lingers.

"Argh!" he shouts as he goes flying backward into the stone wall. It splinters a little, and so does his torso, but he begins to mend almost immediately. His jaw is crooked, and with only one hand, it's hard for him to pop it back into place.

"Well, you really fucked up this time, didn't you, Jake?" I ask him.

He's spitting blood, trying to fix his face, so he can't answer me. He just scoots up off of the wall a bit, trying to sit, but with his mangled body, he's having a hard time of it.

A couple of guards stand outside of the cell, the only witnesses to what will happen here, and if I wanted to ensure no one ever finds out, I could do what a lot of leaders do and get rid of them next. But I won't. We are in the process of rounding up every guard who ever took a bribe from these two assholes and executing them, so I'm pretty sure I'll have everyone's loyalty from now on. I've put Rainer in charge of retraining them. No one will want to screw up and make him mad, no one in their right mind anyway.

Jacob has learned this lesson too late. "I just want to know why," I say, shaking my head at him. He's righted his jaw now, so it's no longer misaligned, though it is swollen. "Why the fuck would you and your sister do something like this? Do you have a death wish?"

"She got away, didn't she?" he reminds me, his voice a bit hard to understand because of his jaw.

"That's true," I agree. "But you didn't. You had to know there was some risk involved in this, didn't you?" He only looks at me blankly. "Were you always supposed to be the one to take the fall when it went to shit? Or did you just come up with the short straw?"

"We weren't supposed to get caught," he spits out, glaring at me. "If your fucking brother hadn't sold us out, we'd be back in our rooms, snug in our beds, while a couple of guards got caught red handed with your bitch feeder's body."

I want to kick him again just for calling Emory a bitch, but I keep my boot where it's at. I'll save breaking him for more important moments, like when he's not answering my questions.

"So this was her idea?" I ask him, and he nods.

"Initially, it was her idea. The two of us talked about it together and came up with the scheme. We couldn't believe it worked so easily. Of course, if Opal hadn't been in your room last night and figured out that you'd tried to fuck the feeder but failed, well, we wouldn't have had the ammunition we needed to design such a believable story. And of course, she came running right toward your open arms, longing for acceptance from you, something she didn't get from her father, obviously."

Part of me hates that he's being so straightforward. It's not giving me the opportunity to bash his head in the way I so want to.

"Why did the two of you want to kill her so badly, though?" I have to ask. "Why not just leave her the fuck alone?"

"Because she is a threat to Opal's queenship," he says, as if that should've been obvious to me. "You clearly have feelings for that woman. Fuck, you might even be in love with her, though I'm not sure how anyone knows that so quickly. Anyway, Opal was afraid you'd latch onto the feeder and make her your queen instead of Opal."

"But Opal can give me a baby, and Emory can't," I remind him. "We had an agreement that was meant to give us both an heir, nothing more than that. She had a number of men on the side, as you know. Why would she care if I had Emory?"

"You don't do shit like that," he spits at me. "You are not the kind of guy who just fucks around with someone when he has feelings for them, so she knew you'd end up wanting the feeder to be your queen. And then what? Opal would be left with nothing. So it was just easier to eliminate her right from the get-go. And she figured we were doing it soon enough that you wouldn't be that attached to the bitch, but obviously we were both wrong there." He rolls his eyes at me, and I can see his point.

That doesn't justify what they did, though. "Do you realize if the two of you would've come to me with these concerns, we could've sat down and talked through them, gotten together with your father, and drafted a new document that insured that Opal was queen of both your kingdom and mine until after our child reached the age of majority, and we agree that it's time for us to both step down and let the child rule? That's what people with morals do. That's what respectful adults who deserve to rule kingdoms do. They don't kill innocent people just to get them out of the way.

Jacob shrugs. "Opal and I have always done what needed to be done to make sure things work out for us. Call it immoral if you want to, but from my perspective, killing is killing, whether it's in a castle or on a battlefield."

"So you don't think it matters whether or not the person you're killing has consciously accepted the risk that they might die by entering into an activity, such as fighting in a war, where there's a possibility they may be killed by the enemy?" Surely, he sees the error in what he's saying!

His response tells me that he does not. "You can die anytime doing anything. Some people are destined to die on a battlefield. Others are destined to die in a library. Really, the bitch should've known better than to leave her room. I know Opal tried to tell you the bitch started the incident in the garden the day before, but we both know that's not true. We weren't going to kill her then, but we were going to fuck her up." He looks away for a second before he swears under his breath. "Shit. Lex really did trip us both on purpose, didn't he? Asshole. And to think I let him suck my dick."

I have to close my eyes for a second to will that image away. "I really don't want to hear about any of your sexcapades, especially not those concerning my brother." So much for Lex trying to tell me he's only into women.

"Anyway, she should've stayed in her room. We couldn't make it in there. Those two bitch maids were always hanging around. Opal wanted to kill them, too, but she thought it would be too many bodies floating around."

I shake my head again, glad they didn't kill Nellie and Helga. Those two women deserve a reward for what they did to help Emory. They will get one, too.

"Well, I guess if your theory is right that some people die on a battlefield, and some in a library, then we can add some people die in a forest when an angry second-in-command rips them apart and others are put to death for their crimes."

It's his turn to shake his head, and I can hear the bones popping as he does so. "My father will run your borders over so quickly, you won't survive the night. I know you think you have allies in the vampire community, but you don't. Not really. Not like my dad does. Unlike you, he sells our young bitches to the other Vampire Kings, so they won't shut him down."

I have heard whispers that King Peter is involved in an underground sex trafficking scheme, but whenever I've spoken to him about it, he's always denied it. Now that I've heard his son say that it's true, I realize I have even more reason not to cooperate with King Peter.

But I also have to think about my own clan, and the fact that I have already signed an agreement with him. The baby that was supposed to be born of this union isn't just important to my kingdom, he or she is important to him as well. He will be furious at Opal and Jacob for this.

But he won't want to see either of them die, so perhaps I can work this to my advantage.

"All right, Jake. I'm going to go call your father. I'll see what he has to say, but you should get used to the idea of finding out really soon what the answer to that age old question is—do vampires have souls or when they are killed, do they simply cease to exist?"

He narrows his gaze at me and says, "Fuck you, Kane. You're just as much an asshole as any of the rest of us. You can't honestly think that no innocent lives have ever been taken by your hand or your command."

I am done listening to him. I signal for the guards to let me out, and I leave him to continue his writhing on the floor in pain. It is too bad that I didn't get more chances to inflict damage on him, but there will be plenty of time for that in the future.

I make my way back upstairs to my office and pour myself a glass of blood before I go to my desk, sipping on it and feeling the energy course through me. I'm not quite sure how to handle this situation with King Peter, but I can't just start making demands, not unless I'm willing to start a war, and while I am confident that I have lots of allies who will come to my defense, so does Peter.

I pick up the receiver and dial his number. I'm not surprised when he answers on the very first ring.

"It's about fucking time you called me!" he demands. "What the hell is going on over there? I've got one of my children showing up her battered and bruised, telling me your guards chased her out of the kingdom trying to kill her, and the other one is in your dungeon, ready to be tortured and executed, for what?"

Anger boils up inside of me as I already hear the twist he's putting on this story. Through gritted teeth, I tell him, "For fucking with the wrong feeder."

31

DEMANDS OF KING PETER

Kane

"WHAT THE FUCK do you mean fucking with the wrong feeder?" King Peter asks me, and I can hear the disbelief in his voice. "Opal said nothing about a feeder, and even if she did, what does a dirty feeder have to do with anything?"

I resent the tone he's taking already. He's lucky we are on the phone, and he's not within my grasp or else he'd look a lot like his son does about now.

"First of all, she's not a dirty feeder," I explain to him. "She's the daughter of an Alpha of a nearby wolf pack, one I paid a great sum of money for. One I gave specific orders to the entire clan and everyone who was staying in my castle at the time not to touch, and your children tried to kill her because Opal was jealous."

"Jealous?" He laughs in my ear. I narrow my eyes, thinking of all the things I would like to do to him. "Why would my beautiful daughter be jealous of a mangy dog?"

"Because... the girl is mine. Because she fulfills me in ways that Opal never will. And despite the fact that your daughter was fucking half of the nobles in my clan, she couldn't accept the fact that I might rather spend my time with another woman." I don't feel that it's necessary to go into all of the details about how I feel about Emory to this man. That should be reason enough for him.

It clearly isn't though, as his laughter rings out again. "I seriously doubt that my daughter could give a damn about who you're fucking, Kane. Perhaps you have this all messed up in your own mind. And as for my daughter's virtue, I believe her when she says the only bed she's been visiting there is yours."

"My bed?" I ask. "That's the furthest thing from the truth. If you are under the impression that your daughter is a virtuous woman, you will need to change your perspective on life, King Peter. No, I'm afraid that your daughter has been in many different beds since she arrived here. In fact, I'm willing to guess she's been in many different beds for a lot longer than that. Your son can attest to that."

"We are not talking about my son at the moment." His words come out through gritted teeth. "Though if I hear that you've hurt a hair on his head, you will find yourself under attack before the sun rises."

"Then... I suppose you'd best give the order to send out your troops. Not only did I make sure Jacob understood how disappointed I am in his behavior, he was hurt severely when he ran from my guards after breaking my laws. Surely, as a king, you can understand the importance of making sure everyone within the borders of your land follows your laws, can't you, King Peter?"

"All I know is that my daughter was terrified when she ran from your guard. She said all she could think about was fleeing with her life before she was punished for a crime she didn't commit. Honestly, is it this feeder's word against my children's? Perhaps she is just trying to gain sympathy in your eyes."

"It seems to me that there's not much I can say to make you under-stand that they are guilty, King Peter, I reply, growing tired of trying to explain myself. Would I have had to have witnessed the incident myself to assure you that they did go against my order? Was I meant to follow them around and make sure they followed all of the rules? Don't you have guards for that sort of thing?"

"Of course I do," he says with a chuckle rumbling from deep in his throat. "But I wouldn't believe a guard or a feeder over a member of a royal family. After all, we have a certain upbringing that prevents us from telling the sort of lies those from lower classes may spout off for any reason."

"You don't believe an Alpha's daughter is the equivalent of royalty?" I ask him.

"I don't know, Kane. In my experience, those wolves are all a bunch of vile creatures. Is she one of your enemy's children? That's what Opal has told me. Perhaps she's meant to disrupt your kingdom and cause you to second guess your relationships with others."

"No, I can assure you that's not the case. Besides, it's not just the feeder who told me what happened."

"Oh? Who was it then? A maid? A butler? A pet dog?" He laughs again, thinking he's being so funny.

"No, actually, the feeder's story has been corroborated by a royal, just as you've requested," I tell him, doing my best to keep a cool head.

"Let me guess? That pitiful brother of yours? You know, Opal told me you were likely to try and say that Prince Lex is holding her accountable for what happened, but my understanding is that your own brother hates you so thoroughly, he's likely to tell you all sorts of lies so long as it messes with your logic."

"Lex was present in the library when the incident took place, so what Opal has told you is true. I have had a full account of what happened from him. He is a royal, and as you've just said, his level of trustworthiness should be held with more esteem than... others." I am using his own argument now, not that I agree with him. "But you see, King Peter, it's not my brother's recounting of what took place in the library that tells me, with great certainty, that it was your daughter and your son that broke my laws and hurt my feeder."

I hear a change in his tone as he begins to speak again. "Oh, really, Kane?" he asks, and I do take note of the fact that he's no longer using my title. "Who, by chance, then was it? Your mother? The ghost of your father? Perhaps I was there, and I simply don't recall the incident any longer."

"It was your son." My words are pointed as I drive them through the phone to his ear. "Jacob told me exactly what happened and why. I'm quite certain, if asked again, he would say the same thing. And before you ask, no it was not under threat of torture that he gave me his version of the events. He found the tale amusing, so he wove it for me."

The line is silent for a moment as he has to mull over what I've said to him. Once again, I wish that we were having this conversation in person so I could see his face. I want to see the man sputter as he attempts to come up with some way of explaining away what I've just told him.

Ultimately, he says nothing to me, and I know that's because there's nothing he can say. He has to believe me, and he has to know that Jacob, in his attempt to spit in my face, would tell me everything. He knows his son better than I do, after all.

"Well, even if what you are saying is true, I'm not sure what you'd like to do about it now. What's done is done. You cannot harm my son any further unless you want to start a war with me, and I will not be returning my daughter to you. I suppose you simply have to ask yourself whether or not the honor of this feeder you're so enthralled with is worth losing your kingdom over. You may think that you have friends in other clans, but I can assure you all of them will choose me over you every time."

I remember what Jacob said about the sex trafficking, and I'm certain that's true. But I can't let it dissuade me. I have more allies than he thinks I do. Some of them may take his young women for purposes I don't wish to think about, but that doesn't mean they won't fight alongside me. After all, we have treaties. I give them lots of natural resources and other items they rely upon for their very survival. That has to be worth something.

"Unless you can think of a fitting punishment for your offspring that tried to kill my property, I am afraid I'm going to have to demand that Opal be returned to me so that I can make sure she pays for what she's done."

"Not only will I not be returning my daughter to you or punishing her for hurting your silly feeder, you can be sure that if you do not return my son to me by tomorrow morning, I will march on your kingdom, Kane, and I will do some with a fury. I want him returned to me—now."

"That will not be happening," I tell him. "I will be keeping Jacob here until he either dies or you send me Opal, and once I have her, she will be punished for what she's done." I hope he hears the sincerity in my tone. I am not backing down from this.

"You would do that?" he asks, scoffing again. "You would punish this woman you're meant to marry, the mother of your unborn child?"

Now, I am the one laughing. "She's hardly the mother of my unborn child, King Peter. Nor will she ever be. I think it's fair to say that the agreement we've made before is completely off of the table now. You will have to find someone else who is willing and able to knock up your hellacious daughter."

He is silent, and I assume it's because he is pondering the weight of my words. Perhaps up until now he hasn't considered what it would mean to go to war with me, that he'd be left without an heir.

But when he speaks, I understand that's not what caused the pause after all.

"Do you not know then?" he asks me, and I'm not sure if he has a hint of laughter in his voice or if it's pity I hear.

"Know what?" I ask him.

"Well, that's rich," he says, chuckling at me once more. "The powerful King Kane, lord of all the vampires, or so he'd like others to believe, doesn't even know the truth of the situation, doesn't even know what's gone on in his own castle."

"What the fuck are you talking about?" I demand.

"I don't have to wait for you and my daughter to get married to have an heir for me, you asshole," he says, and I feel my blood begin to boil. "Opal has already told me what she's failed to tell you, though for what reason, I can only guess. Probably because she knew you didn't truly love her. But you see, King Kane, Opal is already pregnant. With your baby!"

"What?" I ask him, wondering why Opal would make up such a ridiculous lie to tell her father. He will find out in only a few months' time that she's not really pregnant. She can't be pregnant.

I never had sex with Opal….

"That's right," he says. "So perhaps you go making threats about what will happen to my children, you should think about what I can do to yours! I want Jacob back this instance or else your own child will pay!"

With that, he slams the phone down, leaving me staring wide-eyed, mouth agape.

Opal isn't pregnant. She can't be. I'm the only one who could do that. The only natural born vampire in the area who isn't related to her.

The only one….

Except for….

"Oh, fuck!"

32

CONFRONTATION

Kane

I MAKE my way swiftly to my brother's room, doing my best not to lose my cool before I get there. My hands are balled into fists, and I am doing everything I can to keep from slamming one of them into a wall.

In my mind, I go over the conversation I am about to have with Lex. I am cool, calm, and collected, as I ask him if he has any idea how badly he has fucked up this entire situation.

But when Lex opens the door to his room and says, "What?" I am no longer cool, calm, and collected.

I slam my fist right into his face, causing him to splash the glass of blood he is holding all over himself. When he winces and glares at me, I am only upset that most of the blood now dripping down his face is not his own. "What the fuck?" he asks me, wiping at his white shirt that will now be permanently pink.

"What the fuck indeed!" I shout at him as I step over the puddle at the entrance and slam his door behind him. "You are the biggest fuck up I've ever met in my entire life, Lex, and just for once, for ONCE, I

195

was praying to whatever fucking gods might be listening that perhaps you wouldn't manage to fuck something up, but not only did you fuck it up beyond imagination, you literally fucked up the one thing you didn't need to be involved in."

Lex stares at me for a moment before he goes to his kitchenette and grabs a towel to wipe his face off. When he pulls it away, I see I did do some damage to his pretty face at least. His lip is bruised, and his nose is a little crooked. He straightens it, and I just want to punch him again to knock it out of balance.

"What's going on?" he asks me, his tone conveying he is managing to keep his emotions in check a lot better than I am.

"Guess who I just spoke to?" I ask him.

He shrugs. "I don't know. The Queen of Sardania?"

I glare at him. "I wish." Sardania is one of our allies, and the only reason he thinks that might be funny is because the queen is probably six hundred years old and has always had a thing for me. She looks like she's about ninety and smells like mung beans…. "I spoke to King Peter. And we have a problem, dear brother. A fucking major one!" The idea of how the news Peter had given me complicates the situation has me seething again.

"What is it?" he asks, and I see genuine fear behind his blue eyes. "I'm sure whatever it is that Opal has told him isn't true."

"Did you fuck her?" I ask him.

Somehow, his bulging eyes grow even wider. "Fuck Opal?"

"Answer the goddamn question!" I say, slamming my hand down into the kitchen counter and cracking the quartz.

"Yes!" he says quickly. "I did… a few times. But… we always used protection. Wh-why are you asking?"

"Where did the protection come from?" My brother has never been a genius, but he isn't an idiot either, so I don't know why he wouldn't have enough sense not to trust Opal as far as he could throw her, but it is beginning to sound to me like he is a lot stupider than I have ever recognized.

"Uhm… she had condoms," he says with a shrug. "There were other people in the bed…."

"Any other born vampires, brother?" I continue to chew right through him with my eyes, and he is beginning to get where I am going. Slowly.

"Only Jacob. But he didn't have sex with his own sister, of course. Why?"

I take a slow step toward him, not answering him, just waiting.

"Why, Kane? You're... you're scaring me."

When my nose is almost touching his, I say, "You. Know. Why."

He takes a deep breath but then begins to shake his head wildly, stepping away from me. "No, that's not possible. I was careful. I made sure—"

"She fucking tricked you, Lex! You were her backup plan, and now that she's in this situation, she's going to use your own child against us!" I shout at him, watching a plethora of emotions sweep over his face. Realization that he's going to be a father—the fear and elation that goes along with that—dread of knowing his own child will be a pawn in the child's mother's schemes, knowing I am about to rip his head from his body, and he would deserve it completely for fucking up royally in only a way a royal can fuck up.

"But... she could be lying," he says, grasping at straws as he runs his hand through his hair.

I shake my head. "No, she's not. Even Opal wouldn't go to those sorts of lengths. She's too smart for that. She'd be discovered soon enough, and when her father found out she was lying, he'd punish her. Even King Peter has his limitations."

"Well, we can fix it," he says, taking a few rushed steps toward me. "Just because she's carrying my child, that doesn't mean that we are bound to her. I mean... it's not like it's a child I wanted anyway."

I listen to his words and try to hear what he's saying, seeing him grasping for some way to try and justify this, to make it all right. But it's not all right. I won't allow any relation of mine to be abandoned in that kingdom with that woman as his or her mother.

More importantly, this will mean war. I have Jacob as my prisoner, and King Peter is already demanding to have him back. He believes the child Opal is carrying is mine. He will attack if I don't acknowledge that the agreement we made has already been carried out.

I try to come up with a way to explain that to him, that the damage has already been done, and we can't just ignore it.

"He thinks the baby is mine," I say, my words measured. "He thinks that we've already consummated the relationship, and in his mind, that means that I have to marry his bitch daughter!"

Lex understands now, and his eyes are wide as his mouth opens and closes quickly like a wide-mouth bass. "Uhm… it's okay," he finally says, his shoulders up around his ears. "I'll tell him. I'll call him and explain."

I shake my head slowly. "He won't believe you, and even if he does, he won't care. He has what he wants, Lex. Thanks to your balls, he has me by mine."

I am done speaking to my brother about this. There's only one person in this world I want to see right now, only one person who can even begin to calm me down so that I can try to figure out how to handle this. How do I get my brother's baby without having to put up with that bitch who tried to kill Emory?

I don't know, but I'm not going to find the answer in this room.

As I turn to go, Lex is still shouting after me, "Don't worry, brother. I'll figure it out."

I take about five steps down the hallway before I turn to face him. "You know, Lex, for once, I was beginning to feel a little bit proud of you, like maybe you weren't quite as colossal a failure as I'd made you out to be. But now… I can see that I'm wrong. I appreciate your attempt to help Emory, but you are still a long way from being a responsible adult."

He says nothing, only stares at me, and I know that I've hurt him, but at the moment, I can't let it bother me. He's needed to hear the truth for many years, and now that I've told him, I don't feel any better, and I don't think that he will do any better either.

My feet carry me swiftly to the healing center, thinking if I don't see Emory right away, I'll go mad. I don't want to tell her anything that's going to worry her, but at the same time, I have to see her face. It's the only thing in the world that can calm me now.

When I arrive at her room, a wave of confusion washes over me. She's gone. Panic wells up inside of me as I stare at the empty bed.

One of the healers comes into the room. "Where is she?" I demand.

The woman jumps a bit in shock. "Uhm, she's... in her room, sir. She was released a little while ago."

I don't apologize for being so rude, even though I know I should, and I hurry down the hallway toward Emory's room.

As I rush to Emory's room, a thousand thoughts flutter through my head. I had thought she was gone again. Terror had pulsed through me as I stared at that empty bed, thinking about what might've happened to her.

It is clear to me as I reach her room that this woman is special to me in ways I am not yet ready to face. I pause outside of her door, taking a few deep breaths, attempting to calm myself. I can smell her here. I can feel her heart beating beyond the wooden barrier. It's slow, relaxed, and it makes my heart beat slower as well.

I knock on the door, but she doesn't speak, and I wonder if perhaps she's asleep.

Slowly, I push the door open and step inside. My questions are answered as I hear the sound of running water from the bathroom.

I should leave, give her some privacy, but my longing to see her is overwhelming. Against the gentlemanly voice in my head, I approach her closed bathroom door and wait.

The thrumming of her heart increases slightly as she realizes I'm here. I take a breath, and it shutters releasing from my lips.

If I enter that room, I will claim her in every way imaginable.

"Kane?"

My name is a whisper on her lips. She calls to me like a siren. I am powerless to turn away from her.

"Emory."

It's not a question. I love the feel of her name on my lips.

The sound of water rolling off of her skin tells me she's in the bath. I can smell the scents of flowers and oils now, but they are in the background compared to the scent of her I'm longing for.

I hear a soft whimper escape her lips and know she is longing for me the same way I want her.

No longer able to control myself, I push the door open. My eyes meet hers, and everything else in the world fades away.

33

I'M THE KING OF THE WORLD!

Lex

I AM A FOOL.

Everyone knows that. In fact, it's quite the topic of discussion at court. It's a joke, really. Kane is the serious, responsible brother, and then there's Lex, the playful, irresponsible, woman—or is it man—chasing whore who will never be able to accomplish anything of significance in his life no matter how many centuries he may last.

Yes, it's all something to chuckle over while sipping sherry and wondering about the weather.

The possibility of Luther Alexander doing something foolish is almost as certain as a chance of rain at the castle. Both things happen nearly every day.

So… it shouldn't have been a surprise to anyone that I did something that was likely to get me into trouble or get me killed. I didn't find it surprising at all when I pulled my sports car to a stop outside of the massive gates of the Maxwell castle later that same day that Kane had come to me to say that I'd fucked up for real this time.

When the guards at the gate demand to know who I am and what

201

business I have there, I snicker at them. "Just tell His Majesty King Peter that Lex is here. He'll want to see me."

The guard raised an eyebrow but within five minutes, I am strolling down the halls toward King Peter's private office. My stomach is permanently situated somewhere behind my eyeballs, I'm so terrified of what is about to become of me, but under no circumstances can I let it show.

I have to continue to maintain that aura I often have about myself —nonchalance, carefree, playful.

Foolish....

What would my brother do in this sort of situation? Well, he would never get himself into this sort of a situation, but if this were him, he would walk in and demand that King Peter see things his way.

I can't do that, so I have to take a different approach.

When I reach the door, a guard in a regal blue uniform with a large plume attached to his hat that makes him look a bit like a rare bird signals for me to wait there. He goes into the office while two other guards in similar uniforms without the headgear stand at attention.

Unlike the guards in our castle, they are actually looking at me. One of them is kind of handsome, and I might actually do a little flirting under different circumstances. For now, I avert my eyes, keeping them trained on the door.

A moment later, the door snaps open again and the large, angry birdman walks out. "His Majesty, Vampire King Peter Maxwell will see you now."

I arch an eyebrow at all of the unnecessary pomp. This fellow is beginning to make my brother look relaxed.

I walk in to find King Peter situated behind a large desk, a pen in his hand. I wait for him to acknowledge me, my hands folded behind my back. It seems quite clear to me, considering all of the large maps on the table against the wall that he is either about to use this room as a war room or he's been perusing his options alone.

After a lengthy wait, Peter puts his pen upon the table and looks up at me. "What in the devil's name are you doing here, Lex?"

I crack a smile. I'm Lex... that's what I do. "It's a pleasure to see you again, Sir," I say with a twirl of my hand and a bow.

He grumbles at me. "If this is your brother's way of trying to make peace, I'm afraid he's sent the wrong ambassador. I know what an idiot you are. Your reputation always precedes you, you know?"

Inwardly, I wonder if he will still think I'm an idiot when he discovers that his grandchild has half my DNA, but I do not respond to the rude comment.

"I've come to speak to you about your daughter," I tell him.

His stare is heavy as he replies, "Unless you also brought my son along with you, I'm afraid I have nothing to discuss with you."

I shake my head. "No, I'm afraid I did not. In fact, my brother doesn't know I'm here."

"That doesn't surprise me. It does seem like something a babbling idiot would do to drive into what should now be considered enemy territory right after an act of aggression, and my daughter did mention that you were one of the two who pursued her after she was thrown out of the kingdom, unceremoniously."

I clear my throat.

"While it is good to hear that your daughter has given you some information, I'm afraid that she hasn't told you everything, Your Highness, and that's precisely why I'm here. To make amends. To make the situation right."

He continues to glower at me for a long moment before he asks, "Whatever the fuck do you mean?"

I chuckle because I am nervous. "Your daughter has told you that she is with child, yes?" I ask him.

He nods. "That's right. Opal has told me that she is carrying your brother's baby, that they consummated their relationship before the pending nuptials, and that he threw her out in favor of some... feeder or something. While he claims he was unaware of the child's existence, I can't help but think that's not true. I believe he simply doesn't want a child to become the next king of his lands who was conceived out of wedlock."

When I laugh this time, it almost sounds natural because what he's said is almost funny. "Oh, King Peter, I'm so afraid to be the one to tell you that your sweet daughter is not at all who you think she is."

His eyes narrow even further until he's staring at me through little more than slits. "You'd better have a satisfying explanation for slandering my little girl, or else, what you and your whorish brother did to my son is only the beginning of what I will do to you."

Only one word springs to mind, so I let it out, though I may soon regret it. "Orgies," I tell him. "Lots of them. Almost every night. I was present for dozens of them, as was your son. And most of the ladies Opal left behind at our castle. I've had all of them several times, including other people from your kingdom and mine… including your children. Both of them. I'm sorry to be the one to tell you, but—"

"Enough!" Alpha King Peter shouts at me, standing as he sinks his fist into his desk. "This is all fucking bullshit, and I will not hear you speak so poorly about my children anymore!"

"It's true," I say, keeping my chin up. "There are plenty of witnesses back at Castle Graystone that can tell you."

He shakes his head, his eyes sending daggers through me. "This is just an attempt for you to try and weasel your way into power, both in your own kingdom and here."

That makes me laugh out loud, and in fact, I am laughing so hard, he looks about to toss me out as he comes around the desk to stand toe to toe with me. "Believe me, Sir, coming here was about the most dangerous thing I've ever done. I certainly wouldn't do it in the off chance it might give me some power. Why don't we get Opal in here? See if you're good at detecting lies."

He leans in very closely to me so that I can feel his warm, stale breath on my cheek. "You will not continue to sully the name of my daughter."

"Sully my name how?"

Opal's voice from behind me makes my stomach churn. I'd been bluffing. There was no way in hell I expected Opal to take my side.

But now that she was here, I needed her to confirm what had actually happened, and I needed her to see how it benefited her.

"The baby," I say, staring right into her face. She looks a lot more put together than she did the last time I saw her, running through the forest, scaling a wall with her fingernails.

"What of the baby?" she asks me, and her glare is almost as sharp as her father's.

"This poor excuse for a prince has come here claiming that the baby in your womb is his. He's saying all sorts of vicious things about you, darling," King Peter says as he goes over to his daughter and kisses her cheek.

I see Opal's throat moving as she swallows hard.

"It is possible to prove paternity," I remind them both. "Opal, you and I both know that Kane didn't sleep with you, so…."

"That's not true!" she says.

I turn my head to the side and stare at her for a moment. "So you're saying that a man slept with you but prefers a werewolf in bed now instead?"

Her mouth drops open, and her father wears a confused expression. He won't understand why this is so horrifically offensive to Opal.

"Well… he's just trying to hurt me!" she stammers.

I shake my head. "Why? He wants your head for attacking her. He had Rainer hunt down your brother and nearly kill him and was trying to do the same for you. That seems a little unlike love to me."

"That's enough!" King Peter shouts.

"Fine," I say with a shrug. "Go ahead and go to war on behalf of your lying daughter. Risk our child's welfare to prove that a man who does not love you has impregnated you. He won't marry you now. You already know that."

I start to walk away, but King Peter's demanding voice shouts. "Where the fuck do you think you're going?"

I turn to look at him. "Home," I say. "Why would I stay here?"

He is finally smiling at me, and it is a devious grin. "Because… you're my guest now, until I get my son back."

A chuckle escapes my lips as I tell him, "Now, come on, King Peter. Do you really think I'm of more use to you here?"

His head tips to the side. "What do you mean?" I ask him.

I look from him to Opal and see she's already figured out what I'm saying. Her smile is toothy and bright as she says, "I always knew you were the smarter brother."

I smile back at her and wait for her father to catch up with this scheme. When he finally gets there, he chuckles. "Oh, I see. Well, if you're willing...."

Looking at Opal, I force a charismatic look upon my face and pledge, "There's absolutely nothing I wouldn't do for the welfare of my child and the beautiful woman carrying my baby."

Whether or not I'm willing to hold up my end of the bargain will remain to be seen. Perhaps, I'm simply ensuring my way home.

Or maybe I really do want to take over the world.

34

HOW DID HE ESCAPE?

Kane

VAMPIRES DON'T GET FATIGUED. At least, we don't usually get fatigued. Not from simple tasks like the one I am doing now, but as I lean over the desk and stare at the map in front of me, my eyes start to blur out of focus, and everything begins to fade slightly.

I've been looking at this fucking map for far too long, and it's time to just make a decision.

"You could just position them all here," Rainer says, pointing at the border between my lands and King Peter's. "If they never cross into our lands then we won't have to worry about them attacking."

"Yes, but Alpha King Peter is not that stupid," I remind him. "The chances of him actually sending all of his forces in from that direction is very unlikely. I think there's a better chance that he'll send in a diversion from that direction and use a different path to come at us."

I look at our other borders. Our lands share most of our northern border with Scarlett Thunder, Opal's home pack. To the east, we have several smaller neighbors, but on the southeast, rolling around a bit to our eastern border lies the large lands controlled by Vampire King

Myenas, who is a royal fuck-off and someone who very well may be in cahoots with King Peter. I can see the two of them working together to try and bend me over, so I can't leave that border unwatched.

To the very south are two fairly unthreatening wolf packs, but wrapping around to our west, we run into some enemies.

First, there are a few packs that are still angry that I aided Moonraker pack in funding the war Alpha Bernard used to attack them. He wasn't successful, but it still likely cost them both money and men to defend their borders.

Then, there are the Moonraker pack lands themselves. Alpha Bernard is in absolutely no shape whatsoever to attack me, and I honestly don't see him as a threat even if he does. His lands are vast, even though he is out of money and warriors to defend them with. Eventually, other packs will grow the balls to start taking them from him, but for now, I really don't see much of a threat to my immediate west except for the ones mad at me for giving Bernard money. I doubt they will attack me unless they can get organized, but it isn't impossible.

Finally, along the northwest border is a large city primarily inhabited by humans. We have a pact with them that involves feeders for freedom, and a little bit of money exchanges hands as well. They wouldn't want to piss us off, so I have a feeling they will leave us be.

My debate at this point is how many troops to put where, and I am growing remarkably cross-eyed just staring at this damn map.

"You can't split them evenly. Leave the borders as they are, add an extra ten thousand here and here, and you'll be good," Rainer suggests, moving little figures around the map as if to show me what he's talking about, which normally would irritate me, but I'm so cross-eyed at this point, it actually helps.

I'm about to give the order when the sound of fancy dress shoes clicking off of the stone floor tells me someone has barged into my war room, and I don't have to look up from the map to know who it is.

"Oh, Lex. You're back from your adventure, and you're not dead.

How… unappealing." I narrow my eyes at my brother who dared to go and pay a visit to our enemy without asking me first, a mission that was both dangerous and stupid. The devil only knows what he may have said to Alpha King Peter. He will try to tell me, but I won't believe a word he says.

I do want to know how he managed to drive right across the border of a clan territory that is on the verge of waging war on us, enter the castle there, request and be granted an audience with the king, speak his mind, refuse to trade the prince of that kingdom that we are currently holding hostage after torturing him, and then come back here. All without being dead.

"I am back, brother," he begins, keeping his distance from Rainer who has been cursing his name ever since we discovered his absence, and standing near the far end of the table with his hands folded behind his back. "Did you think I'd be incapable of removing myself from the situation with Alpha King Peter? Really? You think so little of me?"

I snickered. "Yes," I said. He glared at me. "What in heaven's name made you think it would be permissible for you to go to Scarlett Thunder without speaking to me first?" I demand, standing up straight which causes my back to pop after all of this time of staring at the map.

His eyes widen. "Whatever do you mean? Why would I need your permission to go there? You told me yourself that Opal is carrying my child. Did you think that would have no bearing on what I did next?"

I do have to give my brother a little credit. He is quite good at twisting a situation so that it appears to favor him. I narrow my eyes even further at him. "Don't be ridiculous, Lex. Of course, I didn't think you'd leave the safety of the castle to go into enemy territory to check on your unborn child and a woman neither one of us can stand."

He purses his lips together and continues to let his eyes bulge from his head. "Well, I never!" he finally says. "First of all, I don't believe that Scarlett Thunder has actually declared war, have they? And have we?"

I don't even bother to answer the question as he already knows the answer.

He also is smart enough to know that it doesn't matter. The chances of him getting out of Alpha King Peter's territory alive were less than my chances of walking outside right now and stepping on a magical leprechaun—slim to none. The fact that he wasn't currently broken and bleeding in a cell below the castle in Scarlett Thunder was mind-blowing to me, especially considering Jacob was still in my dungeon, his leg twisted and his arm missing.

It just didn't make any sense.

And in my experience, when something doesn't make sense, one should question it—completely.

"How did you earn your freedom?" Rainer asks. "I seriously doubt your girlfriend threw herself at her father's mercy and begged for you to be released."

"My girlfriend?" Lex asks, an amused expression on his pretty face as he says, "This from someone who insists I am only interested in boys."

"I don't believe I ever used the word 'only,'" Rainer replies, in his defense, but I am uninterested in a history lesson or one involving semantics.

"How are you here, Lex?" I ask the question in a demanding tone, one that has his head whipping back around to face me.

"Simple enough, my brother, the king, I am smarter than you ever give me credit for, and I was able to trick Alpha King Peter into releasing me. While I was on my way home, I did a bit of scouting, and I'm afraid you've got his positions wrong, though not completely. May I?"

He gestures at my map, and I decide to let him mess with it just to amuse myself. Lex has never been one for paying much attention when it comes to war.

He comes around the table to my right, opposite Rainer, and moves a few pieces that are clearly representing Scarlett Thunder troops, moving some of them further to our northwestern border but moving still more down to the east.

"How do you know they're down there?" Rainer asks. "You wouldn't have come home that way unless you truly do have a death wish."

Lex chuckles. "I used some of my skills with the generals as I was leading to find out."

"You mean you sucked their dicks?" Rainer asks bluntly.

"No. I mean I had a conversation with them, asshole. But I'd much rather suck their dicks than yours." It's meant to be an insult, but Rainer doesn't quite take it that way.

"I'd be too much for you to handle," he says with a glimmer of mirth in his eyes.

I only shake my head, praying they'll stop. Lex laughs, and I wonder if my brother ever thinks about Rainer that way, but I decide I don't want to know. What Lex does in the bedroom only concerns me when it produces unwanted heirs.

"Thank you, Lex. That will be all," I tell my brother, ready to discuss this disclosure with Rainer in Lex's absence.

"But… don't you even want to know how I got out of there?" he asks me.

"I already asked you, and your response was vague. What would make me think you'd be more forthright with your answer now?"

"True," he says. "All right then. It shall remain a mystery—like how Rainer manages to walk in an upright position when clearly his dick weighs ten thousand pounds."

On an ordinary day, I don't find Lex's sense of humor amusing, and I certainly don't now. "I'll talk to you later, Luther," I tell him, and he heads for the door.

The moment he is gone, I ask Rainer, "Do you trust that information?"

"Fuck no," he says. "Why should we? I don't trust your brother one damn bit. How the hell do you think he got out of there? He has something up his sleeve. Or up his ass as the case may be."

I think Rainer might be right, but there's only one way to test this theory. "We should give him some misinformation and see if it makes its way back to Alpha King Peter."

My second-in-command nods. "That sounds like a reasonable idea. Do you have an idea of what to tell him?"

I think for a moment, my eyes grazing over the map, but that's not what I'm thinking about. Finally, something comes to mind. "Yes, I think I have it."

A smile crosses Rainer's face, "Well, then, Alpha King, let's hear it."

I lean in close to tell him my plan, and when I've explained it all in great detail to him, I ask, "Do you think it will work?"

Immediately, he says, "Hell yeah, I think it will work. But there's only one way to find out. Let's put it in action."

I give him a nod of approval. "Hop to it."

35

SAYING GOODBYE

Emory

A WALK in the garden was meant to lift my spirits, but when I return to my room a few hours later, I find that it has done very little. As I come back to my room, I am reminded that at least I no longer have to fear having my throat ripped out while I'm out and about. That is something to be happy about, I suppose.

My hand goes to my neck, and I pause in front of the mirror to look at my scars. Helga and Nellie dismiss themselves into their own chambers, and I barely murmur a, "See you later," as my fingers trace two jagged marks, one on either side of my throat.

I'd healed quickly enough to keep me from bleeding out, but the speed at which my tissue had mended itself also prevented the pack healer from having the opportunity to put me back together with a straight stitch. So now, these three to four inch long tears will always be there to remind me of the horrendous encounter I had in the library.

I've hardly even been able to look at a book since then.

"They will fade, I believe."

Kane's voice behind me has me sighing, and as he comes up behind me, I close my eyes and lean into him. He makes me feel strong, like I can handle anything, even though I don't feel nearly as strong since the attack as I had before.

His lips trace down the scar. I used to flinch, only a day or two ago, whenever he would touch me there, but now, it's like a cool compress to my fleshed skin to have his lips trace that line, and I find myself letting out a soft moan.

My heart feels heavy inside my chest, though. I can guess why he's here, and it makes me feel all alone to know that he'll be leaving soon to fight against King Peter, and I cannot come with him. I must stay behind in the castle where I am safe. If I could shift, perhaps I'd have a better chance of convincing him to bring me along, but as it is, there's simply no way I'll be able to talk him into it, so I don't try.

One hand comes up to cup my breast as the other slides down my belly. I am panting now as the velocity of his kissing increases. I want him so badly, the ache in my core is already beginning to thrum through my thighs, and as his hand slides lower and lower, I am willing him to take me.

His hardness presses against the small of my back, and I can't help but rub against him. Working my nipple through the fabric of my dress is pleasurable enough, but when he slides his hand down my top, tearing away the fabric and pushing my bra out of the way, I lean up and find his lips with mine.

His tongue glides against mine, my hand tangles in his silky hair, and he pinches my nipple harder. I want to consume him entirely, and my hand begs him closer as wetness drips between my legs.

He's managed to gather my skirt out of the way, and sliding the silk of my panties aside, he gently massages my outer folds, taking his time, stroking the outside of my opening without pushing inside.

Instinct tells me to lean down and take his wrist, to force him to finger me fully. I want to ride his hand like he is a stallion and I'm riding off into the sunset, but I keep as much restraint as I can, and eventually, he's pressing inside of me.

Kane releases my mouth and lifts the hand that's been rubbing my breast to my chin. Gently, he turns my face toward the full-length mirror. "Look at you," he commands me. "See how gorgeous you are."

Standing there with this Adonis of a man behind me, his hand causing ripples of pleasure to tear through my body, I can hardly focus on what I look like. I have to brace myself with my hands on his shoulders. I am panting and writhing against his hand, and when he begins to hit my most sensitive area, I cry out, feeling my muscles restrict.

He is smiling wickedly at my reflection in the mirror, and I know he is enjoying watching my wanton ways even if I am not able to concentrate. I come, hard, around his hand, grabbing a fistful of his long black hair as I do so. He laughs and slowly removes his hand from me, and I spin around to face him.

His hands clamp down on my ass, and he plunges his tongue back into my mouth. His hardness is impossible to ignore at this point, his big, thick cock caught between us.

He lifts me and spins me to the bed, pulling my panties off and tossing them aside. I don't even get a chance to discard my torn dress before his pants are undone and falling down to pool at his legs. He has my ankles, my bottom on the edge of the bed, and with my legs spread wide, Kane thrusts inside of me, deep and hard.

My clit is already so sensitive from his finger-work that I am already ready to come again after just a few passes of his hips. Somehow, I manage to fight the urge to come completely undone and focus on his face as I watch the tension build within him.

The Alpha King is a work of art. I wish he would've removed his shirt so I can more clearly see his rippling chest muscles, but even with his shirt on, I can see his abs and biceps working as he continues to thrust into me. His eyes are closed, and his perfect lips are held in an ecstatic pose.

I bite my bottom lip, fighting the urge to explode into a thousand pieces. I can only hold off for so long before I'm shouting his name again, my fingers splayed on the comforter, searching for purchase of some kind and finding none. I'm doing my best to hold onto reality, but with every passing second, the world falls away, and all there is left is my breathless body and his.

When he comes, it's hard, and he fills me completely with his warm essence. He is left panting, which is saying something for a man in such perfect physical condition.

Kane collapses next to me on the bed and pulls me toward him, pressing his mouth to mine. The first kiss is fast and deep, but then, he pulls away, looking into my eyes for a moment before he slowly moves to kiss me again, taking his time, savoring every movement of my tongue on his, every inhale of my breath mingling with the air he breathes.

When he pulls away again, I see a change in his demeanor and can guess what he's about to say to me. "I have to go."

I've been expecting this revelation, so it doesn't shock me, but it still hurts. I nod, though, keeping a brave face on for him—the same way I did for Lola when I told her the same thing. "When?" I ask, keeping my voice as light and innocent as possible.

"Tonight. We're moving out under cover of darkness. It's all part of a plan to see whether or not we can trust Lex."

I arch an eyebrow. "Why wouldn't you be able to trust him? He's your brother. He saved me. Twice."

He shrugs. "The second time he saved you he could've done a better job," he replies, and I don't feel the need to argue with him even though I understand why Lex couldn't have done more under the circumstances.

"Has he done something to make you think he might not be trustworthy?" I reach up and lightly stroke his cheek.

"Yes, lots of them." With a loud sigh, he moves us around so that we are lying on the pillows and kicks off his pants so they are no longer twisted around his ankles. I don't care at all that my skirt is still up around my waist and my dress is torn at the bodice. All I can think about right now is him.

"Something in particular?" I clarify as I rest my head on his shoulder. He is playing with my hair, and the feel of it is so soothing, I am afraid I might fall asleep before he answers.

"We believe he may be working for King Peter. It's the only explanation we can come up with for how he got out of there." I assume "we" refers to Kane and Rainer.

"And what does Lex say about this?" I wonder.

"He says that he told King Peter he would send him information and managed to convince him enough so that he was able to get away."

"But you don't think that's true?" I clarify.

"No. I don't know. Maybe."

I can't help but chuckle a little. I rest my hand on his chest, still lamenting that his shirt is in the way. "Well, I would say, don't do anything stupid, but at the same time, try to trust him if you can. He is your brother, after all."

"True. But… would you trust your brother?"

He has a point. The only person in my entire family that I trust right now is my sister. "No," I tell him.

He reaches down and lifts my hand kissing my wrist. "Then you understand."

I sit up abruptly and stare into his eyes. "Kane," I say, "do you think… before you go… you should… use me for my intended purpose?"

His eyebrows arch as he stares right back at me for a long moment. "Your intended purpose? You make it sound like you had a reason for coming here that involves me sucking you dry."

I shake my head. "No, but I am your feeder."

He leans down and kisses my nose. "No, you're not, Emory. You're so much more than that. I don't know if I will ever feed from you, but if I do, there will have to be a better reason than just putting a label on you."

I'm not sure what to think about that because I want to fulfill my duties, but at the same time, I am grateful that he sees me as more than a feeder. I want to ask what word he would use to describe me.

But I am too afraid.

Resting my head back on his chest, I listen to his heartbeat and hope that this isn't the last time I ever hear it.

3 6

THE SCENE OF THE CRIME

Kane

WHETHER OR NOT MY brother is lying remains to be seen. Our forces drove out from the castle in large transport vehicles that were designed to get us closer to the launching off point, but then, we would travel by foot through the thick forest, moving in on the enemy, using our speed, dexterity, and stealth to try and get the upper hand on another group of vampires attempting to do the same thing.

Lex had been told differently than what we were actually doing, and I'd sent him to a different position than the one we were moving toward. If King Peter moved his main force to our eastern border, then I'd know that Lex had betrayed us. If he continued to go to the locations Lex had told me his insider at the castle had revealed to him, then he was telling me the truth.

Either way, we had our bases covered for what would happen wherever Peter came out to meet us. I'd managed to secure alliances with all of our neighbors. It hadn't been easy because some of them were reliant on Peter's sex trafficking ring to get their jollies.

It turns out that some things are more important to greedy old vampires than sex. Like money.

And blood.

I had promised them so much blood, my own coffers would be empty soon. I'd need to find a source to replace what I'd given away soon, or else my own people would end up suffering for it. I had a few ideas in mind, but I didn't have time to go about that at the moment. It would have to wait until I fought off the initial threat.

Still, thank the powers that be that I'd had the foresight to keep such a massive stockpile of blood frozen in the royal freezers stationed across our lands in secret locations known to only my most trusted advisors.

Not having Rainer with me as I went into battle felt like a detriment, but I'd had to leave the payoffs to someone I could trust, and I didn't trust another vampire in the world the way that I trusted him.

It took a few hours for us to get into position. By then, night had fallen, and the sky was an inky black. Cloud cover kept the stars at bay, and that was a good thing because I wanted to sneak up on Peter if I could. If the bulk of his forces were where they should be, according to Lex, then I should be able to take him by surprise and force him into a position where he would be seriously thinking about whether or not it was worth it for us to continue with this ridiculous war.

The dirt road we were traveling on became less gravel and more dirt until the grass overtook it, and the trees closed in on us. The driver brought the transport vehicle to a stop. "Your Majesty," he said, turning to where I was sitting in the passenger seat, "is this the correct location."

"Yes," I said, my fingers reaching for the door handle. "This will do. Thank you."

"Yes, Your Majesty."

I got out of the vehicle, and the commanders climbed out of the backseat, letting the other warriors out of the back of the transport. Immediately, my soldiers lined up, all of them wearing the black version of our military uniforms. They would be able to move quickly through the trees on a night like this and sneak up on the enemy undetected, assuming he didn't know we were coming.

Of course, King Peter's troops could do the same to us.

Once the thousands of soldiers had poured out of the vehicles and lined up behind me, I took a moment to address them, letting the stillness of the night remind me that we had to move like the wind. We had to strike before we were discovered, and we had to be deadly with the first blow.

"Noble members of the Crimson Peak army, I thank you for assembling here today." I spoke aloud, but I used telepathy to make sure that everyone present could hear me without raising my voice. "This night, we embark upon a mission to preserve our lands and ensure that hostile forces are not able to overcome us."

No one spoke, but I could see in their eyes that they understood the importance of what I was saying.

"Tonight, we will move through the trees unimpeded, inflict mortal wounds on our enemies, and disappear into the darkness before they know what hit them!"

Through telepathy, many of the warriors sounded off in agreement with a loud, "Huzzah!"

"Now, let us forge ahead, let us fight bravely, and let us be victorious. Today, we fight for Crimson Peak and for all of the vampires in the world who stand for all that is good and just!"

More cheers erupted in my head, and many of the troops raised a fist in solidarity.

With that, I turned on my heel and moved quickly ahead, leading the troops into battle, and they followed me, taking on the proper formation to slip between the trees at full speed, keeping our feet light, as we searched the darkness for King Peter's troops, ready to destroy them, demolish his forces, and end this hostility once and for all.

Emory

Kane is gone.

He'd left earlier this afternoon. For some reason I don't quite understand, Rainer is still here, but he's busy, in his office, doing something.

I feel alone. Helga and Nellie are here with me, but it's not the same as having Kane nearby or even being able to spend time with Rainer.

I'd wanted to go with him, but he'd said absolutely not, that since I couldn't shift, I wouldn't be able to move quickly enough to keep up, and he would be too worried with me on the battlefield.

I understand. I do. Still, it's hard to know he's out there fighting a battle to protect the kingdom, a battle that I feel at least partially responsible for starting. The situation between Kane and Opal might not have been ideal before my arrival, but I certainly made it worse.

I decide to use my time wisely while I am waiting for word of Kane and the battle that may have already started since night has fallen. So… I go to the one place in the castle that makes me the most uncomfortable.

The feeders' dungeon would be one such place, though I'm told I wouldn't even recognize it if I went there now, but that's not where I'm headed to.

The hallways are empty as I make my way down the familiar path, my slippers quiet on the stone floor. I'd just as soon do this fully on my own. I don't want anyone to see me and ask a lot of questions about whether or not I'm okay or how I am feeling. No, it's best if I just do this on my own.

Reaching the double doors, I pause for a long moment, breathing in through my nose and letting it out through my mouth slowly. I do that a few times before I push the door open and walk in.

It's quiet, perhaps a little too quiet. The scent I noticed the last time I was here hits me immediately. Paper and book glue. That fragrance when it mingles in the air has always been one of my favorites, but right now, I'm not as pleased with it as I used to be.

I smell something else as well, something that wasn't present the last time I walked into this room.

Blood.

It's not strong. Only the faintest tinge of it hits my lungs every time I inhale, but it's there.

And it's mine.

My blood.

I'm sure that Kane had everyone come and scrub the area where the two vampires ripped my neck apart and slurped up my essence, but it would be impossible to get every trace out. I have to wonder if it's soaked into the wood of the balcony where the reading nook has not been restored. I can see that from the entryway. The bookshelves and seating are all gone. It's just a barren area now, and it sticks out because it's no longer warm or inviting.

I won't go back up there to see if perhaps that's the source of the blood, but I do take my time, walking through the rows and rows of books toward the place where I saw Lex standing when I'd looked over the railing.

Looking up at the balcony at this angle, I can imagine he didn't have a perfect view of what was happening, but he had to have known. He heard my screams. I'd been begging for his help.

At least, when they tossed me over the balcony, he'd been there to catch me. In my mind, I can see that, see my body in that dress that's been disposed of fluttering down from the sky like a bird with a broken wing. Like an autumn leaf, spent, and no longer of any use to the tree that has expelled it.

Where had he been standing when I'd hit his arms? When had the guards burst into the room? How had Opal and Jacob gotten down? I imagine they'd leaped, rather than taking the stairs. My eyes go to the side door. Is that the escape route they use?

"You truly are a brave woman."

I hear him speak before I notice he'd crept into the room, my mind registering his voice, steps, and scent at the same time. I need to be more aware of my surroundings; I can't risk being assaulted again with Kane gone and Rainer so busy.

Lex doesn't come over to where I am standing. Instead, he hovers back by the door.

My mouth hangs open for a second as I lock eyes with him, unsure of what to say. When I finally do speak, I only say, "I don't feel brave."

He smirks, and I notice that his laugh sounds a bit like his brother's. It's about the only thing about Lex that reminds me of his brother. "You are brave. But then... you've got nothing to fear here now, I suppose."

I would almost take his statement as a threat, but I know he won't hurt me.

"You did something brave, too, I hear."

He looks down at the ground between his shoes as I leave my spot by the balcony and cross back to him. "Brave or stupid."

"Kane thinks it was stupid." It's not a question but he nods. "I'm not sure. I don't think you would betray your entire kingdom in the way he's afraid you have."

He raises his eyes and looks at me. "I don't want to be king, Emory. I've gotten a little taste of what it means to have power, and I don't want it. All I want is a little estate by the beach where I can hear the crashing of the waves against the sand."

Images of what he speaks of come to mind. "I think I'd like that, too. But... I have a feeling Kane wants other things."

"Kane was born to want other things," he reminds me, which I understand to mean that he might have naturally wanted other things if he hadn't been born to be a vampire king.

"Well, I hope that all of this works out for you, and you get what it is you are looking for, Lex." I smile at him, and I mean what I've said.

"You, too," he says, and we stand there in amicable silence for a few seconds before the door behind him opens and Nellie comes in.

"There you are!" She's looking at me, and her tone makes me think something is wrong. "You have a telephone call, Miss Emory."

My forehead knits together. "A telephone call?" I didn't even think that was possible. "From who?"

She doesn't answer me, only grabs my arm and tugs me into the hall and toward Kane's office with her, and my heart lurches into my throat.

I pray to the Moon Goddess that he's okay.

3 7

AN IMMINENT THREAT

Emory

I RUN off behind Nellie as she leads me to Kane's office where I see a telephone sitting on its side. I've never been in here before, but I know it's his office because it smells like him. My stomach clenches into a tight fist as I make my way across the room, terrified that something has happened on the battlefield, and this is how they are informing me.

Sitting in his chair, I take a deep breath and reach for the receiver as Nellie turns to go. "Wait!" I say a little too harshly. She spins back to look at me, her eyes wide. "Sorry. I just… will you stay?"

Nellie nods and turns to face me, folding her hands in front of her, but not speaking or sitting in the chairs that are closest to her on the other side of the opulent, carved, gold-gilded desk.

Kane's tastes are not reflected in his office, at least, not from what I know of him.

I lift the receiver to my ear and say quietly, "This is Emory."

"Emory!"

The sound of my own name explodes into my ear through the

227

receiver, and immediately, I burst into tears, holding a hand over my face like a small child, unable to control myself.

I can hardly believe what I'm hearing… the sound of that voice. I'd thought perhaps I'd never hear such a sound again, the melody dancing through my mind and drudging up a thousand memories and all of my pain of the past several weeks.

No response will form on my lips as I do my best to control my tears and get myself together.

"Emory? Are you okay?" she asks, and I hear the concern in her voice.

"Yes, yes, I'm okay, sweetie. I'm okay! Oh, Goddess—how are you? How are you doing?" I'm sputtering now, picturing the beautiful face of my little sister. Nellie comes around the desk and places a hand on my shoulder, producing a tissue from somewhere, and I am eternally thankful for her again, even though it's clear she had something else she needed to do and didn't want to linger in here with me. She is my friend, after all, and she's here for me.

"I'm okay, sissy, but listen, something bad is happening, and I had to call you really quick to tell you before it's too late!" I can hear the panic and desperation in her voice, and it has me sobering up. No longer crying, I prepare to face the problem head-on, no matter what it is.

"What's going on, Lola?" I ask her.

"It's Father. He's got a whole bunch of soldiers ready to march on Crimson Peak. He even got guys from other packs to help. They all know that King Kane is busy right now fighting some other mean vampire guy, so they're trying to get him while he's not looking."

Her words rip through me the same way that Opal and Jacob used their fangs to rip at my flesh. "Are you sure?"

"Yes, I'm positive. They don't know I'm calling you. I know King Kane is a bad man, but I didn't want you to get hurt. Can you hide or something?" Lola sounds so scared, and it makes me long to take her in my arms.

I don't want to worry her either. "Yes, of course. It's fine. And King Kane isn't a bad man, honey. You've been told a lot of lies over the years, same as me, but I assure you, he's not bad, and when I get a chance, I'll prove it to you. For now, you just take care of yourself. Don't do anything silly, okay?"

"I will try not to. I just… Oh, no, someone's coming. I have to go. I love you so much, Emory!"

"I love you, t—" I don't get to finish the sentence before I hang up the phone, praying to the Moon Goddess that she didn't get caught. I can only imagine what my mother or father will do to her if they find out she called me.

Turning to Nellie, I say, "Where's Rainer?"

Her eyes widen slightly as that must not have been the name she thought I was going to say, but Kane is busy, and the last I heard, Rainer was still here.

"He's… out working on gathering blood, Princess. That was your sister?" Nellie is all kinds of confused, and I can't blame her. I would be, too.

"Yes." Taking a deep breath, I blurt out to her what the major problem is. "Moonraker and other packs are getting ready to attack Crimson Peak while Kane is gone. I don't want to draw his attention away from the front, but we need to move quickly to organize the guards that are left here to be able to defend the castle. The wolves won't be able to get over the walls like the vampires can, but they will find a way in."

Nellie's mouth is agape as she considers what I am saying. "Most of our army isn't here, Princess. We have the reserve guard, but… if they attack now…." She stops speaking and simply shakes her head.

She doesn't need to explain to me what can happen. I've seen it enough times with my own eyes.

Not the battle itself, but the aftermath.

Rows and rows of limping, bloodied, mauled wolves stringing their way back to the village, many of them collapsing and dying along the way.

That's what my people see when they think of Crimson Peak. They see a legion of vampires that overran us, that obliterated our once-strong army, tore us to shreds—and for what?

In their minds, it was to get their grubby, claw-clad hands on our resources, our land, and our people as feeders. Not the reality of the situation where Kane was simply trying to get what had been promised to him for the investment that he had made in our pack.

I understand so much more now than I did before. But my people won't, and it doesn't matter whether or not someone from the vampire clan stands up and tries to explain to them the truth of the situation or not.

I know these people. I grew up with them. I trained right alongside them. I was meant to rule them one day, in my head and in theirs. They will never back down just because a vampire spokesperson tries to explain to them that they've been misled.

Images are so much more powerful than words, and coming from an enemy, words are meaningless....

"Princess, what shall I do?" Nellie looks so distraught now that I want to do or say something to make her feel more at ease, but I have never been the type of person to use my words to persuade people. I've been taught to fight, not to debate, so it makes even soothing someone in their distress difficult.

Except for Lola. I always knew what to say to her....

"Uhm, where is Rainer? Gone?"

She nods. "Yes, for a day or two."

I doubted we had that kind of time. The wolves would find a way in before then. If they were already amassing to the point that Lola could see what was happening, my father was already on his way.

"Who is in charge now? With Rainer and Kane—King Kane--both gone?" I blush a little when I accidentally forget his title, not out of disrespect but out of familiarity.

I almost see a smile crest Nellie's mouth as well as she wants to join me in our little secret, that he is more than just a king to me, but she doesn't. Instead, she says, "I will tell you, but I'm not sure it will do us any good."

That answer has basically already been told to me.

Lex.

"Okay... where is the prince?" I sigh and wonder if it's even worth my time to discuss the situation with Lex; I have no idea if he's on my side or against his entire clan. But with him being left in charge, I suppose I have no choice.

"I can summon him, if you'd like." Nellie looks a bit reluctant to do so, and I imagine the only other time she's spoken to Lex telepathically is when I was being killed. The two of them probably had to discuss their plans silently so that Opal and Jacob wouldn't know.

"Please do," I tell her, and then I go to Kane's bookshelf and begin looking for a volume that might help me.

I find it quickly enough. An atlas. I pull it off of the shelf and carry it over to the desk, opening it up to a page that shows a recent map of the border between Moonraker pack lands and Crimson Peak.

Within a few minutes, I've got a pretty decent handle on the topography from the opposite direction—how the wolves will come —and I think I even know where they will attack.

There's a higher portion of land in the middle section of the wall that surrounds the castle.

My father will not bother with the outlying villages when the king is away from the castle. He will strike here while Kane and his army are away; I'm certain of it.

Lex walks into the office, a cautious air about him as he approaches me. "What's going on?" he asks me.

"My father is getting ready to attack," I tell him.

His eyes widen only slightly before he says, "That shouldn't be too much for the remaining castle guards to handle. Your father's army was basically decimated in the last war, right?"

His nonchalant mention of all of those people that I know, people I cared about, dying is a bit like a knife to the heart, but then, Lex isn't exactly known for being polite when he speaks.

"Yes, but he's somehow managed to get other wolf packs to join in with him, probably by spreading the same lies to them that he told me and my family for all of those years."

This has his interest a bit more. "How do you know all of this?"

"My sister called." I don't bother to tell him her age. He might decide it's a made-up story, dreamed up in my little sister's mind.

"I see." He strokes his chin and looks at the map.

"I think they'll come through here," I tell him.

He nods. "Yes, I believe you're right. We only have about a thousand, maybe two thousand troops at the castle, and most of them are much further away to be easily called back, but we need to let Kane know so that he can decide what to do."

I shake my head. I don't think we should do that. I think we need to leave him be. After all, his attack has already begun, correct?"

"Yes, but Emory, I'm not capable of leading a defensive stance like this. I've always just stood back and let others fight. Kane wanted it that way, and I've never been one to argue with him when it comes to putting myself in a position where I might die."

I nod at him. "I understand. I'm not asking you to lead the defensive stance, Lex. I'm just asking you to order it into existence."

"But all of our leaders are out in other parts of the kingdom. If I don't lead it, who the hell will?"

I don't hesitate when I tell him, "I will."

3 8

THIS IS WAR

Kane

OUR INITIAL ATTACK had been a phantom mist that rolled in through the darkness, catching King Peter and his troops completely off-guard. We'd cut between the trees through cover of night and descended upon them before they even knew we were there.

I'd personally taken out fifteen of his warriors, rolling down the line, dispatching one right after the next before they could make a sound or use their telepathy to communicate the threat to one another. Now, back at camp, I had time to reflect upon it as the sun had climbed the sky and we had broken away from our enemies for a bit to regroup.

The first one had been standing there in an unassuming, bored position, likely awaiting orders. I'd come from behind him, grabbed his head, and twisted until it came off. He'd crumpled to the forest floor, his knees sinking into the dew-covered grass as I tossed his head into a nearby bush and moved to the next.

She'd turned to see me just in time, her blue eyes widening as she considered what tactic to take to defend herself, but it was too late. I was already at her jugular before she could even shoot her hands up.

Down the line I went, and after a dozen or so of them had fallen, the others caught wind of what we were doing, either from noise being produced by one or more of my warriors or by someone surviving long enough to get a message out.

It hadn't made that much of a difference once they were made aware.

King Peter's forces were no match for us anyway, especially when they were terrified of the fact that so many of their numbers had been felled so quickly and effortlessly. They'd retreated into a clump in the center of the forest, and we had been about to surround them completely when the signal for them to retreat had sounded in their heads.

We'd followed them several miles, back into their own territory, and now, we were camped in King Peter's lands, awaiting his next move. I had only lost six, whereas he had lost thousands.

Those numbers were very heavily in my odds, and I hoped that he would reconsider what he'd been trying to do.

Sitting in a chair behind a portable desk in my tent, my eyes went over the map. We'd made inroads into other forces that had been set to attack us on other fronts as well, but none of the victories had been as large as here, where King Peter had been completely fooled.

He was under the impression we were still in front of him and to the east when we'd slipped around to his west and come in from the side, charging down his flank.

With such a large victory, I had been continuously congratulated, but I constantly pushed those kindnesses off on the warriors.

They were not the only ones who had served us well, though.

Lex is on our side, after all. He has proven that to me now that I know he didn't give Peter any information to help him. In fact, he'd misinformed the enemy, and while King Peter clearly hadn't completely taken my brother at his word, he had arranged his troops as if he believed what Lex had told him.

He hadn't learned a lesson I had discovered to be true as a young boy until much too later—never trust Luther Alexander....

"Your Majesty?" A voice jars me from my thoughts, and I look up to see one of my seconds, a man called Henri, standing in the opening of the tent.

"Yes?" I say, still in a good mood after our resounding victory.

"King Peter is asking to meet with you this afternoon, sir. He would like to negotiate terms." Henri has a hopeful look upon his face that has me raising an eyebrow.

"Terms? Already?"

He nods. "That's what his courier is saying. He's still outside if you'd like to speak to him."

"Yes, please," I say, covering up the maps I've been looking at. It's not that I don't trust Henri to tell me the truth of the conversation, but I might be able to get more information from the courier than my subordinate.

A few moments later, a short, thin vampire with dark hair and menacing eyes walks into the tent. I'd like to think perhaps he is a courier because of his size. Maybe he's not that good at fighting.

But another lesson I learned long ago is to never assume anything based on appearance alone.

He bows to me. "Your Majesty, I come from Vampire King Peter. He would like to meet with you this afternoon at dusk to discuss terms of a cessation of hostilities."

"After one short battle, the mighty Vampire King Peter of Scarlett Thunder is ready to fold?" I don't mean to jest, but I can hardly believe it.

He clears his throat and taps his heels together. "Your Majesty, we truly only have one request. King Peter doesn't wish to be at war with you, but he would like his son back. Also... he would like to know your intentions toward the child."

I cock my head to the side and study his face in disbelief. "Are you saying that he no longer wishes to fight? No longer seeks vengeance for what has befallen his children while they were in my lands?"

"While the king regrets that his children came to harm, he doesn't see the purpose of continuing to lose lives when he believes gentlemen such as the two of you can work this out on your own terms."

Something about what he is saying has an air of misinformation about it, and I have to wonder if perhaps this is all a trick, a lie to get me to come to him.

"What of the child?" I ask. "Does King Peter now believe me when I say it is not my offspring?"

"That I cannot speak to, Sir," he says. "I only know what I have said so far, that the king doesn't want to fight any longer, but he does want Prince Jacob returned, and I believe, an assurance that you will no longer come after Princess Opal for what allegedly happened in your castle."

"Allegedly?" My dander is up now as I stand tall and stare down at him. He is at least a foot shorter than me.

"His words, of course, Your Majesty."

This guy is good. He knows exactly what to say. That's probably why they send him. Anyone else may have managed to get themselves killed.

"Very well," I say. "I shall think on it. If I intend to come, I will send a courier."

He clinks his heels together again, likely relieved to be on his way. "Thank you, Your Majesty." His bow is low enough that I can see the top of his head before he backs out of the tent and disappears.

I go back to my maps. There's something fishy about this, and I don't quite trust it…. I don't think this war is over yet.

Not by a long shot.

***

EMORY

THE TROOPS we've been left with are sparse, and as Lex and I roam down the line, looking over every soldier we have at our disposal, I begin to wonder if we have any trainees, new recruits, retired warriors, anyone else who can stand with us.

Not to fight, but just to give more sustenance to our line, more support. Otherwise, it will look lean, and a lean battle line is too enticing for my father to resist.

"We have to tell him," Lex says as he follows behind me. This isn't his first statement of such. He's said the same thing about a hundred times.

I am dressed in black pants and a matching black shirt made of the stretchy material the vampires use for their uniforms, though the cut on my garments is not the same as these troops, so I don't think it's officially a uniform. I think it's just similar, and it fit me, so Nellie brought it to me.

I ignore Lex until he says my name in an imploring tone. "Emory, are you even listening?"

I nod. "I heard you, Lex. But I've already told you, I don't think it's a good idea. Your brother is busy. We can handle this."

"But what if we can't? You know we only have about a quarter of the troops one would usually use to defend the castle. If your father is able to get in behind the castle walls, not the barrier around the perimeter but the actual castle walls, we'll never get him out."

His concern is not unfounded. But I truly believe I can do this. I don't want to ruin the whole war because Kane has to come sprinting back here to help.

But then... if I fuck it up, we're all screwed, and Kane will never want to see me again.

I take a deep breath and check the time on a watch I found in the jewelry box in my room. It'll be sunset in about an hour, and I know my father well enough to know that's when he'll begin his attack. It'll take an hour, maybe two, for them to march their way over here. We probably have three hours at most.

I've studied the maps, and I know where Kane is. I'm not sure a messenger can get close enough to him to use telepathy to send him word and then get back here quickly enough. While it might be possible for Lex to contact him right now, my understanding is that telepathy is stronger when vampires are closer, and there are no distractions.

I'm assuming there are distractions for the king right now….

"Fine. Send word to him," I tell him. "Make sure that they explain that we have a plan in place, though. He shouldn't abandon his current situation to come back here."

"We have a plan in place?" he repeats and then scoffs. "What the fuck plan is that? Stand out there and wave our arms, begging them to stop?"

I clear my throat. "Something like that…."

"That will never work in a million years, and you know it. At the very least, please, let me find Rainer."

I look over Lex's shoulder and see a large figure flying at us from a great distance. He's moving so fast, it's hard to see his face. But I recognize the gait.

"I believe he already knows."

39

FAMILY OR POWER?

Emory

RAINER IS PISSED. Still. And it's been a couple of hours since he returned to the castle and I sheepishly told him what was going on.

He'd yelled at me. A lot. Everything from how dangerous this was, to do I not remember that I was almost dead a few days ago to how could I not send for him or for Kane.

I can't blame him. I would be pissed in his position, too, but when I attempt to explain, he accuses me of trying to be the hero, and that just makes me mad.

So here we are, leading the defense against the castle, both of us irritated as hell at one another, knowing we may very well end up dead without being able to hug it out.

He has sent for Kane, even though I assured him we'd already done that, thanks to Lex. I did give the prince credit for being the one to insist that the king be notified.

It doesn't matter now. We are about ten miles from the border between Moonraker pack and Crimson Peak, and I already smell wolf

—in large quantities. It's billowing through the air like someone has emptied a bottle of wolf shifter cologne.

I can tell that Rainer, who insists on staying right by my side, smells it, too, but for some reason, he doesn't look as repulsed as I feel, which is odd considering he is the vampire and I am one of the same creatures whose scent is currently repelling me.

It's strange. The last couple of days, I have been noticing odors a lot more strongly. I hadn't really paid much attention to it until now....

Perhaps the vampire venom that got into my system from the bites is affecting me. At the moment, it doesn't really matter. I need to concentrate on the task at hand.

Before we even left the castle, I went over with Rainer what my plans were, and he'd laughed, shook his head, and said there was no way they were going to work.

He might be right, but it's worth a try. We'll know soon enough how badly outnumbered we are. He thinks we should just try to hold them off until Kane can move more troops back here, but I am afraid if he does that then King Peter will invade in areas where Crimson Peak troops are not present to hold the line.

No, my plan has to work. It just has to....

Lex is on my other side, and we have almost covered the expanse. We've exited the wall so that still lies behind us, between us and the castle, which means whatever my father was planning to do to get over the wall, we may be able to stop him. Ladders, perhaps? That's how we got over it. There won't be time for that when the shifters will have to switch to their human forms, climb, and then climb down the other side. That would only work if my father had the element of surprise, and thanks to my sister, he doesn't.

I can only pray to the Moon Goddess that Lola is all right.

They come into view in the distance, all of them on foot, most of them on four paws. I am guessing they brought transport vehicles and parked a distance away so that they wouldn't be heard by any vampire patrols that might be here looking for invaders of any kind. I doubt they walked all this way, which would've been about twenty miles from my father's house to where we stand right now.

We had taken the train the day that my father sold me....

I push those thoughts aside and take a deep breath. Now that I can see them, it's time for me to enact my plan.

I am certain that Alpha Bernard has noticed the forces standing in front of him by now. I am certain that he thinks we are a minuscule force and can easily be torn apart by his combined forces since I can see even from here that not all of these wolves are part of Moonraker pack.

But I wonder if he sees or smells me yet. I wonder if he knows it is his daughter standing in opposition across the ever-shrinking battlefield from him.

I wonder if he even cares or if it matters.

Well, I'm fairly certain I know the answer to that question already, but I'm about to find out for sure.

"Alpha Bernard, I order you to halt where you are, right now, by the authority of King Kane Alexander of Crimson Peak, whose territory you are currently invading." I use the mind-link, and I am clear, precise, and as authoritative as possible.

Before my father can respond, Rainer asks me, "Did you do it? Are you doing it? Are you trying your little plan?"

"Yes!" I tell him. "Shut up so I can hear!"

He shifts back and forth on his feet while I wait for a reply. After about five seconds, he asks, "Did he answer you yet? What did he say?"

I swat at him as Lex, who is on my other side, says, "Rainer, shut up and let her concentrate."

"But I want to know what's happening!" He sounds like a spoiled child.

In my head, I hear the loud, demanding voice of my father. "Emory Moonraker? Is that you? What in the Goddess's name are you doing out here? You should be in the castle where it is safe!"

I almost laugh. Why would he care about my safety?

"He answered, didn't he?" Rainer asks, leaning toward me. "Did he make a joke?"

"Shut up!" I tell him, and then I respond back to my father. "I am here, and I am warning you, Alpha, you need to step back. This cannot end well for you."

"Emory, darling," he says, more quickly now that he knows it's me. He's using the tone he always uses when he is trying to convince me that something is good for me when it's really not. "You need to step aside. This doesn't concern you. This is between me and the evil vampire king who stole you from me."

"Stole me?" I scoff, but before Rainer can say anything, I stick a hand out in front of him. We have come to a stop about half a mile from the enemy, and they are no longer advancing either as we size each other up across the open field. It's growing darker by the moment, but our eyes adjust to the dark easily, so it doesn't matter. It's just a choice of whether the death will begin with the sun still peeking over the horizon or with the stars in the sky above us.

"I know what you're thinking, but I had no intention of selling either one of you, Emory. I had no choice. He threatened me. You missed all of that." My father still sounds confident but also pleading just a tad. "Step aside and let us go past. It'll be better that way."

"No, Father. Either you turn this army around and march back to your villages or I will tell them all the truth, about the war, the debt, all of the opportunities Kane gave you, and how you sold me, which I'm sure they don't know about."

"It's all lies, Emory! That madman has been poisoning your head and likely poisoning your blood. You simply can't believe him."

My eyes focus on his face. He is in his wolf form, and he is a great distance away from me, but I can see him.

My brother is on one side of him, Darius on the other. They look as if they are trying to look as powerful as he is. I am certain the other older wolves near them are Alphas from other packs, and I wonder if they know the reason for the delay.

"This is your last warning," I say.

"Emory, darling, I will try to spare you the embarrassment, but your pack mates will not believe you, no matter what you try to tell them. You'll be wasting your breath and your energy. Energy that could be spent fighting." He shakes his head, and I see a look of irritation in his eyes. He's trying to stay calm with me, but he's about to lose it.

I have no choice but to play my final card before the battle begins.

"Warriors of Moonraker pack!" I begin, using the mind-link to project my message to every pack member standing in front of me. "It is I, Emory Moonraker, daughter of Alpha Bernard Moonraker! I was to be your next Alpha. I trained with you, served with you, lived with you, laughed with you, and cried with you from the moment I was born until I was sold as a feeder to King Kane by my father not long ago."

I see their heads turn, their expression shift as they consider my words. I decide to start walking forward to get closer to them so that I can be better understood. I signal for Rainer and Lex to stay there, but Rainer throws a fit. "Absolutely not!"

I turn and glare at him. "Just give me a moment."

He mumbles under his breath, but his feet don't move.

I close about half the distance as I continue. None of them move.

"That's right. I was sold. But not because my father wanted the king to have me. No, I was able to step in. To spare the life of my younger sister, Lola."

Now, the murmurs are even greater as the wolves yelp and yip, their way of asking how can it be true.

"You're lying, Emory!" my father barks through the mind-link, but I will not be stopped.

"I am sure he told you some story about me that made you think I had suddenly changed my mind about wanting to serve as your next leader, but if you will look back at the history of my father's choices, you will see many of them are not what's best for our pack. Many of them involve making poor choices and blaming others."

"Lies! All lies!" he says. I see Darius,

"Did you know that my father borrowed millions and millions of Drakes from Kane to attack our neighbors? Some of those pack members are here right now, standing up with him. While I can see why you might be upset at the vampire king for loaning the money, he didn't know my father's purpose at the time, not until it was too late, and then he battled my father to try to get repayment, even after their packs had seen heavy losses keeping us out."

The members of the other packs wouldn't know what was happening because I couldn't communicate through the mind-link with them. But some of the people in human form were repeating my words. I believed they were there to carry supplies, possibly to hoist ladders which might be on the ground behind them. I wasn't close enough to see through the tall grass.

I continued. I could see my father and brother getting ready to give the order to attack me. I was running out of time.

"I have lived at Castle Graystone for several weeks now. I have gotten to know the vampires, including the king, and I can tell you that what you've been told before is all wrong. They are not evil monsters. The members of the Crimson Peak Clan are good people. We can work together, their people and ours. We can finally have peace and unity. I can help facilitate that."

I took a deep breath and said, "But not if you attack today. Rest assured the forces you see in front of you are only a small portion of what is waiting for you. It is true King Kane was gone from the castle when our scouts confirmed you were approaching, but he is returning enforce, and you still have a massive wall to scale. The element of surprise is gone. Only a fool would order you to attack now." My eyes went to my father.

"You don't have to fight. We can have peace. We can have a society where vampires and shifters can coexist—"

"Emory!" My father's Alpha voice boomed. "That is quite enough! We did not come here to discuss the merits of King Kane and the vampires. We came here to reclaim what is rightfully ours, to take back the supplies, the feeders, the money we were forced to give in tribute—it was never borrowed!"

"You are a liar!" I shout the words aloud. "You are a liar and a weak man who will give up anything and everything for power! Including your own child!"

I am moving forward now, not thinking about the consequences, even though I hear Rainer shouting at me to stop and come back.

I stop directly in front of my father's wolf, and he looks at me, snarling, his eyes narrowed in hate. Rainer is coming. I feel him covering the ground quickly behind me, but I'm not afraid.

"Tell me, Father. Tell me the truth. What do you love more? Your family—or power?"

The answer comes in the form of a white-hot pain that burns through my flesh into my abdomen and through my spine as the world spins and I find myself falling backward.

40

THE EMERGENCE OF AN ALPHA

Kane

I WAS ALMOST THERE.

I had almost made it to where Emory was confronting her father. I could see her in the distance as I sprinted across the grass, not even slowing as I passed the line of my own troops that had been standing back, watching.

"What is she doing?" I'd screamed aloud to no one. Why had Rainer allowed her to get so far ahead of him? I see my friend dodging forward now, coming up behind me, but it's too fucking late!

Emory falls backward, the slash of a wolf's claws ripping through her abdomen as blood sprays across his face.

I am there before she hits the ground. I scoop her into my arms as the crowd gasps in shock. I have no idea what Emory had been saying to them, but by their expressions, most of the wolves looked ready to stand down.

All but one.

Her own fucking father.

Blood drips off the claws of Bernard Moonraker as he stands directly in front of me, his fangs showing as he snarls at me… at her.

Never before in my life have I wanted to speak to a wolf shifter more than I do right now. I want to know what the fuck he was thinking.

Rainer is behind me, and he's calling for a healer. Emory's eyes are open. "K-Kane?"

"You're all right, baby," I tell her, but I have no idea what the damage is. All I know is that I smell her blood, and she's in enough pain that she can hardly keep her eyes open.

Rainer insists that I let him have her, and I turn to address the wolf in front of me. "You'd better shift right now and give me a really good fucking reason why I don't rip your goddamn head off, Bernard Moonraker!"

He smiles at me, still snarling, and it's not him that speaks but a woman nearby who is in her human form. "The Alpha says that he was punishing his daughter for trying to get his own army to turn against him."

"Turn against him? He sold her!" I shout. I look along the line of wolves standing in front of me. They are no match for my army that is coming in at full speed from the north right now. The line that is here will hold them, and we will destroy them.

And I'm not fucking afraid of any of them or all of them. Not in the mood I'm in.

"The Alpha says that you are a liar, that you stole her, and that Emory has been compromised." The same woman is speaking to me, but she doesn't seem to believe the words coming out of her own mouth.

"You all know that's not true! And now, he's led you all here to be slaughtered, the same way that he just tried to kill his own daughter!"

A healer is there now, treating Emory, and Rainer is up now, at my side.

I look at her brother and the man that I am certain Emory thought at one point would be her mate. They are both uncomfortably shuffling on their feet next to the Alpha. They know. They are not fools who are so consumed by the idea of having power that they are acting irrationally.

I hope.

We are about to find out.

"I'm giving you all a choice right now," I tell them. "Before I send in my troops. Before you all have to risk dying because of this nasty asshole whom some of you call Alpha and some of you have absolutely no loyalty whatsoever. Shift back into your human forms and pledge your allegiance to Emory Moonraker as your Alpha. If you do so, she will be the Alpha of your pack. She will use the knowledge and skills she's been honing her entire life, ones she worked on in anticipation of becoming your leader, until this man lied to her, tried to sell her sister, and then she gave herself up, to stay here, in a castle full of vampires, people she'd been told her whole life were her enemies, but we're not! We don't have to be. We don't want to be!"

I look down the line and see many of them heavily affected by my words. The ones that are not members of her pack are already backing away. This isn't their fight. Ordinarily, I would punish them just for being here, but I don't have any desire to fuck with that at the moment.

"Make your choice, and make it now," I say. My eyes wander up and down the line, looking for reactions.

I feel something cold brush against my hand and see that Emory is struggling to sit up. She looks a lot better now than she did when I'd handed her over to Rainer. I'm not sure what the situation is, but I'm thankful to see that she's able to take my hand.

If this works, it will be because of the words she said to these people before I arrived. But I am still infuriated that she did this—and that Rainer and Lex did nothing to stop her.

When I return my attention to the wolves, the members of the neighboring packs are retreating. The others are still hesitating.

Bernard Moonraker shifts and takes a pair of shorts from a servant standing nearby, one next to the woman who did the speaking for him.

His eyes are not focused, and he still has that snarl on his face. His hand is dripping with blood, but it's not his.

"How dare you!" he shouts at me. "How dare you spread lies to these people. Stand strong, Moonraker pack! We will move forward with our attack, and we will claim Crimson Peak as our own! These vampire demons cannot stop us! He's lying to you again, telling you that there are more nearby!"

"Father!"

Emory's brother has shifted and is pulling on some shorts as well. "Shut up! Don't you see what's happened? Now, you've screwed everything up for me! These people, they don't want me to be their Alpha, not after what Emory just said to them. They want her! And what of me? She'll likely have me sent to the feeders' prison."

With his words, Emory begins to stand up. I am hesitant to help her because I don't want her to be further injured, but she manages, and I hold her up, my arm around her waist. When she speaks, her voice is quiet because she's having difficulty breathing through the pain. "No, Colt. I would never do that to you. I will need your help. You're my brother. I love you." Looking at her father, she says, "I would never turn my back on my family."

"You little bitch!" her father says, stepping toward her.

"Call her another name and I will tear your throat out!" I shout at him. "You might've been able to take advantage of your daughter when she wasn't expecting an attack, but I assure you those tactics will not serve you well."

He hesitates, stops in his tracks. I can see him considering whether or not he should continue to press the issue.

But I am done.

"All right, members of Moonraker pack. If you are ready to accept Emory as your Alpha, shift now. The rest of you can either take off and try your hand at being rogues or prepare to fight my army." At that moment, they appear over a rise in the distance, twenty thousand vampires, dressed in black, their faces glowing in the moonlight as they prepare to fight.

That was all of the persuasion most of them needed. But they didn't turn and run like I expected them to. No, they all shift and drop down on their knees. Even her brother bows down to her. The other guy, the Beta's son, he does the same.

The only one who doesn't bow down to her was her father.

He takes two swift steps backward before I release Emory to Rainer, knowing he is right there to take her, and grab him by the throat. "You don't get to run away, Bernard," I tell him.

He makes gurgling noises, and I decide not to squeeze so hard, not for his sake but for his daughter's. As much as I want to snap his neck, I won't. Emory can do whatever she'd like with him, but I won't kill him.

"Should we round them up?" one of my lieutenants asks me as another takes Bernard Moonraker into custody.

"No." The answer comes from Emory, but I agree. "No, they did as the king requested. They are free to go back to their homes. Colt, you're in charge as acting Alpha until I can sort through the situation and get some treatment for my injuries. Darius, you're acting Beta. Make sure that everyone has what they need. I will be there to check on the situation as soon as I can."

Her words make me wince a little. She's leaving. She'll go back to her pack, and I'll let her. It doesn't matter that I "own" her. I can't keep her at my castle against her will.

"Yes, Alpha," both of the men Emory has addressed say, and immediately, they take charge of the situation. I single for some of my people to assist them. I'm not sure what the status of their pack is at this point, but if they need something—food, supplies, resources, anything—I will provide it for them. The only thing I'm short on myself right now is blood.

Thinking of that reminds me that I still have King Peter to deal with. He wanted to meet with me to discuss the situation, and I left to come here instead. I know that the troops I left behind are well-led, and they will not lose the upper hand we fought so hard to take, but it's one more thing I must deal with.

Right now, though, all I can think about is Emory. I want to ask

Rainer what he was thinking. I want to yell at her for doing something so dangerous. I want to kiss her.

I won't do any of those things. Especially the last one. She is leaving soon. She's made her decision, and even though I can respect it, I can't help but feel like my heart is being ripped out of my chest.

The healers show up with a stretcher, and even though she protests, she climbs on it. As she is taken back to the castle, the people of Moonraker pack erupt in chants of, "Hail Alpha Emory!" I couldn't be prouder of her, but I have no idea how I will ever let her go.

EMORY

A CLAN HEALER has sewed me up for the second time in just a few days. The attack from my father was deep, tearing through muscle, but it didn't hit any vital organs.

I am thankful that I am okay, but I can't believe my own father did that to me. I trusted him. I know Rainer and Lex both feel awful that I was injured; I just hope Kane hasn't done anything to kill them yet.

He hasn't come in to see me either, and that worries me. I know he's probably busy with everything that's going on. We need to talk about how I will do this—be the Alpha of my pack and still see him.

Assuming he wants to see me. I hope he's not angry at me for going out there without speaking to him first.

My hand brushes over my abdomen. It's a bit sore, but I'll be okay.

I need to talk to him desperately, though. I need to tell him what the healer said to me. I can hardly believe that it's true. I didn't even know it was possible…. She said it had happened once before, a thousand years ago….

The door creaks open and Kane sticks his head in. I smile at him, but the smile he gives me back is forced. "How are you feeling?" he asks me.

"Better, thank you. I'm sorry I didn't tell you. I just thought you'd be busy, and I could handle it."

He comes to stand next to me, but his hands are folded behind him. "You did handle it. I only… reinforced what you'd said."

I can't help but smile at him. "We have a lot to discuss."

"Do we?" he asks me.

"I think so. Being an Alpha over there and living here…."

His eyes widen, and I am confused. "Living here?"

"Well… yes." I pause. "Unless you don't want me to."

"Do you want to?" His tone is cautious. "Because you don't have to. I'm not going to force you to stay with me, Emory."

Confusion washes over me as I'm not sure what he means. "You own me," I remind him.

He shakes his head. "No one owns you, Emory Moonraker." Finally, he reaches over and touches my arm. "I only want you to make an effort to stay with me if you want to."

My hand slips down to his, our fingers interlacing as I run my palm along his smooth, cool one. "I can't imagine being without you." We've been through too much for me to be anything but honest, even if the truth leaves me feeling raw and exposed. I feel so drawn to him, so intoxicated by him, I can't imagine a mate's pull being any stronger, but I'm not old enough to have experienced that yet.

If I never meet my true mate and this is the closest I ever get, I will not know what I am missing.

Kane's smile is content. He seems to be breathing easier as he says, "I can't imagine being without you either, Emory. In fact, I love you."

His words make my heart swell as an ache of longing shoots through me. "I love you, too," I tell him. He leans down and gently presses his lips to mine, like he's afraid I might crumble and blow away in the wind.

When he pulls away, I say, "I want to be with you always, but even more now that you and I will forever be tied together."

His forehead crinkles as he caresses my cheek with his thumb. "What's that now?"

I grin up at him and say, "Kane… I'm pregnant."

His reaction is the same as mine had been when the healer told me. "Wh-what? But... how?"

I shrug. "I'm not sure, but it has to be yours. I have never been with anyone else. The healer says I'm not very far along, and this has happened before, long ago, but... we're going to have a baby."

"A baby?" he repeats as a look of pure joy has his face glowing from within. "A baby with the woman I love? What could be better than that?"

He leans down and kisses me again, and I know that nothing in the world could ever be better than this.

Mated to Four Alphas

Threats Against the Breeder

At War for the Breeder

The Stolen Breeder

Four Alphas, Four Babies

Becoming the Luna Queen

Descendants of the Breeder

Desired by the Devil series

Whispers of the Devil

Banter of the Devil

Murmurs of the Devil

The Mafia Kings series

Indebted to the Mafia King

<u>Loved by the Mafia King</u>

Claimed by the Mafia King

Secrets of the Mafia King

Burned by the Mafia King

Kidnapped by the Mafia King (coming soon!)

Dark Stalker Romance series

Tempted by Sin

Fated to Sin

Secret Billionaires series

Finding the Secret Billionaire by Olivia Bhelle Kildare

Falling for My Secret Billionaire by Bella Moondragon

Driven by the Secret Billionaire by ID Johnson

Wolf Shifter Alpha Kings series

Ravens and Ruins

Sundrops and Shadows

Snowflakes and Sabotage

The Vampire King's Feeder series

Claiming the Alpha's Daughter

Loving the Alpha's Daughter

Finding the Alpha's Daughter

Bewitching the Alpha's Son (coming soon!)

Writing as B. Moon

The Boy Who Died

Sign up for Bella's newsletter here.

*Or get a free novella from The Alpha King's Breeder series when you sign up here:
The Beta and the Maid*

Follow Bella on Facebook here.

Follow Bella on Bookbub here.